# TULUM

# TULUM

## DAVID SETH MICHAELS

iUniverse, Inc.
Bloomington

# TULUM

iUniverse books may be ordered through booksellers or by contacting:

iUniverse
1663 Liberty Drive
Bloomington, IN 47403
www.iuniverse.com
1-800-Authors (1-800-288-4677)

ISBN: 978-1-4620-6922-4 (sc)
ISBN: 978-1-4620-6923-1 (ebk)

Printed in the United States of America

iUniverse rev. date: 11/22/2011

For Benjamin, Jeremy and Cassandra

"A writer should never know the whole story. He imagines one part and asks the reader to finish it. A book should never close. The reader should continue it."

—Carlos Fuentes

Sunday. October 14. 4 pm. In this country, a day off for everyone. For me, it's like any other day. First, a small tequilita from the freezer. And then, my book, my plastic chair under the flowering tree, and a cold bottle of beer with a piece of lime in it. A perfect day for the yard. A perfect day to read. A perfect day to be a lizard.

To no one's particular surprise, when the bottle is empty, I find that I cannot keep my eyes open, the book becomes heavy in my arms and it sinks through the warm humidity into my lap. My eyes close slowly. The beautiful siesta I invited gently sneaks up on me. Initially I can still hear the birds, the soft clacking sound from the cocos, the hum of the town. These fade gently, and then a dream.

An elephant has escaped from its handlers and has run down the beach to escape the intense heat and to frolic in the ocean. It floats in the surf, blowing sea water through its trunk onto its back, enjoying the surf. On the shore, its handlers grow impatient for it to return. They yell at it, "Come bank, Sweetness, come back!" Sweetness, if that is truly her name, ignores them. She wallows in the cool water, she swims around in circles, she sprays sea water with her trunk. "Sweetness," they shout. "Come back." Evidently, she's not yet ready to return to land, to heat, to servitude, and to them. She ignores their shouts and continues her bath. The handlers become more impatient. And angry. One of them shouts at her and in frustration throws a coconut toward her. Sweetness apparently doesn't care for this. At all. She trumpets loudly and swims slowly down the beach, farther away. The handlers run down the beach after her, kicking up sand.

Some of the sand hits me. It wakes me up. I expect to see the wide beach and the handlers and the escaped elephant basking defiantly in the turquoise water, but when I carefully prop open my right eye, there's no ocean and no elephant. I'm in my yard. And there are two sweaty people, people I don't know, standing there, standing in my yard, near my chair. I reluctantly pry both eyes open. I look at them. I know very well why they're standing there.

"Excuse me," the bearded one says in English. "I'm sorry to disturb you, but I wonder if you could help us."

I consider saying that I don't speak English. This would have its benefits, but it will probably prolong their unwanted visit. They will pantomime to me. We will play charades. I consider telling them directly, please leave my yard. Instead, knowing this directness will seem unnecessarily unkind in a country where seeming politesse is so important, I say, "Yes?"

"We're looking for someone," he begins. "We're looking for the curandero. And we wonder if you know where we could find him? If you'd tell us where we can find him."

I knew it. Same as always. How many times, I wonder, am I going to have this conversation? How many people are going to show up with this very same question?

The question, I think, deserves a consistent answer. So I tell them my usual lie. "I'm sorry. I don't know who you are looking for. Perhaps some of my neighbors could be of assistance to you, but I don't know who that is."

"Oh," they both sigh. Crestfallen, they mumble gracias and wander off into the heat and humidity to continue their search for the curandero.

I return to the elephant. There are only Dream Elephants in this part of Quintana Roo. I have no idea what they are doing here. Or where they come from. Or why.

Look. I'm not exactly like all the other lizards in Tulum. Not really. Like me the lizards sit still in the yard and the sun warms them. They don't move at all. In the late afternoons I sit in my yard. We share the sun. We listen to the birds and the sounds of cooking. We smell the dust and the onions and chilies, the charcoal, the blooming flowers. They have their thoughts, their wonderings. And I have mine. We can't talk to each other, although we're aware of our common activity. I suspect that their thoughts are few and far between. Unlike me, they don't remember enough of the past ever to recall it. And I don't know whether they have any dreams. They have only their lizard thoughts, which have a very short life before they are forgotten. I, of course, have my dreams. And the many things I wonder about. My dreams, my thoughts occupy me often. In my memory events of decades ago are sometimes more alive than this morning's newspaper. But it's my wondering and my dreaming that fill my days with vivid colors and the brightest of lights.

In the late afternoon I like to smoke a little cigar, if I have one, or I have a glass of wine or two. Or a cold bottle of beer. I like Pacifico beer best. Especially if it's very cold. With a slice of lime. But I'm easily pleased. I don't have much brand loyalty for anything. My simple pleasures are not infrequent. I'm quite content. Mostly I just sit. I just hang out. It's all very simple. I sit in a white plastic chair with a beer logo on the back in the shade under a flowering tree with purple flowers. I enjoy the warmth, the humidity, I think my thoughts. I dream. I wonder about the world. I imagine things. I breathe deeply. I listen to the sounds of kitchens and muffled voices and the children playing in the street. I hear the sounds of the many insects. The barking dogs. Occasionally, I can faintly hear music from the bar around the corner and the humming and growling of the traffic a few blocks away on the main street. If my hearing were better, I might hear more, but I'm not complaining about that. My hearing is just fine. Mostly, I'm alone with my dreams and my thoughts, and mostly, I'm content. I like being by myself. Mostly, I amuse myself with thinking. Wondering. And with my imagination. And with the stories I find.

There is a rich delta, a river delta where the river of dreams nourishes the ocean of stories. That's where I like to set up my chair. I cast slowly, and I watch what my net brings in. Sometimes the catch is some distant memories, seemingly insignificant recollections from decades ago in distant places. Sometimes it's just an old boot, disquieting, disappointing. And sometimes a story in the net sparkles and glows, filling me with admiration and delight, moving me to feel my heart thumping in my chest, reminding me to find a notebook with some unused paper in it. Or an envelope. Or the back of a bill. And a pencil. Then I write down something about it, I make some quick notes. Just so I won't forget it. I sit in my chair, watching, breathing, traveling, following the twists and turns of the story slowly to wherever it might end up. Scribbling occasionally. Making illegible notes I will later have trouble deciphering.

My thoughts are in my original language, English. This is the language I learned from my parents. And these thoughts all seem to have a mild New York accent. I was never Cervantes, and Spanish remains harder for me. Especially when I am absorbed in thinking. Or dreaming. I enjoy dreaming. A lot. And sometimes my dreams are in Spanish, especially when I'm dreaming about my present life. And then they are filled with the mumbled, chuckling, joking slang of my neighborhood. But sometimes my dreams come from unknown places as if they were messages from far, far away, as if they were a faded letter inside a wine bottle that has been afloat in the endless Caribbean for decades. And sometimes my dreams take me to places I cannot even recognize.

And then there are the stories. The stories come from the ocean, and some seem to come from the clouds. Of course, the sea carries stories here. They float and drift, sometimes sticking to each other. If you look carefully, you can see them in the turquoise water. They look like round bubbles, small, shiny spheres. Some stories also seem to come from the clouds. I don't know where they originally come from, but there they are in the clouds. The wind carries them to the Yucatan. You cannot see these with the naked eye. At first you can feel them lying on your skin. The sun is ever so slightly blocked. As if a thin cloud were standing in front of it. The stories fall from above. At first they feel like the other sea breezes, damp, sweet smelling, but when you pay attention, you find the story lying on your arm or forehead. These are the most delicate, airy, gossamer, beautiful stories. Once in a very great while you might even discover one of them hiding on your face. You think you are wiping away mist, or the sweat from your brow, or even tears. But when you open your hand, you can see it. It's a little, bright story. It's on your hand, shining there, opening for you, pulsing. But otherwise you cannot see these stories, not really. Especially because unlike me, you probably aren't ever looking for them.

To you I may appear to have turned into just another of Tulum's lizards. A garrulous one, to be sure, an odd one, yes, but, alas, a lizard nonetheless. I sit motionless in the yard. I move infrequently. I'm happy to have occasional visitors. I don't ask for or expect much. My neighbors who visit call me "the Don", even though I own very little, and certainly no finca, and they occasionally bring me little cigars or rum or tequila or a piece of flan or white, sugary cake with white icing for dessert. I love sweet things. And this is a country that loves very sweet. The sweeter the better.

I think there is a rumor that I once owned a huge parcel of land, a ranch even, and tragically lost it. I neither deny nor spread this story. I do like its melodramatic flavor. It somehow reminds me of the respect the people of the fictional Cuernavaca in *Under the Volcano* try to show the narrator. They knew he used to be important. That he was once somebody. And now, well, now he's just gone to seed. He's just an old drunk has-been. A nobody. In this world even being an old gringo doesn't disqualify you from a certain, required, formal respect. The formal respect comes automatically with aging and being around here for a long time.

"How are you, Sir?" they ask, probably knowing the rumors. I approve of the deference in the inquiry, as I should, and I like being asked. Unfortunately, I don't have much to say in response to these questions. Most of the people near me have heard my opinions and all of the stories I am willing to disclose to them already. In fact, sometimes I think I may have told them some of my anecdotes too many times. So when temptation in the form of beer or wine or boredom overcomes me, and I do begin again to tell an old tale, thinking I haven't told this particular one yet to this particular person or that one, I have to check very carefully. I try to see whether they roll their eyes, meaning that they've heard the story at least twice before, that I'm a forgetful old gringo, one to be respected, patronized, perhaps, by not interrupting and with brief but silent nodding, and with a tiny, obligatory smile. If I see that, I drop the story, I just say, "Oh, never mind. Forget about it." Usually, though, to avoid any imposition on my listeners, I just say I'm fine, how are you, and I leave it at that. Sometimes I say that nothing's new. But sometimes, like now, I just want to tell a story. Actually, my story. I think I will enjoy telling you this story. And anyway I know neither you nor anybody else has heard this entire story before. I know I haven't ever told it all in one piece, all the way through before, from the beginning to the end, though I've talked about parts of it while it was happening. And I've scribbled some of it down on the back of old envelopes and blurred cash register receipts.

Unfortunately, when I'm finished, you probably won't be able to check up on any of my facts, to see whether what I've told you is actually true. Or whether I just made it all up. You probably won't be able to tell whether it's fact or fiction. I would prefer, if you must think about that dichotomy at all, that you think of anything I tell you as just my fabrications, my inventions. When I'm finished, I will probably have moved on, and my sweet Tulum will have transformed itself into

5

something almost unrecognizable to me. Maybe you'll still be able to come here and find some of the places I mentioned. And maybe some of the people will still be around. But by then the places won't look or be the same. They can't. Depending on their fortune and time, they will be shinier or encrusted in rust. Some will have collapsed. Or disappeared into thin air. Some will be completely changed and replaced by who knows what. I don't know what will happen to the places I mention. And the people. The people, if they ever existed, will have scattered or died or moved or been replaced by new arrivals to Tulum or they will have changed themselves into someone or something quite different. And now unrecognizable to me. Someone new. And certainly different. I would like to preserve them all, as if in amber, so you can see them. And visit with them. But I can't. So I prefer that you think of all of them as entirely made up. That will be better for them. And maybe for you, also, because you can always return to visit them in your mind.

Sometimes young people come to my house, even people from Europe and South America. They see me sitting alone in the yard under my tree. They think I'm not doing anything, and they approach me. I assure you I am not doing nothing. They walk around the side of the house, uninvited to enter the yard, and they clear their throats or excuse themselves and then ask me strange questions about this neighborhood and the curandero, who they suppose might be my neighbor. They want to know whether what they have heard about magical miracles (is there any other kind?) and amazing healing might be true and whether I can tell them where they might find him. They act like they are in on a big secret, that they are insiders and that others don't know about him. Of course, they're fooling themselves. Their quest is filled with contradictions, looking for the secret but famous person, discovering the newest of ancient wisdom, finding anew something that is age old. Of course, I know him, that's completely true. I've known him for quite some time. And I know him quite well. I've spent a lot of time with him. But when they ask me these questions, I don't let on. I sometimes make believe I just don't understand their language. I'm not rude about it; I just don't understand. I smile. I say I just don't know, I'm sorry. "Perdon, no se, lo siento." I shake my head. I know that the curandero isn't amused by these visitors, that he doesn't want them to visit him. He's been very clear about that to me. And to quite a few of them. So I help him out a little.

Sometimes I fall asleep in my chair. There is no harm in this at all. This is not doing nothing, either. This is actually a luxury that is vastly underrated in the First World. North Americans don't really understand this well. I take a small siesta whenever it comes upon me, whenever I might feel like it. On good days, it's a drowsy beer or wine siesta and my eyelids become heavy like sacks of wet sand. Other times, it's just a siesta. My eyelids close, and I just drift off. Whatever I was thinking about makes me briefly close my eyes, and then, as I enter the veiled, hidden land of inventions and illusion, myths and symbols, there are those ephemeral, bright dreams, sparkling insights, wonderful ideas. What a huge world it is behind my eyelids. Sometimes I end up startling myself awake with my own snoring. And sometimes the people seeking my neighbor try to wake me up by standing near me and clearing their throats, or far worse, touching my arm. Can you believe that? This always surprises me. Their touch makes me startle. I absolutely hate this abrupt wake-up. It makes my heart pound for no reason. It unjustifiably unleashes powerful fight-or-flight chemicals in my brain. You would think I could enjoy a beautiful daydream or peacefully travel far and wide in the world of dreams during a sweet siesta in my own little yard without being disturbed by these uninvited people. But that's not the case. They believe in the urgency of their adventure, their mission, if that's what it is, and to them it is much more important than what they think, at the most, is just a nap. My nap. They're wrong, of course, it isn't more important. And I'm not just sleeping. I'm not doing nothing. They could just as easily wait for me to wake up. There would be no harm in that. What, after all, is their rush? Listen. There's no real rush around here. Ever. But they won't wait. To me they seem impatient, out of place, maybe even disrespectful. A minor, irritating nuisance, like a cloud of pestering gnats or a hungry mosquito or two, but a nuisance nonetheless. I am sure they are excited about searching out their treasure, my neighbor, and they think they might get my help to find him.

The funny part of this is that they have no idea what the curandero looks like. For all these visitors know, I myself might be the curandero. Anybody they pass on the street might be the curandero. In Tulum all of us, every single one of us might be the curandero. This isn't central casting. The guy they are looking for is not wearing a special costume with plumage made of quetzel feathers and face paint and the skin of a jaguar wrapped around his loins. Or a mountain lion's hide around his shoulders. He's not wearing some beautiful, ornate, bejeweled designer creation from *Apocalypto* as a tiara. He won't have a gigantic lip plug. Or a special robe. Or face tattoos. I expect these visitors to be surprised by how short, how square, how thin, how ordinary the curandero is, but for some reason, when they meet him, they never let on about his appearance. When they meet all 5 feet 4 inches of him, dressed in a faded t-shirt and frayed jeans and a greasy baseball cap, they never gasp in surprise. Or show disbelief. They never question that he's who he says he is. More important, they never question whether he can actually do whatever they think they want him to do for them.

Actually, I don't know whether I myself appear to these foreign visitors to belong here or not. I don't know how observant they are. I'm curious whether I appear to be an anomaly, which on some level I am, or whether I now fit so well in my neighborhood that it's like Basho's haiku, "He who appears before you now is the toad of this thicket." Anyway, nobody ever seems to suggest that I don't belong here, even though, years ago I didn't, and probably even now it's still a gigantic presumption for me to make believe that I do.

Because of this I have developed a special appreciation for starlings. These birds are not native to the Americas, but there are now so many of them that they and their bad manners appear to belong on every branch in every tree on this continent. Everywhere. By now they, like me, probably think they belong where they find themselves. Wherever they originally came from is just another distant, tentative memory. They've been here for long enough that going back doesn't seem to be an option. Same for me. The connection, however, is not completely severed: where I came from will still be something interesting to include in the second paragraph of my obituary in a sentence beginning with the word, "Originally."

It might even be a presumption for me even to tell this story that I've apparently now begun. If it is, please forgive me, no offense is intended. I doubt that my talking about my life here really hurts anything or anyone. It certainly won't hurt the curandero, who will simply not be found if he wishes not to be found, and it won't hurt Tulum, which by the time you read this will likely be entirely different in all important respects from how I am describing it. And it won't hurt my neighbors either, because they will never read this, and it's entirely possible they won't ever even hear about it. Especially if it's in English.

Anyway, over time I seem to have become less of a gringo and more like Tulum's many lizards. Caterpillars become butterflies; here, gringos like me desiccate after a long time into seemingly dozing, barely moving, sluggish lizards. Maybe slightly eccentric and mysterious, maybe not exactly what I seem to be, but you can be the judge of all of that later on. I'd be the last one to tell you that you were wrong in whatever you may decide about me.

When I first came here, Tulum was a dusty, little Mayan town and appeared to be just a wide spot in the narrow two-lane blacktop running from Cancun to Chetumal and then on to the Belize border. Beyond Tulum, it seemed, there was nothing but jungle for miles. The vegetation and the mangroves were thick, the mud was often deep, and the plants were tall and grew right up to the side of the road and reached their branches out into it. Vines rubbed the sides of passing cars. Some aggressive, flowering vines even tried to enter the windows of passing cars and grab the occupants or snatch them from their seats. When the wind blew, the plants swayed into the road. Suicidal birds ran squawking and flapping their wings from the narrow sides of the road directly into the sides of passing cars. The speed of the cars didn't prevent these unfathomable, suicidal assaults. Fierce mosquitoes hovered in shimmering clouds waiting for warm flesh. Insolent lizards stood on every flat surface, basking, glaring, flicking their pointy, black tongues, refusing to move or startle, staring defiantly. In the late afternoons there was a bird that sang a tune that sounded like an Ornette Coleman improvisation. It repeated and looped beautifully back on itself. You could always smell burning brush in the air. And charcoal. And the scent of evaporating muddy water.

Throughout the dense mangrove, and partially buried by vegetation, are stone ruins the Mayans built more than a millennium ago. Hardly any of them have been found, much less unearthed. The few that have been unearthed are tourist destinations and designated archaeological zones. Tulum's Mayan ruins are among the largest, and they have always attracted many visitors. They were built without the benefit of the wheel by many very determined people. Some people think extraterrestrials lent a hand with the construction. I haven't decided about this one way or another.

The town, the pueblo—it was more a rickety one-story assemblage of weakening concrete, faded and patched paint and rusting, corrugated tin—didn't have restaurants and European bars and tourist shops. It didn't have banks and Internet cafes and places to make telephone calls. It didn't have the Spanish and Italian tourists, or North Americans in designer sunglasses, or tattooed Brit backpackers, or people with dreadlocks. Some hippie backpackers came through every once in a while. They didn't stick around for very long. The town was not particularly romantic. Or artistic. It was exotic, in the sense that it was a Mayan town, as opposed to a Mexican one. That should have been clear to anyone who cared to look into the situation. Most outsiders came to Tulum for the exquisite Caribbean beaches and the ruins and then just passed by like waterlogged coconuts floating drunkenly in the waves, floating with the tide to somewhere else, to the next exotic, Latin American beach, to some other World Heritage Site.

Even though beach goers don't care about it at all, Tulum has a remarkable history. I like to tell about parts of it, because it's surprising, and to me much of it sounds like fiction. Until 1935 the Mexican central government didn't really control Tulum; the Mayans had run the place for several centuries, and there wasn't even really a contest about who was in charge until the 1840's when the War of the Castes broke out. After that the Mayans tended to kill Mexican soldiers and other people who showed up uninvited and didn't seem to belong. The Mayans traded directly with the British in Belize, which was then British Honduras. The map may have said Tulum and the state of Quintana Roo was part of Mexico, but Mexico City was definitely not its real capital city. And Mexico City was definitely not in charge of Tulum or of the rest of Quintana Roo.

The capital city, a town south of Tulum and with a similar unusual history, was Chan Santa Cruz, a name that blends a Mayan word meaning "small" with two Spanish ones. This place is now named Felipe Carrillo Puerto. It is inland It is not a port even though some road signs used to abbreviate it "Pto." These road signs were a manifestation of historical contempt by the then ruling Mexican party, the Party of the Institutional Revolution (PRI), for the socialists who formerly ran the place. The town is named with all three names of a martyred, Mayan, socialist governor of the early 20th[h] century who was shot by Huertistas. It is a place where crosses once spoke in Mayan urging continued armed insurrection against the Mexican central government and where for decades the resistance to Mexican control of the Yucatan peninsula was firmly entrenched.

You won't be surprised to hear that Tulum and its people were until very recently extremely isolated from outsiders. Until late in the 1960's there were no real roads in the entire state of Quintana Roo, and you could get here from outside only by swinging a machete and slowly slogging through hot, mosquito and snake infested mangroves and the thick selva or by sailing to the coast from Cozumel or Belize. It helped to be familiar with where paths had already been cut through the mangrove and the forest, which was a matter of birthright. And the people who lived here weren't telling anyone about that who didn't already know it. Especially the various, rare species of wandering gringos. The Mayans didn't speak Spanish. Or English. They spoke Mayan. They had contempt for the Mexican government and what then seemed to be its imperial language. And they weren't exactly thrilled to see others arrive who looked a lot like the small pox and syphilis bearing Spaniards who had decimated them half a millennium before. I should mention that the Mayans don't really give a hoot about scholarship on the epidemiology of these diseases. To them, precisely who was responsible for which of the many fatal diseases that appeared in the 16th century and killed so many thousands of people is beyond the need for any scholarly research. They know very well where the deaths came from. And how. And they remain not at all happy about it.

Tulum was not a plausible destination for those from the outside world until relatively recently. And the people who come here now, especially those looking for my neighbor, have no idea where they really are. Or that this place, just beneath its surface, has strong roots to a very old, very different, very unusual world. A world in which the unseen is at least as important as the visible, if not more so. A world in which energy is more important than matter. A world in which the care of the earth, mother earth, Santa Tierra Madre, is of primary importance. And they have no clue what has happened here in the past and how it has grown Tulum into what it is now. Yes, they know it's exotic. And uncrowded. And it might seem sweet to them in a laid back, artistic, post-hippie way. But that's about it.

It probably doesn't matter what these travelers don't know, but it's important to me. Those are the roots of where I am now living. It explains some things about this place. And how I might fit into it. And how the curandero and my neighbors fit into it. After all, there's a reason why people from halfway around the world are standing in my yard and looking for the curandero. And seeking an even older, mythic, indigenous Tulum than the one that is selling tourists things on the main drag. There's a logic to it, too.

The creation of the state of Quintana Roo was actually a punishment. Because the Mayans besieged Merida in the middle of the nineteenth century, the Mexican government divided the Yucatan Peninsula into three states, one of which was called Quintana Roo. Quintana Roo got it's name from Andres Quintana Roo, who was part of Mexico's struggle for independence from Spain. Compared with the other states of Yucatan and Campeche, Quintana Roo had nothing. Campeche in Mayan means "a place of serpents and ticks." Quintana Roo, at the beginning, had, if possible, even less. It was impenetrable mangrove with thin soil that wouldn't really support more agriculture than the Mayans' small, slash and burn milpas, their corn fields. It had cocals, coco farms, on the coast and chickle trees and dense forest with no roads in the interior. The cocos were cultivated; chickle grew wild in the jungla. Convicts, runaways, fugitives, madmen from elsewhere wandered the interior and gathered the chickle, which they sold on the beach to the agents of chewing gum manufacturers from the United States. The law among these outsiders was a machete. Or a gun. They were very dangerous, unrestrained people. And there were no police or judges or procedural niceties. Like arrests or trials. When things got out of hand, they had to be resolved with either sudden, brutal violence or immediate flight.

Just below the surface the entire state was limestone. The world's largest underground rivers ran under it, and there were many sink holes, cenotes, deep, fresh water pools, created when limestone dissolved and the surface soil fell in. The Mayans considered the cenotes, which held clear, cool, drinking water, sacred, and they used them in their many rituals. They bathed frequently in them. They drank their water. And there were many dry caves as well. Nobody until relatively recently had thought about the possibilities of making cement from the limestone and building with it. That would come much, much later. Until quite recently, Quintana Roo was truly a lost world.

I'm not trying to scare you or make Tulum sound especially perilous. Or unruly. I'm just saying that until very recently Tulum was a wild frontier, one with its own, unique rules, and in many ways, it still is. The new Palacio Municipal, a beautiful, stone town hall, in the middle of the pueblo in my view is intended to give quite another impression. It's an attempt to make the local government seem important. And legitimate. And in line with the mainstream of present world governance. But I'm not completely convinced. And I'm pretty sure my neighbors aren't, as well.

But enough about history. For now. In the interest of being truthful, which is something I'm not always dedicated to, I have a disclosure to make. I have quite an excellent, friendly relationship with my neighbor. He is a teacher and a friend to me. And he has been for quite some time. I know him well. I spend a lot of time with him. I do things for him; he teaches me. And he is very important to me. I have worked with him on all kinds of things. I think both our lives would both be better if he weren't attracting all of these people from wherever they were hanging out before, to Tulum, to seek him out, to pursue him, to ask his advice. It's a little complicated why. I'll get to telling you that. And, by the way, it's not that I have no sympathy for those from far away who show up here, who don't really understand how it is, and who end up staying for long stretches of time, or even forever. That's not it at all.

Look at me, for example. I'm over 60 years old. Pardon my vanity about how much over. I've been here for more than 20 years in this little house, painted the color of mango and the color of papaya, with the flowering tree and its purple flowers in the yard. Depending on whom you ask, I'm more or less just another crazy gringo. When I first got here, the main virtues of this place as far as I was concerned, were that it was not well known elsewhere, I could remain here without contact with the authorities, and the climate was hot and humid. I like hot and humid. I didn't want to get sent back to the States, where I had some legal problems I wanted to forget about, and I didn't want there to be too many questions from the authorities here. What I discovered was that if I minded my own business, which I do instinctively, and laid low and occasionally paid some small bribes to the right people at the right times, I could be quite content here. At the time la mordida, a bribe, was just a way of life, it was nothing extraordinary or even upsetting. Bribes were cheap because people including me had very little to pay las mordidas with. And we weren't fooling ourselves about what we had or trying to impress anybody with our prosperity. We were generally impoverished. We were not trying to appear glamorous. In Tulum back then, there wasn't really much evidence of "upwardly mobility."

My neighbors and I were friendly; we'd help each other out; and we'd keep a respectful distance. We'd privately marvel at how different we were. They, for example, will eat pork and fat and caldo I find really frightening. And they delight in eating tons of botanas, which translates as "junk food." Junk food in Mexico makes United States junk food seem like it came from the solely vegan and raw health food store. And they will drink harsh aguardiente straight from a plastic bottle at room temperature. This is enough to poach your eyeballs. It tastes to me a lot like paint thinner or sterno. I, on the other hand, seem overly fastidious to them. I am afraid of the various forms of large, buzzing, fearless flying cockroaches that live here, and I am quite particular about what I eat and especially what kind of oil it might be cooked in. I am trying to keep my liver and kidneys in working order. I am trying not to have daily heartburn. My neighbors find these idiosyncrasies utterly incomprehensible and laughable. They might even consider them a form of hypochondria. They laugh at me when I flinch from being crashed into by the buzzing, flying elephants. They have learned not to be insulted when I sometimes turn down their offers of food. Instead, they make fun of me. And they laugh out loud. This kidding is all good natured, thank goodness. It's a form of affection.

Some of my neighbors revere the curandero. Others consider him a species of vermin or bothersome insect. For reasons only he understands, he doesn't have a single place where he stays. He has a hammock, and he ties it up in various places in the neighborhood, either in the yard or in the house. Once I asked him where he lived. He responded, "In my body." So he's chosen to be unaffixed, a nomad of sorts. Look, even if you have no money, there are still places all around town where people can and do squat until they are ready to go elsewhere. They arrive on decades old, exhaust belching buses from impoverished, depressed places in the interior with virtually nothing, hang out until opportunity visits, and then they move on to take advantage of whatever might have shown up. This is a common occurrence. Many people have left their impoverished pueblos in the interior to find work on the coast. But nobody I know is a nomad quite like him. His drifting appears to be completely voluntary, and he also perpetuates his rootlessness with his constant refusals of anything that potentially might feel like an offer of stability or look like something to possess or tie him down or delay his moving about. He's not waiting for anything. He wants to wander.

And he's going to turn everything down so he can continue doing what he does exactly as he now does it. And he's not going to change his mind about this. No matter what. This, as he's told me at least twenty times, is how he does what he does. Period. It's a part of being who he is. And doing what he does. This is his life. People, he tells me, need him to be just like this if he is to be of service to them.

The neighbors who like him invite him to stay with them, they feed him, they do his extremely limited laundry, and they try to provide the few extra things that he might like. They let him hang his hammock in their yards or houses and hold his consultations with the many people who search him out. This is a large number of people. Not a crowd all at once, but a steady trickle of all kinds of people. Those who house him are always disappointed when eventually he decides that it's again time to move on, to move to another yard down the street, or around the corner, or across the highway to another neighborhood, as he always does after a while. It is not a surprise when he moves. He's moved scores of times. After he moves, they continue to seek him out, wait for him, visit and talk with him, ask him questions. And after they ask his advice, they cheerfully do whatever he tells them to do. Maybe they hope he will leave some of the gifts he receives behind, but I don't think that's what's important to them. And anyway, he probably drinks and smokes or eats most of the gifts as he goes along. The rest he probably abandons or gives away, because he doesn't seem to carry much with him except a small sack and his hammock.

I should add that the curandero doesn't have any fixed ideas about what to eat, drink or smoke. He gladly accepts what he is offered. He abstains from nothing. Well, nothing except judgment about other people and having material possessions. That's about it, as I understand it.

The neighbors who dislike the curandero shun him, talk about him behind his back, and spread terrible, defamatory rumors about him. "Did you know that he raped a woman?" "Did you know that he killed someone?" "I heard he is hoarding a great deal of money, have you heard that?" They don't even say hello to him when they pass him on the street. They don't mumble "Buenas" or even nod or smile or wave. This is rude. It's especially rude in Tulum, where manners require at the least a brief eye contact and a mumbled, "Buenos Dias," upon meeting anyone in the street. He doesn't seem to care about these affronts. He certainly doesn't appear to take offense at any of this mistreatment and he never responds to it.

Personally, I don't think any of the negative rumors about him is truthful. He freely wanders from place to place, and if he had done anything as awful as many of the rumors claim, by now the relatives or friends of the wronged party, or other freelancers, or even "concerned citizens" who might have had too much to drink, would have exacted their sudden, bloody, midnight revenge. The Federales would probably be a much smaller problem for him than outraged, alcohol fueled citizen vigilantes. And if he had tons of money, I doubt that he'd still be utterly shoeless, wearing his faded clothing, and shuttling from house to house, from yard to yard. There would have to be something, some tiny, almost imperceptible indication that he had just a little money socked away someplace. I know that doesn't rule out that he's filled a secret cave in the selva to the ceiling with crisp 500 peso notes, but that just doesn't seem very likely to me. After all, where would he get this fortune? Certainly not by extracting it from my neighbors, even a little bit at a time for many years. Yes, my neighbors give him a little money. But it sure isn't all that much. It cannot be that much because sadly my neighbors don't have that much to give.

My neighbors who consult with the curandero and unquestioningly follow his advice are constantly trying to enlist others to visit him, to solicit his views, to follow his advice, however strange it might be. It's as if they were proselytizing, as if they were Jehovah's Witnesses going persistently from door to soon to be slammed door. Something good happened for them, they claim, so they want to share their good fortune. And they go on missions to get others to consult with him. You can't say anything about your life to these people without being told that the only possible, good solution is to see him about it, that he's got the answer for you. Got heartburn from years of eating chilies and swilling Coke and eating Bimbos? See him. Got a toothache because you eat too much junk food and sugar and don't brush and it's rotting your teeth? See him. Feel depressed or listless or have undefined but troubling spiritual issues? See him. Want to be freed from sorcery, evil magic, a curse of bad luck, the evil eye, malo viento, or just plain, garden variety physical illness? See him. Unrequited love, unhappy marriage, sexual dysfunction, difficult in-laws, straying children? He's your man for the full spectrum of human complaints, they say. Their faith in him, however, tells you nothing. None of these people appears to be living in a perfect paradise or to be perfectly happy, or even to be close to those goals, so they're probably not great, living advertisements demonstrating the dramatic efficacy of his services. No matter. None of that, however obvious it might appear to outsiders, matters to any of them. The fact is that they wouldn't keep coming back to him if he weren't doing something for them. They'd try to find something else. Something that worked better. Evidently, they remain satisfied with what he does for them.

Their faith certainly doesn't come close to explaining why backpackers from halfway around the world are standing in my yard, touching me, waking me up, interrupting my dreams, disturbing the stories I was following and making notes on, searching for a man they've never met and don't know anything about. Yesterday, for example, there were two young people here with an Australian flag sewn on one of their gigantic, tall, red backpacks. No, I didn't talk to them. No, I didn't ask them where they were from. I just cannot believe that somebody has traveled 10,000 miles to stand in my yard and ask me about how to find the curandero.

No, the local "referrals" cannot explain this profusion of foreigners. So I suppose that before I go any further, I have to reveal something else. I don't want to mislead anyone. It galls me slightly to have to make these kinds of admissions repeatedly in the course of just beginning to tell you my story, but I will nevertheless, just for the sake of clarity. So I don't mislead anyone. I had a very minor, unintentional role in bringing some of these bothersome people to Tulum. I regret it, it wasn't really predictable, but it's nevertheless so. You might even find it funny. Especially if you're a charitable sort of person. Or are interested in unintended consequences.

About fifteen years ago, as Playa del Carmen, about 40 minutes north of here, was growing on tourism from a fishing village of 12,000 people to a thriving, bustling city of 100,000 or more, I was running out of money. In fact, I badly needed an immediate money transfusion. The funds I had brought with me when I first arrived were just about all gone. I needed some serious dollars to stay afloat. So I wrote a few travel pieces for US magazines and newspapers about the growth of Playa del Carmen, and what was then first being called "the Mayan Riviera." The Mayan Riviera is the Mexican Caribbean coast from south of Cancun to Tulum (the "Costa Maya" runs from south of Tulum to the Belize border). One particular piece was about a yoga resort on the Tulum beachfront, which was then called "Osho Oasis." And not being satisfied with talking glowingly only about the simple comfort of the resort, its beautiful setting, its gorgeous, wide beach, the centuries old practice of Yoga, the excellent teaching by world class yoga teachers, and this exotic and beautiful setting for a spa or retreat, I got a little carried away. This happens to me. Sometimes I restrain myself, sometimes not. It depends.

I took the creative liberty of adding a few things, what I would call "non-factual elements" to the story I was writing. To make it more exciting. I know what some people think about this kind of journalistic lapse. At the time I was aware of the potential ethical issue, but I admit that it didn't phase me in the least. Put another way, I needed the money. Badly.

Anyway, I invented that there were some indigenous Mayan healers in Tulum, and that they had achieved astounding and even miraculous results. They were very modest about their achievements, even secretive, but I personally had talked to them and to those they had healed of numerous miserable conditions, and those who were healed had nothing but extreme gratitude for the healers and praise for what they had accomplished by their traditional, Mayan practices. But that's not all. I couldn't leave it at that. No. I couldn't stop myself. This was too good not to fill out. So I expanded it. I made up a small interview with a curandero in which he refused to deny that he knew how to make himself invisible (I did not say he could "disappear," which is different) and that he had cured all kinds of dreadful, life threatening, chronic, wasting diseases. I didn't specifically mention HIV or cancer. I do see how some people thought I had, but I really didn't. Honestly. It was a hell of a story, even if I say so myself. It was just amazing. Literally.

I made this story up. It was not reportage, it wasn't the truth. I knew it was fiction that I was writing but I decided that I would nevertheless pass it off as fact. At the time, I didn't care whether there were actually indigenous healers or even creatures from another planet living in Tulum. I didn't really know who might be residing or visiting in Tulum. I just wanted to be paid well for the articles, and if I departed from strict writing ethics, whatever that might have meant, it was just fine with me if the check cleared. I repeat for the sake of clarity: I had no idea whether there were such people, and I certainly didn't know specifically who they might be. Because I hadn't really met them. Not yet, anyway. Not back then.

OK. I can sense your skepticism. You don't believe this. Then let me explain this a little bit more. Maybe that will help. I knew, given how Tulum is, that there might very well be such a person or persons living somewhere in or near town, but I didn't know then exactly who that person might be. I suspected there might be at least a couple of such persons. I did suspect that. But I'm lazy. I wasn't trying to search anybody out; I wasn't going to do actual research. No. It was a lot easier and more consistent with my habitual sloth to dream up the entire, astonishing story. My neighbor, a tiny Mayan woman about 85 years old, badly bent by osteoporosis, frail as a small bird, virtually toothless and about 3 feet tall, who gave me some herbs in a poultice to heal a bruise and infection was not who I was talking about. Her poultice, foul smelling as it was, worked like magic. It was astonishing. But that would have been insufficiently miraculous for the fabulous travel article I was intent on writing. And selling. Smelly poultices, however effective, aren't good, profitable journalism. Good, profitable journalism, as you've probably noticed on your own, has to be surprising. It has to exaggerate. Forget, if you will, whether it's true or not. That doesn't matter that much at all. This is obviously as true of print as it is of all other media.

I just took some anecdotes I had heard or maybe even dreamed up and expanded them a bit toward the otherworldly, toward the intriguing, the miraculous. And lo and behold, I had a story I could easily sell. And I did. It was accepted immediately for publication. Definitely. And I was well paid for it, which was the reason I wrote the story in the first place. Perfection on my part, I thought. That should have been the end of it, but it wasn't.

Apparently, because fiction is so much more in demand than fact, and because people aren't particularly adept at telling the difference between the two, or another possibility, they just don't care, many people who came to practice yoga on the Tulum beachfront went looking during their afternoons off for the famous curanderos of Tulum, hoping to find an exotic, powerful Mayan healer, who they supposed would be willing to spend time hanging out with them and answering their many questions. Talk about presumption. Look. At the time doing sun salutes and standing on your head and being devotedly vegetarian was not exactly common, mainstream behavior. And I hope I won't offend anyone if I say that I considered these people, these seekers, these yogis, naive optimists. In a word, gullible. Suckers, if you insist. So I made up a story I presumed they in particular would find extremely compelling. And, of course, they did. I admit all of that. If I did something that was wrong, and I emphasize the "if", I apologize for it.

But there's also definitely a limit to my responsibility. Think about it. Usually an article like this is around for a month or two at the longest and then it disappears from the face of the planet. People, of course, go on to something else, unless they are in a medical or dental waiting room or some other archive. So I couldn't really anticipate that the article, which was extremely favorable to the resort and to Tulum, would be duplicated by the resort and by several others in that tourist area, namely, the many small resorts all the way down the Boca Paila Road to Si'an Kaan, and handed out gratis to hundreds and hundreds of patrons for several years. Or that the article, and the false assertions in it would find its way past legendary fact checkers, past wise editors, past basic common sense and into major United States newspapers and magazines, which would mindlessly repeat each others' reported, but thoroughly unscrutinized "facts", and refer to each other, if they ever had to, which is questionable, as "sources". And, of course, I had no idea that later on, the same baloney would be repeated over and over and over again without attribution or credit on the Internet. Someone who researches Tulum on the Internet now is sure immediately to find, in addition to advertisements of spectacular places to get married in Mayan ceremonies and beaches to die for, anecdotes about these amazing, but entirely invented curanderos. And even photographs purporting to be of them. And of ceremonial limpias. And of ceremonial offerings. There are even videos of interviews with curanderos on Youtube. And let's not even think about what's on the blogs. If anybody ever read the article and raised a question about its authenticity, I'd be really surprised. I don't think that ever happened.

Tulum was and is quite small. Seekers came into town and asked shopkeepers on the main Ginza about the curanderos. Who else could they ask? Tourists don't usually explore more than one block from the main street into the actual town. They don't talk to people who are not selling something. Most of the shopkeepers refused to answer questions in foreign languages, or said they didn't know, or simply shrugged.

Some, however, and I have some very definite ideas of who these were, acknowledged knowing a person who seemed to fit the description of what the yoga students were seeking. And so the yogis, in addition to be given what was referred to as a "really good price" on whatever they were looking at, were told maybe they should try to seek out my neighbor, which they, of course, dutifully and hopefully did. The point is that they were curious, even hopeful, but they didn't really know what they were looking for and they certainly didn't know what they had found after they found him.

My neighbor was initially surprised when gringos—as far as he's concerned, everyone who isn't 100% Mayan and from Tulum or the interior is one—began to seek him out. After all, he wasn't the author of the public relations campaign, and he had done nothing to encourage it or to commission any other advertisement of himself to the outside world. He was content enough doing just what he had been doing all along. The people from far away were, he felt, just a nuisance that was somehow being visited on him as a result of Tulum's growth or because of other unseen influences he could easily track down and eliminate if he really wished to. He apparently believes that nothing happens by accident, so if he was suddenly having visitations from brigades of backpackers, there was a discernible reason for that. The reason, the cause for these visits, I think he suspected, might have something to do with me. And my laziness and my incapacity for telling the truth. He never confronted me about this directly. That's not how he does things. But I wouldn't be so silly as to claim that he didn't know full well what I had done and why I had done it. And that I had a role in creating this unusual series of what he would probably consider home invasions, if he had a home.

Apparently, he wasn't all that interested in multiculturalism or the New Age. And he wasn't talking about the Mayan Calendar, Harmonic Convergence, or the significance of the year 2012 and the End of Time with these people. After the first few people, who were initially quite a novelty to him, he realized that he didn't want to deal with any more of them. Ever. They all looked to him to be doing quite well, thank you. They were all quite healthy, extremely prosperous in comparison to people living in Tulum, amazingly kind and, also, very, very time consuming. They looked at him with a respect he considered akin to idolatrous. He, he would later admit, though not in these words, recognized that he didn't have previous experience with the complicated neuroses and obsessive introspections of post industrialized, First World, information societies. The "issues" these people had weren't at all what he was used to. In fact, he wished that Mayans living in Tulum could trade in all of their generational, historical, persistent, vexing problems for some of these great, new, improved "issues." That, he thought, would be akin to dancing beneath the Original Yax-che Tree, the Mayan version of the afterlife Paradise. Put another way, these First World neuroses would be an absolute delight and a complete gift and a supremely wonderful blessing for most of his clientele. Evidently, he thought, one society's neurosis could be another's blessing. If only it could be so. If only such a trade could actually be carried out. Even if just briefly.

The visitors could have been an opportunity for him to make money, if he had wanted that. But of course, he didn't.

And he apparently didn't care about fame either. He didn't want to get into the international guru or lecture circuit businesses, the other, nascent opportunities these people presented. Evidently, he didn't want to be famous. He didn't want to be on Oprah. He didn't know who she was. To be truthful, he had no idea that there were such things in the outside world as celebrity gurus and teachers. He was entirely content living just in his body, moving his hammock around, and serving his community in his own way as he had before. However, something had to be done, he felt, to turn off whatever faucet was bringing him this flood of time consuming visitors.

He didn't know exactly what to do. Maybe he could refuse to see the visitors. He decided at first just to tell them he couldn't or wouldn't help them. But that failed miserably. In fact, this made the situation even worse. A blonde, blue eyed, very tall couple from somewhere in Germany sat patiently for a week living out of their backpack on the hot, dusty curb in front of a lot where he had hung his hammock. They repeatedly begged him in Teutonic Spanish to speak with them. They had some questions about "entities" that they suspected had attached themselves to them, and about events of some kind that might be transpiring in their Underworlds. He couldn't get them to leave. No matter what he said. They thought his refusals were just part of an esoteric ritual of some kind, that he had to refuse to talk with them for a long time, and they were, of course, obliged to persist, no matter what, to show their devotion until he ultimately relented. This, they heard, was a tactic that had worked well with reluctant gurus in India, so why, they wondered wouldn't it work here as well? An obvious answer to this question might have been that Tulum is not India and that this curandero had no intention of being anyone's guru.

Once when he heard a news story about a guru who owned hundreds of Rolls Royces, he asked me what a guru was. I suspected he thought it was some kind of luxury car salesman. I told him it was a revered teacher, a teacher with a lot of followers, with devotees. Devotees, I explained, followed what their guru thought was a path that led to enlightenment. "Oh, hum," he said. Then he wanted to know how it came about that someone attracted so very many people to follow him. Those words didn't make sense to him. I couldn't satisfactorily explain it to him. Why, he wanted to know, would anybody need or want more than two, at the most three helpers?

Eventually, when their hovering like gnats became intolerable to him and their living on the curb was bothering him, he spoke with the Teutonic Invaders just so they would go away. It took a very long time to convince them that all was well in their Underworlds, that there was no problem with "entities", that none had attached themselves to either of them, and just to please go away. He obviously needed a better, more effective strategy for dealing with those he considered intruders.

It was about this time that I broke out in yet another rash in my crotch. I'm not telling you this to be lurid or sensational. It was red and itched like crazy. And it burned. I have no idea where this pestilent body invader came from or why. Or even what kind of invader, vegetable or micro-animal, it was. Yes, I had had it before. Yes, it had gone away before. Yes, I had previously taken all kinds of remedies, both indigenous, as you might call them, and prescription. And they had worked. But obviously, not permanently. The scourge had returned. This time, I tried all of the usual plants. I listened again to all of the old, Mayan plant ladies in town and all of their suggestions about bathing it in rosemary tea and then putting juice from the leaves of the purple maguey plant on it as a salve. That didn't work. This time nothing worked. Nothing at all. Sitting in the Caribbean, exposing it directly to the sun, something that had worked before, only made it burn. And made it angrier. And then, when it dried, it chafed and it itched even more. It was making me very uncomfortable and quite crazy and very short tempered and quite upset and desperate and irritable. It was giving me a torrent of negative adjectives. So, having nothing to lose and a galaxy to gain, I thought I would pay my neighbor a timely, professional visit.

Before this visit we had a passing, nodding acquaintance. I said hello to him; he responded. We nodded Buenas at each other. Even though we lived so close to each other, we didn't have much more contact than that. He traveled in the circles of a Mayan curandero; I was an American expat, one with obviously shady dealings in his past. These two circles don't really intersect in Tulum. They may rub shoulders, they may share with each other, but they don't really connect in Tulum or elsewhere in Latin America. In the rarest of cases, when they do connect, it usually has something to do with making money or violating the law or both. But at least we knew who each other was, and we both were curious about each other. After all, we had both been hanging around the same neighborhood for quite a long time.

When I went to see him, I noticed that there was a 11-year old kid who was running errands for him. The kid, who was wearing a red and white striped Toluca futbol t-shirt and playing with a handful of stones, said he'd talk to me soon, that I should wait there. The kid then ran and got him. I didn't really have to wait. I wondered briefly whether the kid might be the real curandero, and the older guy just a prop, but I didn't get far with this distraction. He arrived instantly.

He came to the front of the house quickly. He was about 5' 4" tall and very thin. His hair was long and graying. I'm not sure how old he was; he was somewhere between 40 and 70. He was wearing faded khaki pants and a t-shirt that said something on it about Christmas at Posada Margherita, a wonderful restaurant on the beach front, and flip flops. He had a gold tooth. The veins on his hands were prominent. "Can I help you?" he asked.

I showed him my sarpudilla. He said something like, "Oh ahum." Then he delighted in cleaning the area with alcohol. He gave me no warning. At first, I was lying face up on a cot on top of a blanket. Then I flew to the ceiling. While I was hovering in the air, shaking all over, with my chest pressed against the hot light fixture on the ceiling, my body covered me in a thick, sticky sweat. A sweat like honey. Then gravity took over again. I fell to the blanket where I was freezing and shaking and moaning. He gently put a salve on me and told me, when I stopped moaning and I could again breathe easily, to go home. I admit that it immediately did feel a little better. Maybe the feelings of relief were just the contrast with the alcohol burn. I certainly didn't know.

As I was leaving, I asked him, "How much should I pay you." It seemed a natural enough question to me.

He said, "I didn't do anything. Nothing."

This to my vestigial gringo mind was clearly not correct. He had done something. The question was whether it would work. I didn't understand.

"No," I insisted. "In the US the doctor gets paid even when the patient dies. How much should I pay you?"

"You're not going to die," he said. "Is that true about the US? That's quite crazy. You pay nothing."

He had a point. I gave him some money for at least trying. We shook hands. I was surprised at how thin and small his hands were. I walked into the sunlight. I privately hoped he had somehow healed me, but maybe his remark was his way of telling me that he didn't think he had. I banished these negative thoughts of failure from my mind and walked home on a cushion of sweet, but still quite tentative relief.

Later that evening, when I was still not itching, I began to think I might have paid him inadequately. What, I wondered, would be an adequate payment for the person who brought me such wonderful relief? I went out and bought him a very good, small bottle of crystal clear, 100% blue agave tequila as a measure of my belated but heartfelt gratitude.

It was then dark outside. There was dim light from a street lamp across the street. I found him sitting on a tire in a vacant lot eating tortillas. He brought out two plastic cups. I sat down on an adjoining tire. We split the bottle in half down the middle, threw the empty into a rusted trash can at the back of the lot. My neighbor held up his finger, to stop, to wait for a second. He then stood up, took his cup and poured some of the tequila on the ground. He said something in Mayan. He then held the cup up to the sky and said something else. "Good," he said. He sat down. Then we drank to health.

Before I could bring the cup to my lips, we had company.

I was surprised by this. It was October, for goodness sake. The tourist off-season in Tulum runs from August to late November because of the possibility of hurricanes and because most children in the Northern Hemisphere are in school or getting ready for it in those months. Nobody wants to arrive for a visit only to be told by police or the army that they have to fly home immediately or go to a shelter in a school gymnasium and that these, amigo, are the only two options.

October, I think, is the most beautiful time in Tulum, it's hot, it's humid, there are gorgeous, heavy thunderstorms, and things are incredibly quiet. In October I don't really expect to see any tourists in the back streets of Tulum, but there he was.

"Are you the curandero?" It was a skinny kid with two, left eyebrow piercings wearing a red Che Guevara t-shirt. Maybe he was 25 years old. His Spanish revealed that he came from Memphis or Wichita or some other benighted, twangy, gringo place; the interruption, that he had no manners and no respect for his indigenous or imported elders, who were trying to have a peaceful, quiet drink and a conversation.

My neighbor, who I now realize had been drinking for quite some time before I arrived with my gift and was already perceptibly intoxicated, said to me under his breath, "I have a great idea." He slurred the words, and he unleashed a crooked smile. His gold tooth shone. He tilted his head to the left.

He stared at the kid. "What can I do for you, amigo?"

"Well, I heard you were powerful. I want to know if you would help me and use your power for me. I have a relationship issue."

"A what?"

"A relationship issue."

"I don't know what that might be. But it doesn't really matter what you might choose to call it. As you can see, I'm very busy right now. Very busy. I don't have time to talk right now. Please come back here tomorrow morning early, 5 am. And when you return, I need you to tell me precisely what you are most afraid of in the world. The biggest one thing, at the very most two things like that. And bring me one or two small stones, also. Two stones about this big." He showed his balled up fist. "Do you understand me? Bueno? Hasta manana."

To my surprise, there was no further discussion, no negotiating. No questioning. No explaining. The kid immediately left and wandered off down the street. "It worked," he said. "It worked." The curandero smiled a drunken smile. "I have such a good idea." We toasted again. We clicked the plastic cups, some of his drink got spilled. My neighbor continued to smile anyway. "I have such a good idea," he told me again. He smiled. His gold tooth sparkled.

I didn't stick around until 5 am to see what would happen next. I couldn't. I was tired. I went home and slept a deep, non-itching, somewhat Tequila sleep with vivid but crazy dreams in both English and Spanish. When I woke, and to my disappontment, I didn't remember any of the details of the dreams. I did remember that they were exhausting, convoluted, unrecoverable dreams. But that wasn't important. The salient fact is that I was not itching. There was no itch to be found. Anywhere. I waited for it to return. It was apparently gone. I had a very slight, dull, quite manageable headache. I appreciated starting the day with such a mild, kind headache. It was already a very good, very wonderful, very joyful day for me. A day beginning with utter relief. And no itching.

You might think I'm not a very good person to be commenting so negatively, so critically about others like the kid with the Che shirt, that I'm probably not very reliable, or maybe even that I'm again being dishonest. Or maybe just biased. Those points of view do have some applicability to me. I just want to tell my story, but like everyone else, there are, of course, times when I've been dishonest. If you weren't born earlier today, this shouldn't be much of a shock. In addition to the things I've already told you, I've done some other things in my life that if you knew about them, they might make you distrust me, and what I'm telling you. Or they might not. I probably should tell you what those things are. That way you can follow what I'm telling you and you'll understand why some things happened. And you can make up your own mind about whether you accept what I'm telling you. Or don't.

Before I came to Tulum, I was a hippie of sorts and profitably employed in the wholesale ganja trade. I drove a truck with some secret compartments from place to place. The truck looked like it belonged to a construction supply company, and it carried various tools and things. These were all props. I picked up a few hundred pounds of marijuana in one place and I delivered it to several other places. I was extremely careful. I then returned home with an empty truck and waited for a call telling me to make the next trip. I didn't touch the money, and I didn't arrange any of the deliveries. I didn't call anybody on the phone. I didn't even load the truck. Others did all those logistical things. I also had a straight job, a business, which paid me some money, but it too was essentially a prop. My part in the mid-70's, early-80's marijuana trade was something I actually liked, driving long ways on interstate highways, avoiding scales and traffic tickets, sleeping in motels, keeping under the speed limit, being alert and careful and observant, listening to the radio, playing music cassettes. Does it date me if I tell you that at one time I had an 8-track player in the truck? Or that I talked on the CB radio?

Because I liked my employment and was quite good at it, I continued it for many years, actually decades. This turned out, as I was always sure it would, to be a problem. Almost nobody, myself included, gets out of these enterprises soon enough. Almost nobody can pick up their chips, take them to the cashier, cash out, really retire, and never, never, never come back. Fake retirements abound, but that's just the same as taking a long break and then returning. That's like going on vacation. Real retirements are few and far between. In fact, I don't really know of any. Most people are doing their best imitation of Bret Fahvre, oscillating between being in the game and out of it.

Eventually, one of my suppliers who was much more involved than I was in what would shortly be labeled a large, federal, marijuana distribution conspiracy got arrested. These things roll down hill as if gravity applied. Somebody else who had been arrested, who was even more involved in weed than my supplier, a big shot in the trade, set him up in an effort to get leniency from the Feds. Of course, this guy only told the Feds about people less important and less guilty than him, but he made believe they were all bigger operators than he was. Telling on people who were more important or more powerful could be dangerous: it could be a problem when you were locked up, or it could be a problem for your family. Why do something like that? Why take chances? Why try to re-invent the wheel? You'd be amazed at the willful ignorance of law enforcement and their complicity in this. They don't seem to care about this. At all. At the time of his arrest, my supplier was holding tons of weed in a garage, a huge stack of folding money in a closet, and a few guns for good measure in his car and in the closet with the money. The Feds told him that he was on tape making deals in two different languages and that if he didn't quickly make a deal with them in their snitch language, he'd do 30 years and get some additional time on top for the guns. He was 40; he'd collect his social security in prison. If he survived that long.

After thinking deeply and meditating about the situation for about 3 nano seconds and then spending 45 minutes with his lawyer in a windowless back room at the courthouse making valedictory speeches about what a "stand up guy" he really was and how it pained him even to be asked to snitch on anyone at all, he conveniently decided to roll over on me and some other minor players like the guys who loaded my truck. And some but not all of the guys to whom I made deliveries. But, of course, not on anybody of equal or greater rank in the business. So much for stand up guys.

Snitching, as you probably understand, is not all that ethical in the first place. But it's extremely common. In fact, law enforcement depends on it. It is, after all, the cornerstone of the US War on Drugs. If you get caught, you have to snitch. You'll do less time. Won't snitch? There is virtually no way to limit your prison time. Nobody wants to do even one extra day of time. Even if that would be the honorable thing to do. Honor among thieves might exist. But among drug merchants, it turns out, it doesn't exist. This should not really be a huge surprise.

At the time of my supplier's initial misfortune, in fact, on the day of his arrest, I was on the road with a full truck. I was on the Interstate headed North, bound first for Chicago and then to the east coast and Boston. I got very lucky. My girlfriend received a phone call from the supplier's wife looking for him, she hadn't seen him in two days, was I around and did I know where he might be?

That evening I stopped at a Howard Johnson's Motel just off the Interstate and decided I'd call my girlfriend to see if she missed me yet. I don't know why I wanted to make this call. I'd only been on the road one day; my trips were commonplace; I didn't usually call home. Usually, I just didn't feel like calling in. This time I was just lucky. For some reason I decided to call. She told me about the call she'd received. I told her not to tell anybody where I was and that I would be home as soon as I could possibly get there. I left the truck filled with pot in the motel parking lot, got a cab to Hertz, rented a car, and zoomed back down the same Interstate highways I had just traveled, this time headed south toward home.

Maybe it's hard for you to understand why such a simple telephone call could be so cataclysmic. Lots of people in various illegal, contraband businesses don't really pay attention. I am not one of those people. I would rather lose the truck and its cargo than be arrested. I do not want to be told by a judge that I have been involved in the business for decades, that I have distributed tons and tons of pot, and that therefore I have to do a very long stretch in prison. I am totally unwilling to have that experience. So when I hear that something happened that really wasn't supposed to, I know something's gone very wrong, and I have to protect myself. And quickly. I am not going to overlook something that's important just to maintain my routine. I'm not going to spend a lot of time thinking about it. I am not big on ignoring the obvious or wishful thinking or making believe. Especially when my future is involved.

Lots of people in drug businesses spend every nickel they get. They buy flashy cars, expensive women, shiny jewelry, airplanes, Rolex watches, even beach houses. When they get caught, the Feds take it all. Then they bitch that the lawyers want tons of money for their defense and that they don't have it so they're going to have to end up in prison. This outcome should not be a big surprise to them. Virtually all these people would be locked up anyway, even if they had trucks full of dough to spend on their defense. Even if their lawyer were Houdini. Some of these people have put their profits up their noses. Others were just impulsive or stupid. None of them made contingency plans. None except me. It's not that I'm smarter. I just realized early on that I needed to hang onto some of the cash just in case there was an emergency. Actually, I considered the cash my defense fund. I wasn't any more proud to have it than you are to have homeowner's or car insurance.

As I was driving the rented Buick home in the dark, I had an epiphany. I realized that there was no earthly reason to give my $50,000 plus to a lawyer. Au contraire. That was a crazy idea. I hadn't been arrested. I was driving on the Interstate. I had a much better idea. The money would be better used to escape before I was arrested and to set me up somewhere else. If the Feds could put people in their witness protection program, I could put myself in my own potential defendant protection program. So I thought I'd just quickly get out of the country and disappear. The phone call I received, and leaving the truck and its cargo in the parking lot made it clear to everybody who needed to know it that my former occupation had definitely terminated.

I didn't know anything about extradition laws, and I didn't know anything really about Mexico, but I knew that I could probably figure it out once I got myself and my luggage to Cancun. No, I did not take my girlfriend. Or my dog. I chose Cancun because it was the first international flight leaving from my home airport and I was in a very big hurry to leave the States right away, right then, no intermediate stops. I could easily have ended up somewhere else. Cancun was the hand the fates, the airlines and I dealt myself.

Eventually, I found my way from the twin Cancuns, the tourist Cancun and the City Cancun, down narrow two-lane Highway 307 to Tulum. There were lots of menacing green plants growing right up to the side of the road, a single Pemex station near Puerto Morelos, and then the vast, inhospitable mangrove through and beyond Tulum. After I left, the Feds managed to take my car, the truck, the pot and my house. My dog moved in with the neighbors. My girlfriend went looking for another, younger gangster. I am sure it was easy for her to find one she would like. I moved into the little mango and papaya colored house with the tree with the purple flowers. The rent was unspeakably cheap, later I bought it. And I busied myself with reading and writing. What else was I going to do?

When you move into a place like Tulum, where you don't seem to belong, people are initially curious about you. They want to know where you came from and why you're there. I told everybody who asked that I was a writer, that I wrote stories for magazines and newspapers, that I wrote books. No, they probably hadn't read any of them because I wrote only in English and they hadn't been translated into Mayan. Or Spanish. I picked Tulum, I told them, because it is so quiet and so peaceful and I could be productive here. The idea of productivity in Tulum was a contradiction. They smiled at it, but they let it easily pass. They probably didn't believe me, but, nodding their heads and smiling politely, they said they too liked that, yes, it was really beautiful. After all, I was not the first, nor was I the last person to flee from something and end up in Tulum. It remains quite common. I put the cash in the mattress and under the floorboards and in the wall, I got some pencils and some pads at the papeleria on the main street, and later I got a computer. So I started out being a writer. As it turns out, I had always wanted to be a writer.

But, also, as it turns out, I have some definite problems as a writer. If you're observant, you may have noticed quite a few of these already. I'm sure you'll find more as I go along. That's entirely OK. The single thing that hurts a writer's feelings most, if I may give myself that title, that hurts my feelings the most is when a reader confesses to me, "Well, I didn't finish reading what you wrote. I stopped." Ouch. It is another matter entirely when a reader says that she read the entire thing but that it wasn't enjoyable. Or that she hated it. Or that I'm a jerk. Or that I'm arrogant. That I can live with. Easily. The best is when a reader sends me a note saying she liked what I wrote, she enjoyed it, it made her smile. Or cry. Or laugh. Or made her mad. That is an utter joy to behold. A treasure. That cannot happen often enough. I love it when that happens. And I have a sense of dread of filling line after line in a notebook with prose that will be read by no one, or worse, having been only partially read, will evoke resounding silence. Or utter indifference.

Before I got to Tulum, I wasn't entirely sure I could really differentiate between what's fact and what's fiction. Being in Tulum doesn't seem to help me with this problem. In fact, being in Tulum tends to merge fact and fiction so that one is virtually indistinguishable from the other. It's as if you blurred a charcoal drawing by rubbing it with your thumb. Or immersed it in water. The boundaries, the borders get very fuzzy and bleed into each other. Sureness about what's real and what isn't just takes an incredible beating.

Examples abound. During the War of the Castes in the 1840's, certain crosses in Chan Santa Cruz started talking to the Mayans, urging them to continue fighting for independence against Mexico. Some Mayans believed then and believe to this day that these crosses actually spoke out in Mayan throughout that period of time. Others, including particularly some historians who don't seem to be Mayan, insist that the talking crosses were actually a parlor trick: a Mayan priest and ventriloquist, Manual Nahuat, they claim spoke lines dictated to him by Jose Maria Berrera, a Mayan rebel leader. Regardless, symbolic crosses in groups of three, to remind of the talking ones, were placed in churches in many Mayan villages, including Tulum, and the war continued for 65 more years. I prefer to think, as many of my neighbors do, that it is a fact that the crosses actually talked. That this was a miracle or a mystery.

Another example: apparently, fighting in inhospitable mangroves against people who knew what they were doing wasn't all that easy for the Mexican central government, and in a moment that must have foreshadowed the fall of Saigon in 1975, the Mexican army finally quit the War in 1915. The Mexican army simply withdrew after 70 years of fighting. The Cruzob Mayans, the ones who believed in the talking crosses, ran this town for two more decades, until 1935. Then, in 1935 the Mayans held a ceremony in Tulum in which they recognized the central Mexican government. The ceremony was briefly reported in the *New York Times*. It reported that the war was officially over. The story was one inch long and was buried deep on an inside page.

The three crosses still remain in the Mayan churches, including the one in Tulum. Some of my neighbors believe without a doubt that the Mayans are destined to take over the town and the rest of the Yucatan peninsula. Again. They don't say when they expect this to happen. I didn't make any of this story up.

Another example: the subject of the limestone. The fresh water around Tulum comes from rain and from underground rivers and cenotes. Some of my neighbors assert that all Mayans are short because there is limestone in the water they drink as infants and that this impedes the growth of their bones. I have no idea whether this is true. I don't have the slightest idea how to find out. I've never met a Mayan who is six feet tall. I have no idea why the Mayans have a "reason" for being short and powerful that is neither genetics nor nutrition. I have no idea what the "facts" are about this.

Which brings me back to the curandero. My neighbor is almost 5 feet 4 inches tall, greying, very thin and square shaped. I don't know how old he is. I think he's in his 50's or 60's, but he could be older. Or younger. His black, long hair has some grey in it, but not a lot. He has a single gold tooth in the middle of his smile. He does not like to wear shoes, though he does wear a baseball cap, and the clothing he wears is always worn out and faded. He does not, apparently, want any new things; he wears his clothing until it falls apart and then replaces it with something else that is already on its last legs. He does not care what his frayed t-shirts may say on them. In other words, he's quite ordinary. And quite invisible. There is nothing obvious about him that identifies him as a curandero. Nor is there anything I see that differentiates him in appearance from so many other people living and working in Tulum. Except the number of people who come to find him and meet with him.

When people arrive to see him—there are no appointments—they are greeted first by the boy who always seems to be with him and runs his errands. The Kid, or as I call him, "El Kid," interrupts whatever games he might be playing with sticks or plants or stones to announce that another client has arrived. He always returns to tell the client that it will be soon. Sometimes soon is a minute, sometimes a few hours. No matter. It's soon. The people who want to be seen always wait patiently, whatever ails them. Some squat; others sit in a chair if there is a vacant one. Some check in and leave to return later on. If you want to be seen, you have to see El Kid, and then you have to wait. The lack of appointments or keeping to a schedule is not a concern. If you want to be seen, you'll eventually be seen. The curandero does not run on Eastern Standard Time. He does not work 8-hour days. If he has a schedule, it has not been announced.

A few days after the modest celebration of my having lost my sarpudilla, I saw El Kid in town. He was alone. I was surveying the cigars in the glass cabinet at Super Mar Caribe, the original supermercado on the main street. This locked cabinet is not a real humidor. Maybe it relies upon natural, central humidity. More likely, the ownership does not want its cigars to walk off without payment: there were several kinds of expensive Cuban cigars that were obviously for the tourists. They seemed oddly out of place. I saw El Kid standing at the end of the check-out line to bag groceries. I asked whether the few tourists—nobody else would be shopping at 1 pm in October because it was way too hot for shopping—understood that they are supposed to tip a few of the smallest coins, just a couple of pesos for this service, one that is probably expected to be received gratis in many gringo places. He rolled his eyes at my question and shrugged. I understood this to mean that the custom was observed too infrequently by gringos, but that he remained hopeful. I should note before passing on, that the poorest, Mayan patrons are religious about giving this small propina, this gratuity.

While I was musing about the tipping practices of the rich and poor, El Kid turned and to my surprise began to talk to the guy with the two, left eyebrow piercings who had just arrived out of the glaring sunlight. The guy was still wearing the same red Che Guevara t-shirt.

Maybe you can understand my curiosity about their conversation. I just wanted to know what had happened. I admit it, I love to eavesdrop. I decided I'd just stand there and listen in. Why not? How could it hurt anything?

"Did you do what he said?" El Kid asked as he folded a plastic bag.

"Well, I tried."

"Well, you're not supposed to see Don Obdulio again until you've done what he said. That's his rule. So you cannot see him until then. Until you've done it, whatever he told you to do. I'm sorry." El Kid was quite matter of fact about all of this, and he was not at all perturbed. He was just being factual, just stating the well acknowledged rules. Just saying exactly what he had been told to say. Nothing more. Nothing less. Just the facts, Sir.

"Maybe I could talk to him and explain to him what happened to me so that I couldn't do it, that might change things," the guy continued. But El Kid stood his ground and restated in the same courteous, mild tone, "No, I'm sorry, not until you do exactly what he said can you see him again. It's a rule he has for himself. He's very strict about this. Very strict. He makes no exceptions. He won't see you a second time unless you did what he told you to do."

At this, the guy with the piercings stopped talking, frowned, turned on his heals, and walked slowly out of the store. He stopped on the glaring, sun drenched sidewalk and turned to face El Kid again, as if he had something more to say, but El Kid was attending to putting a customer's six pack of beer into an unneeded plastic bag in yet another effort to get a 2 peso tip and couldn't see him.

I was more interested in this story than the cigars, most of which were Mexican, made by Te Amo. To me, on that day even these more modest cigars seemed excessively expensive for what they were, so I strolled up to the guy. He was still standing on the sidewalk in direct, searing sun. He was sweating. His face was red and sun burnt and he had mosquito bites. "Remember me?" I asked in English. "I was with Don Obdulio when you first met him."

"I don't recognize you."

"But I recognize you. It's probably none of my business," I began, "But I'd really like to know what happened that morning when you came back to Don Obdulio's. It was way before my usual wake up time. I like to wait until the sun comes up before going out. So I wasn't there when you returned."

"I'm not really supposed to talk about this. He told me not to talk about this at all. Ever. To anybody. I don't know if it's right for me to talk with you about it, even if you say you're a friend of his," he said. "I really shouldn't."

Of course, I know what to do when I'm confronted with these kinds of obstacles, issues of confidentiality, issues of supposed morality, issues about keeping agreements, ethics. So I offered him a small, hopefully adequate bribe. OK, I understood completely, but could we sit down in a shady, cool place I know, and I'd buy him a cold Sandia or Fresa flavored paleta (a watermelon or strawberry flavored ice pop) in exchange for his telling me the story of what happened? He, I'm sure, would find this local treat quite refreshing on such a hot, humid day. After all, he didn't have any important, pressing places he had to go right then, at that very moment, did he? It was too hot for that, wasn't it really?

Actually, by Tulum standards the day wasn't all that hot. Most October afternoons the town is broiling, extremely humid, and full of glare. Brits call the heat ghastly. The usual midday weather is a harsh mix of squinting and sweating. The main street has only a few small trees, which make virtually no shade, the four lanes of roadway are a skillet, and the buildings block any breeze from the sea and squash it like a bug. Sane people, I consider myself one of these, do not usually visit the main street during the traditional siesta hours. Especially in October. My plan, before I got diverted from it by my curiosity and eavesdropping, was ever so quickly to slip into the air conditioned store, quickly buy a cheap, suave cigar, immediately return home, drink a very cold beer rapidly and pass the afternoon in the shade under my tree contemplating in half sleep all of the myriad things for which I have feelings of gratitude, dreaming, harvesting the available stories, wondering about eternal questions. And their forever elusive answers.

Fortunately, my bribe was sufficient, so after perusing the forty different kinds of available pops—there was a remarkable one for 30 pesos with chocolate shavings and Cocoa Crispies on the outside and strawberry ice cream and actual strawberries on the inside—we sat in the rear of the Paleteria Michoacan under the fluorescent lights and a large fan. The front of the store is just a wide opening on the street. The table was yellow Formica and the chairs were white plastic. A telenovella, I'm not sure which one, was playing. It wasn't *Peregrina*, which is set in Playa del Carmen. None of the characters was rich enough for that. It was playing with intense emotion on a television at the back of the room with no audience except occasionally the two women who worked the counter. There were two people at the next table, who I think, judging from their clothing and manner were Italian. They were slowly slurping down some smoothies, smoking cigarettes, and talking quietly, their faces revealing that they were still newly sunburned and nursing the slightest tequila hangovers they may have acquired last night. Probably they arrived yesterday.

"At first I didn't know anything about Don Obdulio, but then I thought that he might help me get back with my girlfriend. I mean, she doesn't want to be with me right now, we're broken up for about three weeks, but I really want to be back with her. Anyway, some guys

I smoked a joint with the other night on the beach told me they heard there was a really powerful and incredible shaman, so I thought it couldn't hurt to stop off and see if the shaman might be able to help me out. I mean, I'd like to get back with her. That would be really so great. I would really like that. The guys said I should try it, and wouldn't it be really something special if he cast a spell or did some secret magic that made her actually want to be back with me? Like maybe he had some kind of special love potion or something like that for me?

"He was really pretty easy to find. I just asked everybody where he was, and they gave me directions to where to find him. I was shocked at how he looked, I mean, he was so small and, well, nondescript. He was so ordinary looking. At first, based on how he looked, I didn't believe he could do anything. Maybe those guys were actually putting me on, sending me on a wild goose chase. Anyway, he told me to go away, which wasn't a huge surprise, and to come back early the next day.

"I had to figure out what I was most afraid of and tell that to him. And bring him two stones. All of that was pretty easy. I'm afraid of extreme heights. I'm also afraid of drowning. More the heights. Maybe there are other things I'm afraid of, but that's what came to mind first. So I told him I was afraid of heights when I went back to see him early that morning. I didn't sleep much before I got there. I mean, I didn't really sleep at all. I was worrying about why he wanted to know what I was most afraid of. I mean, what's that got to do with getting back with my girlfriend? It seemed really strange. And scary. But what do I know about how he works? Or what he does?

"I arrived at the place with the tires, I guess it's where he was living, though I didn't see a house or anything, and I told him I was afraid of heights. He got this weird smile then and said I should wait a minute. He walked away. After a few minutes, at first I thought he wasn't coming back and I was just wasting my time and waiting for nothing, being really stupid at 5 am. Then he did come back, only from the other direction. He told me about a deep cenote in the interior. He wanted me to go there and jump from the top of it into the water. It sounded too simple, and also pretty scary. It sounded like something some people might actually like to do. Not me, though. It didn't sound at all like something I'd like. I was pretty sure I didn't want to do it.

"I told him I just couldn't do it. That it was crazy. I told him more than fifty feet was too much of a jump from the top into the water, and

I'd probably get hurt and drown if I was crazy enough to jump in the first place. And, I told him, there was probably nobody there, so if I got hurt, there wouldn't be anybody to help me get out. Or to go and get help. I told him it sounded like somebody could die doing this.

"He got this incredible grin on his face. He said, 'You wanted my help. I'm giving you my help. Just go and do exactly what I told you to do. Throw the two rocks into the cenote first. And when you hear the splash from the second one, you jump in right after them. Then come back and see me and I'll tell you what's next. But do not come back to me if you don't do what I'm telling you to do. Really. Do you understand me?'

"Then he stood up and walked off. It was still really early in the morning. It had to be 5:30 or so. No later. The sky was just starting to get a little purple color at the horizon. I was sleepy and tired and I didn't want to find the cenote and I definitely didn't want to take this jump he was talking about. Anyway, I didn't know what else to do, it's not like I have to work or have some place I have to go, so I figured I should at least go and find the cenote in the jungle to see what might be involved in doing what he said. I could go, I thought, and just check it out, just look and see what it was like to do this.

"A friend of mine had rented a car at the airport when he arrived. He was staying at a place on the beach, so I wandered over there to see if I could borrow the car from him. One thing leads to another, and as you know, everything takes incredibly long here, so I finally got the car at about 1 in the afternoon. I thought I'd drive out to the cenote. My friend had no interest in this trip: it was really hot, he just wanted to hang out on the beach, swim, drink beer, and smoke some joints. I told him I'd get the car back to him by 5 or 6. So I ended up going alone.

"It was unbelievably hot in the car even with the air conditioning on. The sun was really intense. At first I had some trouble finding the road to the cenote. A few miles north of town, there was a narrow road from the main highway left into the jungle. It didn't have a sign, but it was across from a cement memorial, the kind to somebody who had died on the road, a little cement house with a statue of the Virgin of Guadeloupe and some plastic flowers in it. I passed this spot about 4 times going back and forth before I realized that this was the road I was supposed to get on. It was not much of a road. There was no sign for it. It didn't look like very many people went on it.

"It was really narrow. It had deep furrows and a high center. I had to drive very slowly on it. I didn't want to rip the bottom out of the car. The branches on the trees and plants scraped the side of the car as I drove. I was worried they would scratch the paint. It was muddy in some low places and deep, dry sand in others. I worried about getting stuck in mud or in sand if I went too slow. Or too fast. There was no place to turn around or to pull off. Or to stop. I started to think I shouldn't have tried to drive this car up this road, but there was no place to stop without getting stuck so I kept going. I drove for about 45 minutes or an hour. I don't really know how far I drove or for how long. It was a long, long way. I saw nobody. There was just jungle the whole way. The road was really bad. I was afraid the car would overheat, or I'd get stuck, or, worse, somebody would come toward me in a truck and we'd get stuck facing each other and nobody would be able to turn around. I was getting really nervous and stressed out and sweating the farther I drove.

"Eventually, there was a big downed tree across the road, blocking it, so I turned the car around and parked it. Turning it around was almost impossible: I must have gone back and forth 25 or 30 times, angling slightly each time. My arms ached from twisting the wheel side to side so many times. I was ringing wet. The air conditioner wasn't doing anything. Then I climbed over the tree and I started walking up the road.

"The mosquitoes immediately found me and ate me alive. I got dozens of bites on my arms, neck, legs, face. Look. You can still see how many I have. They all itch. They ate me alive. I hope I didn't get dengue or malaria or something.

"Anyway, eventually, after I don't know how long a walk, I finally came to the cenote. The road stopped just feet from it. It was next to a huge ceiba tree with big spikes on its bark.

"The cenote's opening was maybe 30 or 40 feet across, and you could see that there was clear water down about 50 or 60 feet or so. Way down below. I lay down on my chest so I could put my face over the edge and look into the hole. I could see the bottom of the pool, the rocks and all, the water was very clear and clean. I don't know how deep the water was. But there was no rope or ladder to get out if you fell or jumped in. I guess to get out you'd have to climb up using some of the roots from the trees that were sticking out of the walls. Or you'd need to have a rope. Something like that. I had no idea whether anybody could actually climb up the walls on the roots. You'd have to be really strong, I mean in your upper body, and I wasn't sure you could even reach high enough up the walls to get to any of the roots if you were down in the bottom in the water floating or swimming around. And I couldn't tell whether you'd actually be able to climb all the way out even if you ever got to the roots to hold on to them. There were clouds of mosquitoes hovering inside the hole, they were buzzing. It was definitely not a good idea for anybody to jump in. Including me.

"Once I saw it and had a chance to think about it, I realized that there was just no way that I was going to drop my stones in and jump into this cenote. It was completely crazy. It was really deep and there was no way out from the bottom. There was nobody around. It was boiling hot, and the mosquitoes were fierce. I thought about it for a few minutes, about whether I would do it. I had driven so far. It had been hard to find the cenote. Maybe it could be done safely. Probably not. I really didn't want to jump. I decided I definitely shouldn't. It was way too dangerous. Then I walked back to the car and left. I felt really bad about this, I mean not jumping and all, but there was just no way I was going to do it. It was way too dangerous. For some reason I felt very bad about it, that I couldn't do it, couldn't do what he said to do. But there was just no way."

I found myself first nodding at this story and then shaking my head. The curandero really had figured it out how to deal with these outsiders: he'd get rid of these pesky seekers one at a time because he'd pick a task they just wouldn't do. Or he'd pick a task like this one that might kill them off one by one. I didn't ask the kid how long he thought he could tread water. I doubt Don Obdulio did the same thing with the local people, but he was definitely right, he did have a great idea to stop the invasion of gringo travelers from returning and bothering him. It seemed a particularly effective idea, because the travelers probably would never make a precarious jump. Or do any of the other dangerous things he would invent for them and then ask them to do as a precondition to talking with him again.

I asked, "What are you going to do now?"

He shrugged, frowned, thanked me for the paleta, and walked out into the bright sunlight rubbing his sticky hands with a shredded, wad of paper napkin. I had the idea that he would never come back. Maybe, I thought, he'll try it again. No, I decided. He definitely won't. I decided to skip the cigar and go straight home.

I sat under the flowering tree with a cold beer bottle in my hand, and to my surprise, I saw a bird on the ground near the cement wall. It was unable to fly. When I approached it, it tried to get away, it flapped its right wing awkwardly, and fell pathetically and defenselessly on its side. Then it tried desperately to scramble away from me. It wasn't able to. Its wing was broken. It had a greenish tint to its ruffled neck and was otherwise plain brown. I don't know what kind of bird it was. I imagined because its body was so ordinary and its color was so dull that there must be compensation, that it must be one of those birds with a beautiful, melodic, heartrending song. Maybe this is what the bird looks like that sings the Ornette Coleman song. I left it alone, hoping that maybe it would regain its strength, or it would be rescued by its mother, or it would somehow fly or walk away. I hoped that the neighborhood dogs wouldn't find it. Or the lizards. I would keep an eye on it. I wouldn't let anything bad happen to it. I could protect it. But I didn't know what I could do that would actually help it.

I wondered whether it had fallen from its nest in the wind or had been hit by a swaying branch in mid flight. I wondered about hope. "Hope is the thing with feathers, that perches in the soul, and sings the tune without words, and never stops at all." I fell asleep in the heat in my white plastic chair. I don't know how long I slept.

Some time later, I saw that the bird had died. It lay on the sand. It didn't move when I touched it. It was still warm, soft, almost weightless, shiny and motionless not far from where I first saw it. I buried it in my yard. It didn't need a very big hole. I didn't give it much of a send off. No eulogy. I just asked for it to rest in peace.

I wondered what this meant, if this inexplicable, silent death and burial might be a coded message of some kind. But I had no idea what it could mean or who would have sent it or even if it were addressed to me. I didn't think any more about the poem. Or why I was thinking about that particular poem. I didn't know what the message might be. I felt a grim sadness. I felt it in the depths of my stomach.

When it got dark, I was still thinking about the kid with the Che Guevara shirt and the bird. Did they have something to do with each other? I didn't know how they could be connected or why I thought they might be. Also, to be truthful, I still didn't feel so great. I felt sad, anxious, disturbed, uneasy, slightly sick. I didn't know what was the matter, but something definitely was. I decided I needed to change the subject. So I thought I'd go out. I had a strange thought given the circumstances: I would like to have a pizza.

My favorite pizza was at La Nave, a hole in the wall on the main drag run by Italians. Italians were slowly and quietly colonizing Quintana Roo. Quintana Roo had been colonized overtly and violently by Spaniards about five hundred years ago. The Spanish told the Mayans to give up their gods, stop human sacrifice and cannibalism, and become Christians and subjects of King Philip. And to turn over all their gold and silver. Or die. The Italians have a different, covert, probably much more effective strategy. They'd just arrive, open their businesses, the businesses would succeed, they'd raise their families, they'd speak Italian and Spanish, and they'd stay and thrive. They'd gradually turn Tulum into an Italian-Mayan town.

The pizza at La Nave was wonderful, thin crusted, delicious, cooked in a wood fired oven that made the place swelter, unless you sat on the main street and watched the never ending parade of people. That was a little cooler. In October, the town was not as crowded as it would be in high season: each person could be watched carefully. I enjoyed making up stories about each of them. Some appeared to me to be characters who had escaped from various novels or short stories, others had practiced various arts of nonconformist appearance in the hope that they could be in a novel or movie later on, some were auditioning for a role in a telenovela, and others were attempting to make themselves invisible by wearing the global, inconspicuous uniform: t-shirt, jeans, baseball cap.

My arrival at La Nave determined what language I would end up using for the rest of the evening. The staff and proprietor knew my face, but we weren't familiar enough that we had had revelatory discussions, which might acknowledge our origins. Sometimes they think I'm part of the occupying Italians, and they speak to me in that language. Maybe I look Italian to them. I have enough restaurant Italian to get by. Sometimes they think I'm a local and speak to me in Spanish. Maybe I look like I'm from Mexico City to them. I don't look Mayan. And if I'm with others who to their discerning eyes are dressed or act like gringos, they speak to me in English. Whatever language they choose, I respond without hesitation in that language. They are, thus, never wrong. And I make sure that once I begin, I don't slip or change languages.

Tonight they apparently thought I was a local. I ordered a pizza and a glass of red wine and settled in to watch the parade on the sidewalk.

After a few moments of enjoying the tattoo on the lower back, and the posterior of a young woman carrying a watermelon under her arm, and wondering where she was from and what she was doing there and where she might be going, there was a pat on my shoulder. I turned to find a smiling, fiftyish man wearing a pale yellow Hawaiian shirt, jeans, a ball cap, and a thick gold chain. He had salt and pepper hair and a droopy salt and pepper mustache. He was browned by the sun. And his eyes twinkled.

"Don't I know you?" he asked.

I wasn't sure whether I knew him. He spoke English. Maybe he was from the US, I wasn't sure. He had a very attractive, small, early thirty-ish woman with a navel piercing with him. I definitely didn't know her but I immediately wished I did.

"We used to work together, right?" he continued.

I still wasn't sure I knew him. "I'm really sorry," I said, "I just don't recognize you yet. Anyway, come have a seat, sit down, join me. We'll see if we can figure it out."

As he sat down, I immediately recognized him. From his smile. From his eyes. They hadn't changed in all those years. "You're from New Jersey, from Newark, right?"

He nodded.

"It's been quite a while. You're lucky: you look about the same. Only just a little bit older."

"And you look about the same. Also just slightly older. And much more tan. Much more. And a little thinner. I'm surprised to find you here."

There was, of course, an enormous question to be discussed after these pleasantries. I wanted to get it out of the way. I thought I'd just ask him about it immediately, "If it's not prying, tell me what happened to you."

He took a deep breath. "Probably I should have expected it, that I'd end up making license plates or breaking rocks and banging a tin cup on the bars like James Cagney, but frankly, I was surprised, shocked actually. I ended up doing a little more than 3 years for talking on the telephone. I pleaded to a telephone count, I didn't offer any assistance to them. Couldn't do that.

"Being inside wasn't good. But it also wasn't as bad as I initially expected. Some of the other guys were unusual, and almost all of them were white collar guys or like me, other drug business small fry. I played tennis occasionally, and I played goalkeeper when we played soccer. We did a lot of that. I tried to keep in shape. I had a job, if you can believe this, doing accounting, keeping track of the supplies. Kind of like Shawshank Redemption. Boring. Without the access to money or any of the abuse, thank God. Anyway, I got out years and years ago and I haven't seen any of the old guys in decades. None of them. I guess I'm living an entirely different life. Until now. And now I've stumbled on you. I know you got away in time, you were really quite lucky. Is this where you came? Or did you go someplace else first?"

I was amazed to see him. He was John Coltrane Ramirez, and I used to deliver to him in New Jersey. He had a warehouse in a nondescript, grimy corner of Newark, if that isn't redundant. He himself was a product of Newark and was always bragging about how Newark was America's true but unacknowledged literary capital, having given birth to the likes of Philip Roth, Stephen Crane, Allen Ginsburg, Sarah Vaughan and Jerry Lewis. He used to say that everybody in Newark was as tough as cockroaches and at the end of the world in nuclear winter only people born there would have the right genes and nurturing to be able to survive. If you looked at the city and believed in evolution, you could see why he could say that and mean it. But, most important, he was extremely discreet, and quite reliable. We had done business for more than a decade. He and the girl—her name turned out to be Mari Estrella, a moniker I immediately admired and doubted that it was really her birth name—were in Tulum, they said, because of the green turtles.

They too were ex pats. They lived on an odd-named island in the Southern Caribbean I had never heard of before. And they said they were in Tulum investigating ways to preserve the endangered green turtle throughout the Caribbean.

I didn't believe this for a second. If they said they were lovers on a holiday, or were fleeing an arrest warrant, or involved in some kind of fraudulent land development scheme, or money laundering, or something like that, I would have accepted that and congratulated Ramirez for his good fortune to be with anyone as stunning as her. That would have made much more sense to me than the preservation of turtle ecology. I know that may sound cynical, skeptical. I actually strongly support preservation of the turtles, but I just couldn't believe they were in town for that, to encourage ecology. Yes, things change. And maybe people do too. But I didn't believe it.

It is true that the green turtle, which nests on the Quintana Roo coast and many beaches around Tulum, is endangered. And local people have done what they can to preserve the turtles. Some of the steps have been big, cultural changes, including no longer harvesting and eating turtle eggs, which used to be a common, Mayan food. Other preservation actions have included marking and protecting the nests containing eggs on the beach and tagging the turtles so studies can be done. And requiring adequate septic whenever buildings are erected near the beach. And saving the eggs in safe, secure buildings when big, tropical storms approach that will destroy the nests, and then releasing the hatchlings in mid-October when the storms have passed. And preventing lights on the beach from disorienting the turtles in nesting season. The turtles navigate by the stars, apparently, and white, electric lights on the beach overwhelm their internal direction finders.

Akumal, in Mayan "the place of the turtle," just to the north, was a center for all of these activities, that was true. I supported all of the preservation activities. But I wasn't buying any of this particular tortuga story. Ramirez used to always have secret, complicated, ambitious plans. Or maybe he was just here because of the girl. Times do change. People too. Sometimes.

"Are you kidding me?" I asked. I made sure I was still smiling.

He smiled back. "The pizza's good here, right?" He apparently took no offense. "In desde Desdemona"—that was the name of the island—"we really care about protecting the green turtles and making sure they survive. We celebrate them, we show them to the tourists, and we do what we can to keep them healthy and safe so they can reproduce. We want to make sure that they continue to thrive on our island and all across the Caribbean. And especially here, where there used to be so very many of them. Development here can hurt them quite badly. I'm sure it already has.

"I'm sure you already know that the green turtle nests here. Years ago, in the late 1970's, Mario Villanueva, who was then governor of Quintana Roo and was supposed to be involved in cocaine distribution and other schemes, tried to sell the public beach near here, at Xca-cel, to a foreign company to build a resort. The beach was public and a primary nesting area for green turtles. It had been federally protected

45

before the sale. The hotel, which was planned by a Spanish company, would have destroyed the turtle habitat and made the public beach into a private resort. Greenpeace and others fought against the deal and eventually the good guys won. The lawsuits are still alive, I think, but dormant."

I vaguely remembered this. The event was at the very beginning of my time in Tulum, and at that time I wasn't worried about somebody else's legal problems, let alone the turtles. At the time, the species I was trying to keep off the endangered species list was me. I knew that Villanueva had gone to Altiplano, the Mexican Sing Sing, for drug trafficking and corruption, and that the US wanted to deport him after that for drug crimes, but I also know that there are some gigantic, all-inclusive hotels very near the beach at Xca-cel, just 12 km north of Tulum. There was no way I could decide whether this story was fact or fiction, and I didn't have any idea how to find out.

There was nothing to do in the circumstances but to toast the continuation and fertility of the turtles and to enjoy Mari Estrella's smile. She was a real beauty. Her smile was radiant. I found myself wondering what I could say or do to keep her smiling. And trying to do so.

After more small talk, some more efforts to prolong Mari Esrella's smile, some pescatore pizza con queso (anchovies, shrimp, garlic, and cheese), and about three quarters of a bottle of a nondescript, Mexican vino tinto, the waiters were still talking to me in Spanish even though they heard all of us speaking in English. Such is the global economy and such is Tulum.

"When I think about our former business," Ramirez began, "I think there was a basic problem with our business plan. Noticing this language I'm using now? It's the language of economics and business planning. Very useful. Especially in discussing risk and return, those kinds of important business issues. Essentially, in our former business, we had to continue to make deliveries to continue to make money. Each delivery had additional costs and, of course, ever increasing risks, so eventually, since we wouldn't ever just quit, we stupidly continued until, well, until we got caught. That was bound to happen if we continued long enough. 100%. Definitely. A certainty. Couldn't be avoided with our business plan if we continued to work. Had to happen eventually. A certainty.

"I've been thinking about something else, that if we had just one, unique thing to deliver, and we delivered it only once, just one time, the risks would be fixed and the profits could be so much greater. Am I right?"

What in the world was he talking about? I couldn't imagine it. I looked in his eyes to see whether this was some kind of joke he was playing. Mari Estrella smiled again. Her lips too were really fantastic. So was the rest of her. Her eyes were sparkly. She had exquisite, thin fingers. Ramirez on the other hand didn't seem to be talking hypothetically. Was he proposing something? I nodded my agreement at him, though I think my mouth might have been slightly ajar. Nobody had made this kind of overture to me in several decades. In fact, for quite some time nobody was making overtures to me about anything, let alone crimes. I almost laughed. Wasn't I too old for this? Hadn't I given this up? Wasn't I living a different life now?

"Are you being theoretical?" I asked.

"But anyway you're retired, right?"

"Semi retired is how I like to think of it. I survive day to day. I'm not living the high life. Far from it. My needs, my expenses are really tiny. I manage to get by these days mostly on proceeds from my writing, if you can believe that. In all, my life is now very simple and although it's not at all luxurious, it's comfortable enough for me. You wouldn't believe how frugally I live."

He grinned and suggested we meet and talk the next day. He'd outline what he had in mind then. He didn't want to talk it over now. We could meet at the beach, have a little lunch, a couple of drinks, talk privately, enjoy a delightful afternoon in the sun by the turquoise Caribbean. What could be better?

I think I was flattered. Of course, I was an original G. Not. Well, of sorts, I guess. I didn't think I really wanted to get involved in anything, and I didn't need any unnecessary legal complications, especially the kind he seemed to be suggesting, but, I thought, it couldn't hurt to hear what he had in mind. I was curious about what he might have dreamt up. I was also very sure that I wanted to see Mari Estrella again, and, of course, I would see her if I showed up at the beach. I'd definitely be there, even if I thought what he would propose would be too adventurous for me.

Playa Paraiso is one of the widest, most beautiful beaches near Tulum. It might be one of the most beautiful beaches in the world. It's north of the fork on the Boca Paila Road. There are little beach clubs and small hotels and small resorts on the water from the Tulum ruins in the north until the start of the Sian Ka'an Biosphere Preserve far to the south. These beaches have a huge expanse of white sand and the smallest, most gentle waves. The water is warm, sparkling turquoise when it is shallow, bright blue when it is deep, all the way to the horizon, punctuated solely by the line the barrier reef draws from north to south just before the horizon. The sun is extremely bright, making the beach extremely hot and the sea a totally refreshing contrast. There is very little shade on the beach, but you can rent a beach bed or an umbrella or a chair. Or you can find shade under one of the many coco trees.

I have seen some of the worst, most dramatic sunburns on this beach. Fair skinned, red haired tourists from northern Europe are quickly and unceremoniously flambeed here. For some reason, maybe it's the gentle, warm breeze, they don't notice that they are bright red and crisply fried until it's too late and finding shelter will do them no good at all. This is a beach that was designed for SPF 30 and above suntan products. And hats.

At the north end of the beach, past the many small boats pulled up on the sand by the Tulum Fisherman's Cooperative after the morning's fishing, is a cliff. And crowning the cliff, overlooking the vast expanse of turquoise sea and blue sky, is the tall, famous Mayan ruin, El Castillo, from around the Ninth Century. The view of El Castillo from the beach approximates what the first Europeans may have seen at this site centuries ago. Maybe. This is another point on which facts and fiction merge, and there are, of course, contradictions.

If the first Europeans were Norsemen, and many people including me think they were, they may have arrived just after the Tulum Castillo was completed. In fact, some have argued that the original incarnation of the plumed god, Quetzelcoatl, called "Kukulkan" in Mayan, was actually a Norseman with a red beard who arrived in a Norse sailing ship from the East. The ship arrived from the open sea, and its occupants greeted the Mayans with joy and in friendship. There was no violence. The Norsemen had steel, and various crafts that the Mayans lacked. The Norsemen freely gave the Mayans whatever knowledge they had, the Mayans returned the favor. And the Mayans helped the sailors survive and replenish their ships. When Quetzelcoatl died, he was returned to the sea in a burning ship, in a Norse funeral. But being a god, it was prophesied that he would eventually return, again from the East, on a ship coming again from the open water.

This possibility of the return of Quetzelcoatl actually smoothed the way for the Spanish conquest 500 or more years later. Some of the Mayans, who had a very good calendar and very good, written histories, as well as an excellent cultural memory, believed the invading Spanish might be none other than the returning Quetzelcoatl. Both had sailing ships. Both arrived from the East. There might have been celestial similarities as well. Wasn't the return part of the prophesy? Some of the Mayans thought it was, so they didn't immediately resist the landing and instead decided to welcome Cortez, saying he was the returning god. Later it turned out that he most definitely was not. But by then it was already too late to drive him and his soldiers back into the sea. Or sacrifice them. And eat them.

On the other hand, if the first Europeans were the Spanish, and quite a few traditional historians think they were, they first arrived on this coast in 1511 after the shipwreck of the galleon Valdivia near Cuba. Setting a fearsome precedent, some of the refugees from the wreck who made it ashore near Tulum after several weeks on the open sea—many died on the sea from starvation, drowning and exposure—were immediately eaten by the Mayan inhabitants of the area. Others were caged to be fattened. Some of these Spaniards, whom the Mayans were treating like prime veal, escaped and went into hiding with rival Mayan groups. They hid for about seven years.

Only one of the Valdivia refugees, Jeronimo de Aguilar, a priest whose remarkable claim to fame was that he had remained devout and celibate for the entire seven years of his stay with the Mayans in Quintana Roo, ultimately returned to Cortez and assisted him in his armed invasion, plunder and annexation of the area. Aguilar could by then, of course, speak Mayan and was valuable to Cortez for that reason.

Another of the original Spaniards, Gonzalo Guerrero, who I think had exactly the right idea, became a Mayan, tattooed his face, pierced his ears, married a Mayan woman, had three children, and actively fought against the initial Spanish exploratory invasions. He knew exactly why he was fighting. And against what. Invited by Aguilar to return to Spain, he gratefully declined, probably because once he reached Spain he would have been hanged for treason, specifically for helping the Mayans fight the initial Spanish invaders' exploratory landings.

I imagine that the Mayans felt on Aguilar's later return with Cortez some years later that they should have kept him penned up better and eaten him while they could. I imagine they also felt he was a complete and utter lunatic not because of his consistent, ceremonial praying, which they would have respected, but because of his ostentatious and to them incomprehensible chastity. That they would never have understood. Maybe it would have affected how he tasted.

Now tour buses arrive at Playa Paraiso filled with Italian tourists from all-inclusive hotels. These travelers are oblivious to virtually all of these historical events. Why shouldn't they be? The All-inclusive hotels are, I think, like Caribbean cruise ships that don't move from port to port. They provide the kind of excessive food, entertainment, pampering and service you'd expect on a cruise, but you never leave for a new port and another shore excursion. People who visit AI's tend to want bright sun, lots of alcohol, and floating in the sea. Period.

Maybe a very few of the people spending time in AI's who have taken the bus to Playa Paraiso know that in many of the Tulum ruins quite near the Castillo there are smaller temples with stone murals of descending gods, Dios Decendentes, that some think are actually depictions of visits to the Mayans by extraterrestrials. How else, the discussion goes, did the Mayans manage to build such elaborate pyramids and temples without using the wheel? El Castillo, the story goes, is actually a landing strip for the space travelers.

The buses deposit their passengers on the beach just below the ruins. The Italians call out excitedly to each other and pose for pictures against a particular, well known leaning palm tree near a dune. The palm has weathered innumerable hurricanes and it has called out to people to stand with it for many years. The Italians seem to hover, uncharacteristically forming an informal line, waiting for a turn to approach the important tree. There, the men stand on the trunk and pose as Tarzan; the women are sultry mermaids who recline against the curving trunk and pose as voluptuous Italian film stars. Think Sophia Loren in *Yesterday, Today and Tomorrow*. Throughout Italy there must by now be in dresser drawers thousands of faded photographs of sunburned people leaning against the bent palm tree at Playa Paraiso. Some of the photos are frayed at the edges, and their faded, Kodachrome reds and oranges remind older viewers of their distant, past youthfulness. In these photos there is a brief whiff of the intoxicating perfume and the taste of a piquant paradise beside the Caribbean. The memories evoke smiles. "I remember that so well, how wonderful it was." Even as the photographs fade, the tree continues, weathering the hurricanes and the constant wind.

I found John Coltrane Ramirez and Mari Estrella in the Playa Paraiso bar, a building on the beach with a palapa, a roof made of palm fronds, a small spot of shade beneath some tall coco trees. She was radiant in a small, green bikini and drinking something called "Miami Vice," a mix of a strawberry daiquiri and a pina colada. He had a green Dos Equis bottle in his hand and was wearing a baseball cap. I looked for clues about whether they were a couple. I did not see them touch each other. He announced that he and I were going for a short walk, we'd be right back. She smiled at us. He did not touch her. She had a wonderful smile. I was immediately happy I had come.

We started to walk North on the beach, toward the fishing boats and El Castillo. When we were away from other people, when we were away from a speaker playing iconic Bob Marley tunes, Ramirez was extremely direct with me. "I have someone, a client let's say, with a great deal of money who wants a certain artifact. It doesn't belong to him and, unfortunately, it is not for sale and never will be. He will pay a lot for it and he wants it badly. I'm not sure why he wants it, or what he intends to do with it once he has it, but the project involves, in the first place, going to Cuba to see whether we can obtain it for him. My client will, of course, pay for this exploratory investigation and the entire trip. I think it will only take a few days. Definitely less than a week."

I was enjoying the walk. As usual, it was quite bright and very hot, the warm water occasionally covered my feet, the sand was white and soft, and there is always the promise of topless women on this beach. I am unable to tell whether their breasts are real or fake, but I admit that I am quite curious about that. And on this occasion, to no one's particular surprise, I was not disappointed. There were a few topless tourists on the beach. Were they German? Their breasts seemed real or fake enough, depending on whose you were talking about, but they were in serious danger of brutally burning not only their breasts but also the rest of their bodies. Tonight they would definitely suffer.

We walked past a small soccer game, in which local players were doing their best to show off some of their moves, perhaps for the benefit of the topless Germans. No rational person should think of mechanistic German soccer, something akin to an infantry assault, as "the beautiful game." Effective, yes; beautiful, no. So all the beach futbol moves

51

probably were not going to be adequately admired for their being good futbol, if they were, though the players' youthful, muscular, tan bodies might be admired for other, more obvious reasons. Who really knows about this? Who knows how these elements might come together? All of that might be a different story, a long digression for a different day, the start of yet another tale.

I was also wondering about Gonzalo and the way that five centuries before me, he did essentially what I had tried to do when I came to Tulum, to fit in unobtrusively, to thrive, to stay. I also thought about Ken Kesey and the Merry Pranksters who fled the US for Mazatlan in circumstances similar to mine in the late '60s. Unlike me, they eventually gave up. They left Mexico, they returned to the States, and they faced the judicial music. The punishment was not onerous. Unlike them, I just stayed on. And on and on. By now, I was probably forgotten, a loose end, a cold case lacking any interest, a very thin file in a decades old, locked filing cabinet in a federal warehouse somewhere. The file would probably become relevant only if I ever showed up in the US with a new crime.

I tried to understand Ramirez's proposal, if that's what it was, but it just wasn't clear to me exactly what he wanted to do, what he was really talking about. It wasn't making any sense to me.

"You want to do a some kind of burglary in Cuba, is that it?"

He didn't respond. I continued. "Why do you want anyone else who is not Cuban, specifically me, to get involved in this? As you can see, I'm retired, or semi retired, and I've never been a cat burglar or anything like that. Or a second story man. I mean: I haven't done anything at all. In decades. And I've never been to Cuba. Remember, now, before when we knew each other, I just drove the truck and tried to be invisible. You had a warehouse. I don't know if either of us is particularly suited to what you're suggesting, but for starters, why me?"

"Well, we know each other, right? And I trust you, and you can trust me. You know that I didn't say anything about you when I was in trouble, right? Look. Let me tell you something. I didn't even think of involving you in this, didn't think of even bringing up the subject until we met last night fortuitously. Our meeting was a complete surprise to me, and then it jumped out at me that there might be a reason why we ran into each other here. Why did this happen? Why did fate bring me to you? Is it just a coincidence? I immediately thought to myself, well, he might just be perfect for this. Maybe that's why I ran into you just now. That's what jumped right into my mind. It seemed that you might be the right person for this. And it seemed to me that maybe I was very lucky to have found you so unexpectedly, somebody I hadn't thought about at all for the job. Listen. I need a second pair of eyes and a second brain just to evaluate this. It can be quite a big money maker later on, I think. But who knows? The initial trip, the exploration will still bring a good fee anyway, even if the job we're looking at isn't something that we can actually do later on. And there's no risk to you at any point. You don't have to get more involved in this than just coming to Cuba and looking at it and checking it out with me. Really. You've never been to Cuba, right?"

Again, I was flattered. And surprised. I don't have a lot of people in my life telling me how valuable I am to them. Or offering me things that will make me money. Or talking about how I can evaluate or analyze or think about things. Or offering me trips to places I'd really like to visit. In fact, I'm usually pretty much alone, pretty much by myself, pretty much in my routine. I don't really go anywhere, except in my mind. I usually sit under the tree, harvesting stories, dreaming, seeing what falls out of the sky. I did have a question though. "Is anyone else involved in this?"

"Nobody else, except my client."

Well, I thought, at least Mari wasn't involved in planning international crimes. That was good. I wondered again about their relationship. Were they together? I thought they might be. I wondered whether I should go to Cuba. The two topics, Cuba and Mari, both were new and exciting. And somehow connected. "I'll think about it. Let me sleep on it. We can talk tomorrow."

When we returned to the bar, Mari was gone. Her seat was occupied by an obese American woman twice her weight with arms like tree trunks and bright yellow nylon hair. I said goodbye to Ramirez and watched Mari, over his shoulder, emerging from the surf. I definitely liked what I saw. She was truly a beauty. I waved goodbye to her. She waved back. I liked that. I smiled.

When I finally got back to my house it was early evening, and twilight was disappearing into the darkness. I was getting hungry. The sky was streaked dark purple and orange, and the mosquitoes had begun massing in preparation for their quotidian evening banquet. The neighborhood smelled of cooking, and I could hear a television and the voices of people on the street. I was looking forward to a peaceful, quiet evening and some food. Maybe I would spend the evening reading. I wanted to begin Augusto Roas Basto's book, *I, The Supreme*. I just love reading novels about Latin American military dictators, especially obsessive, talkative, brutal ones. These books—there are many great ones in the genre—fit so beautifully here. And best of all, it's still completely safe here to read them, there is no risk here, nobody's coming to round me or anybody else up for reading. It's unlike many other countries in this hemisphere at various, recent, scary times, when these books would have been deemed subversive. And those who insisted on reading them might be disappeared or arrested or beaten. Or worse.

Sitting on the steps to my house was El Kid. He was obviously waiting for me. I had no idea how long he had been sitting there. Or why.

"Buenos tardes, Senor," he said. "Please, Senor, Don Obdulio wants to see you."

"What for? I've been out all day. I'm tired. I'm hungry. Can't it wait? I'd like to eat." I was surprised to hear myself whining.

"All I know is that he wants to see you. I'll take you right to him now if that would be all right. He told me he wants to see you right away. Please come with me, Sir. I'm sure you'll be back here in no time."

I didn't refuse. Maybe this could be quick. We found Don Obdulio in a vacant lot a few blocks away. He was sitting in a white, plastic chair next to a grey cement block wall and had a beer bottle in one hand and a piece of tortilla in the other. A beautiful, large bougainvillea plant was in bloom over his head. There were a few other chairs near him. Some of an old, blue, wheelless, engineless Nissan Tsuru with a tree growing through its rusted side window was at the back of the lot. It had probably been there for years. He motioned with the bottle for me to sit down.

"What's up?" I asked. "Is there an emergency of some kind or something? How come you invited me over?"

"Do you know what tracking is?" he asked with a mouth full of tortilla. He was staring at me while he chewed.

"It's how you follow the trail of an animal when you're hunting. But that's not why you had me come over here, is it?"

"No, not that kind, the other kind of tracking," he said. "The other kind. You don't know anything about that other kind, do you?" He was still staring.

I shrugged. I had no idea what he was asking me about. He continued to stare at my face, looking directly into my eyes. He smiled. "That's why I had to bring you over here right now. Right now. It's not an emergency, but it also couldn't wait. It's important. You haven't been in real danger in years and years. Actually, you've been really safe for quite a while, in fact, the whole time while you've been in Tulum. But, amigo, today I have been tracking you. I have been tracking you into your immediate future. I want you now to be especially careful. Be very, very careful. Do you know what I'm talking about?"

I said I didn't. I said I had no idea, but, of course, it was obvious that whatever was going on with Ramirez was showing up to him as a potential, big problem for me. That was the only thing that was new in my life. Ramirez and Mari. I really didn't want the curandero getting deeply involved in my life. I really didn't want to become one of those people who's so involved with him. I was willing to listen to him, and to think about this warning he was giving me, but I didn't want to tell him anything about the last 24 hours and what I'd been thinking about doing. It wasn't really any of his business, I thought.

He looked in my eyes. Then he shook his head. "Look, my friend, I'm telling you something. This is really important to you. I really don't want you to do anything bad. That could be very dangerous to you. Very dangerous. Amigo, if you do things that are bad, bad things in turn could happen to you, things that would put you in grave danger, things that might really hurt you." He paused and stared at me for a while longer. He ate another bite of the tortilla. He chewed. He stared. Then he shook his head again, and said, "Do you understand what I'm saying?" I shook my head that I didn't. He frowned. "Do you want a beer?"

I did, but I said I didn't. He looked in my eyes again. "Look," he gestured, "I'm telling you. I'm seeing what can happen to you in the near future. And I know, I see it. I can track this. And I'm telling you that if you do bad things, bad things in turn will happen to you. Those things, those bad things, could be very dangerous for you. So I'm telling you to be very, very careful. I want to be sure that you understand me." I said thanks, I understood. "Don't you want this beer?"

I did, I really wanted it, but again I said I didn't, goodbye, and I left.

On my way home, I was wondering about this odd summons from the curandero, and how he could possibly know anything about the future, in particular, my future, or what Ramirez was just talking to me about, if that's what he knew, and more obviously, how what Ramirez was talking about could possibly show up as something dangerous to me. I mean: I was just going to look, that's all. Just to look. That was the deal. That was what I was offered. Nothing more. I also wondered why the curandero knew about all of this so quickly and decided to call me over and tell me about it. I really didn't believe all the old stories about him and how much he supposedly knew about what people were doing and thinking. But, at the very least, it did seem extremely alarming to have him warn me in such a dramatic, explicit way about something that had not yet happened. Or been committed to. Maybe, in fact, definitely, what he was saying was that I really shouldn't go to Cuba. That that was a bad idea. How, I wondered, could that be? Am I going to listen to him about this? I didn't think so. I didn't think I would rely on what he said. Why would I?

As I was walking home there was loud, constant thunder in the distance, but the sky overhead remained clear and I could see tons of stars. This kind of rolling thunder is a standard October phenomenon in Tulum. By the time I got home, it had started to rain, and then it rained hard and thundered all night. The rain in Tulum in October is sudden and dense and remarkably tenacious. The rain finally tapered off in the morning. There was a streak of bright orange light at the horizon.

When I awoke at dawn, the power of the curandero's warning seemed to have faded, to have almost disappeared, and it seemed to me that, well, I've wanted to go the Cuba for a while, and this was a chance to go, so I might as well visit Cuba. No matter what Don Obdulio told me. After all, it would cost nothing, I'd make a few dollars, and maybe I needed a brief change of scenery. I hadn't been away from Tulum in a very long time. How could it be dangerous to me to do just that much? I mean, I was just going to have a look-see, right? I wasn't really going to do anything. Or to agree to do anything more than just look at whatever might be there to look at. It was just looking. Solo mirando. Solo. Just. How, I wondered, could that ever turn into a problem for me?

There are flights every day from Cancun to Havana on Clic and Cubana Airlines. Gringos, because of the idiotic, half century long blockade, are not supposed to fly to Cancun and then to forbidden Cuba on the forbidden airlines. That is completely forbidden. And illegal. But they do anyway. Constantly. It is an official non-secret secret. If you're a gringo, it can be a big financial problem to be caught coming from Cuba. Because there are big fines and penalties. There can be all kinds of ridiculous, unanticipated expense.

Ramirez and I stood in the long line at Cancun Airport waiting to be checked in on the Cubana flight with US people, Mexicans, Cubans, and Europeans. I had no idea how many of these people were spies or informants of one sort or another. At one point I thought everyone in the line including Ramirez and excluding only me might be a spy or CIA covert operative. Some, I thought, were supervisors, there just to spy on and supervise the other spies. And of course, all of the spies had to spy on each other. And make notes and reports. The line hardly moved at all for an hour. As we were reaching investigatory stasis, the limit of our patience, and we had run out of other passengers to talk to or speculate about, the agent informed us that he was very sorry, but we couldn't go today. No. Not today. Sorry. The plane that came here from Cuba was too small, smaller than the usual one. We could go tomorrow, but not today. They'd put us up in a hotel in downtown Cancun, if we'd like, or we could just come back tomorrow, same time, same gate, same line. Some people in the line made disappointed, quarreling, angry, frustrated or sad sounds. Some sighed their resignation. A few seemed to shrug off this change as if it were a daily occurrence. Were these unaffected people all of the spies? "Hotel?" Ramirez asked me.

"I don't want to go back home and start over again early tomorrow morning. I don't think downtown Cancun is going to be very posh. Not at all. The hotel zone would be great, but that's not what they're offering us, is it? Let's just try it out. At least we'll still be on the trip even if we're not really going anywhere yet."

The hotel turned out to be across the street from the main Cancun bus station on a crowded, traffic choked, broiling, bustling street with the strong smell of diesel exhaust and stirred up dust. It was not picturesque. Not in the slightest. It was not in a tourist area. The exterior was faded; it had a thick patina of dust, car and bus exhaust. I wondered how many of the rooms were reserved for prostitution, and whether the others were always reserved for Cubana's delayed passengers. But the hotel did have a swimming pool, in which Mexican families were then standing waist deep in water eating their botanas and drinking beer. And it had a betting parlor with a bar on the first floor with dozens of televisions tuned in to all kinds of sporting events. And it had a restaurant in an open-air courtyard near the pool where a wedding party was being set up. In all, it was not all that bad. In fact, it was adequate for what it was, and what is was, was a place to spend one night while waiting for the next day's flight to Cuba.

We sat in the betting parlor and ordered beer, some totopos, guacamole. Some more beer. Some more totopos. Mas salsa. More beer. We were well on our way to a gentle, sleepy intoxication.

"Not exactly an auspicious start," I said. "Kind of starting off on the wrong foot. I guess we'll get off tomorrow. We'll see."

"Remember. We're just going to look. This delay doesn't have anything to do with us. This is just what happens sometimes when you travel." He ordered another beer and began to watch two or three football games simultaneously. He had not bet on them although he could have. I watched him drink about half of his third beer.

"Can I ask you a personal question?" I asked.

He smiled. "Depends."

"What's your relationship with Mari?" As soon as I said it, I wished I hadn't. It sounded really awkward. I heard that as I said it. It was too late to stifle it. The question was too abrupt. It should have been more disinterested, cooler, less avid. And I asked it too soon. It wasn't time to ask it. Maybe after the third beer or the start of the fourth would have been more auspicious. The question sounded discordant, somehow dissonant. I really didn't want to reveal my interest to him so obviously. I watched him carefully.

He laughed. "Turtles, Green Turtles, *Chelonia Mydas*. We care about the turtles. That, my old friend, is it. That's what we do. It's about las tortugas. That's all. I've now told you in two languages. Three if you count the Latin. Nothing more. Have another beer, ok? Try to relax. We'll be off for Cuba tomorrow. Why do you ask?" He smiled.

"You know very well."

He was still smiling. "I don't know what she thinks about older guys. Guys like you. I mean you're about 20 years older than her, right? And you don't seem to be really rich. Not rich. Interesting, eccentric, picturesque maybe, unusual perhaps, maybe fun, I don't know, but definitely not rich. Rich, I think, would probably help. A lot. Rich would be a very good thing. It seems to help in most cases like this, I think. I think rich helps a lot. But I don't really know, I haven't discussed it with her. And I haven't talked about you with her. Maybe she doesn't mind that you're not rich. I don't know. I don't know what she thinks." He was being generous about the age difference.

I didn't like how this was going. Not at all. You'd have to be blind not to notice what a beauty she was. And virtually every man would find her attractive, wouldn't he? Of course. And anybody would ask the same questions about her. Definitely. "What about Garcia Marquez? You know, his last book, the one about the 90-year old guy and the 14 year old girl. Or *Love in the Time of Cholera*, the age differences in the last part of that book, I mean. Age differences don't really have to be all that important, do they? Right? I mean it's fundamentally about attraction and desire, about feelings, about curiosity, lust, love, not the demographic statistics, right? It's about the many, many intangibles, right?"

He looked bored by this argument. "I really have no idea. I don't really know all that much about any of that. I just can't say. From my experience it's hard to tell what can happen. Often, with women, whether I get what I want or not, I'm surprised." He shrugged his mild lack of comprehension, smiled and went back to watching the games. And his beer and the chips. Clearly, any interest I had in Mari definitely wasn't a very big deal to him. It didn't seem to matter to him at all one way or another. And that, I thought, was good. Or at least good enough. For now.

I still wasn't buying his story about the turtles. But our frank discussion held out some faint hope to me. I had no intention of saying more about my interest in Mari, and what he said made things seem a little bit better, a little more hopeful. Although she didn't really have anything at all to do with the trip, his answer made it seem to me like the trip might be worth it after all. I decided I'd have another beer. To celebrate. When I think about it now, I'm not sure what I thought the occasion to celebrate might have been.

The next day after being rousted from the hotel in the morning and again standing in a long, winding line at the airport, we boarded a gigantic, Russian, pre-Gorbachev airplane headed for Havana. The air conditioning in the plane released a thick stream of visible mist into the cabin. All of the signs on the plane were in Russian and Spanish. The engines were deafening. The old plane vibrated and lumbered down the runway for an eternity before miraculously becoming ever so slightly airborne at the last possible second. A flying, rickety, aging, thundering elephant. Ramirez leaned over to me and said in my ear, trying to be heard over the plane's noise, "Welcome to the dictatorship of the proletariat." I had never before thought of that dictatorship as so fundamentally scary.

59

Hah. The proletariat. We spent two days ensconced in the Melia Hotel in Havana floating on a magic carpet while our foreign currency produced an opulence unattainable by any real Cubans, who were definitely not welcome to visit the hotel unless they were there to clean up after us or work hard or sleep with us. The Cubans were definitely not invited to participate in any of our divisa purchased luxury. They were also not supposed to express the discontent, if not the outrage our luxury might have caused them when it was contrasted with what they themselves had. Expressing that was evidently strictly forbidden.

The breakfast buffet was extremely varied and unbelievably sumptuous, but in the shops immediately outside the hotel all the pickings were incredibly meager. Exchangeable currency, divisa, bought lobsters at amazing paladar restaurants, nearly worthless moneda nacional bought nothing but sympathetic, though exasperated frowns and shrugs. Rum and cigarettes and cigars and a huge variety of women were all quite inexpensive, and the lines in relationships between hustling (jiniterismo) and friendship, between prostitution and courtship, between legality and illegality, as far as foreigners went, were quite blurred. Jiniterismo, which El Maximum Lider had made a crime, is simply an occupation that for a commission connects foreigners' plentiful divisa currency to the bountiful, covert, illegal Cuban markets. It's just a kind of brokerage or options market. It's just nascent capitalism.

A remarkable paladar, La Fontana, was recommended by the concierge at the Hotel Nacional as the only paladar restaurant to which they ever refer their guests. After all, he smiled, we have high standards to maintain. The fountain for which the restaurant is named is in a courtyard, and it has turtles living in the bottom of it. Are they for turtle soup? Are they pets? Are they a decoration? "Are you interested in these turtles?" I asked Ramirez.

"They're not sea turtles," he responded. "So I'm not really all that interested. I don't think they're for eating, but they might be. I'm staying away from them. I don't really like small, brown turtles. I think they transmit severe, contagious diseases."

The Malecon like much of Havana was gorgeous and in a romantic state of almost total structural collapse. The problem was that almost none of the buildings seemed to have been maintained for the past five decades. They had been divided and re-divided and subdivided and people lived on their roofs. But not maintained. Never cared for. Yes, the architecture was unbelievable, if the buildings didn't crumble and fall down before your eyes. The United Nations was evidently putting some funds into making sure that didn't happen.

Ramirez and I wandered the famous streets. The Prado. It was as if we were characters in a story written by Alejo Carpentier or Ernest Hemingway or Guillermo Cabrera Infante. We decided to stop at the Hotel Inglaterra for a drink under the portico at the sidewalk café. A combo was playing boleros. It seemed appropriate to order mojitos. I was delighted to stop: the kitchen of the Inglaterra was an important location in a novel set in the early 1900's. It was not clear to me exactly where the back door to the kitchen might have been, the door through which in the novel Enrico Caruso fled from mobster gunmen intent on killing him or collecting a long overdue debt.

I have always been curious about places that appear in works of fiction I have read. When I read, the places take on an appearance in my mind's eye that is a collaboration between the author and me. When I then actually see the place, I see what the writer was working with. Sometimes I am quite surprised. When I tried to imagine what the Hotel Inglaterra would have been like a century before my arrival, it was surprisingly clear how grand it was, how important, how busy. It was a place in which the present only slightly obscured the past.

Similarly, there's Tulum. You can visit and see how it is now, but if you want to see how it is for me, you'll have to remove some sidewalks, tear down some buildings, close some roads, break some plate glass windows, remove the stainless steel. You'll have to add dust, and corrosion, and rust. You'll have to scratch its surface. Or dent it. Or hammer on it until its facade begins to crumble and fall. Underneath, I hope, you'll find my sweet Tulum. Strong, growing from its deep roots. Still wild. Still untamed. Living with all its contradictions. Imperfect. And completely lovely.

In Havana, I wanted to sit and talk about and enjoy what a remarkable event it was for me to be there, in Cuba. I was full of delight. It was my desire to indulge in a long, literary and musical tour of the City, to eat and drink and smoke the best the City could now offer, to hear all the stories Cubans would so readily tell me with so little prompting, and to marvel at the wonders of the island's music and culture.

But when I thought about what had actually brought me to Cuba, uncomfortable questions began to arise. Particularly because of the curandero's warning. How could my being here become a problem for me? I didn't see how that could happen. "Are you ready to tell me about what we're doing here?" I asked.

"Partially."

"Is there a problem?"

"I just don't want to go into all the details yet. I'll tell you this: tomorrow we're going to fly to Santiago, and we're going to rent a car and then we're going to drive. I'll tell you more after we get the car and get on the road. We're leaving Havana tomorrow."

"It's just a treasure hunt, right? I always wanted to visit Santiago de Cuba."

He nodded. "How are you enjoying it so far?"

I laughed. I repeated how delighted I was actually to be in Havana. I had wanted to visit for decades. I had wanted to see the places I had read and dreamed and heard about. I ordered another drink. "Why," I asked, "are we drinking Hemingway's favorite drink just down the block from La Floridita, Hemingway's favorite bar?"

"So we can compare."

The next day, extremely hung over and still delighted to be there, we returned to the airport to put our headaches and queasiness through exacting Cuban domestic airline security on our way to yet another antiquated, hulking Soviet airplane with fierce air conditioning and an even more informal departure and arrival schedule. Even though we were in no real rush and on no real schedule, the tedium of constant waiting and standing patiently in long lines was almost overwhelming. How many postcards of Che and Havana architecture and the heroes of the Revolution, how many pamphlets and books of tepid political polemics, how many Che t-shirts can one look at before completely exhausting the airport's very limited distractions?

I had hoped to find a cache of books by Alejo Carpentier in six languages, the complete works of Jose Marti, seven different biographies of Che. And if there were some kind of detente in the persistent battle for the security of the Revolution's ideology, of which there was none in contemplation, the airport could even have been the point at which the books of Cabrera Infante and Severo Sarduy and Carlos Franqui and God knows who else in the enormous, talented, prolific, Cuban literary diaspora could finally come home and join the works of Jose Lezama Lima, even if their authors had already passed on. Maybe the batalla de ideas couldn't live on a shelf in an airport store, but the batalla de novellas certainly could. Its many voices could be a wonderful, rich cacophony of disputation. But, alas. Paz.

That was not to be. The blockade and the corresponding State had stanched the variety and abundance of capitalism and reduced the airport's shops to unhappy, threadbare parodies. Bare shelves abounded. The State was apparently not interested in trying to sell things to its travelers, to its many visitors, even if that would provide more foreign exchange. Maybe it just didn't have anything to sell us.

We arrived in Santiago in a heavy, misty rain. The roads were like rivers. The people apparently lacked umbrellas. As in Havana, there were lines for entry into shops with people standing under the dripping eaves. The taxi driver took us to the venerable Casa Granda Hotel, where Fidel stayed when he came to this city just after the Revolution. In an odd display, the bellboy gave us a special key to turn on the lights in the room. Said he, "Be sure to turn the key on when you are in the room." Ramirez shrugged at me, "Is it to turn on the cameras?" The bellboy smiled and shrugged.

Ramirez decided his hangover would benefit from two aspirins and an immediate nap; I decided go out and to explore Santiago. After about twenty minutes of walking, the sole of my sandal began to flap with each step, making it impossible to walk comfortably. A bystander saw this, called me over and said to me that his brother was a shoemaker who could fix my shoe, did I want to come with him? It was quite nearby. This seemed to be a genuine enough offer. Maybe it was a hustle of some kind, but I needed my shoe to be fixed. I'd take a chance. Flapping my right foot and walking like a circus clown, I flapped and slapped down a side street for a block following him. I was ridiculous, and it was hard to walk like this, but for some reason I wasn't going to walk down the street barefoot or with only one shoe on. I don't know what the reason might have been. Ultimately, we reached our destination and the man banged on the front door of a small, white adobe and wood house with blue trim and a red door.

The shoemaker looked at the shoe and said it would be easy enough for him to fix it. It would only take a few minutes. He had some special, strong glue. It would last for years. Great. I imagined that it was entirely toxic and couldn't be sold in Mexico or the US because its lethal fumes caused horrible lung lesions and terrible skin diseases. And birth defects. He offered me a chair, took my shoe and headed for the dark, back room. His brother leaned against the wall. A third man, very old, black, tall and thin, with short white hair, very long fingers, dressed entirely in white, sat opposite me. He too had no shoes; he must have been another customer. He looked directly at me and held my eyes with his.

"Where are you from?" he eventually asked. His voice was very deep and gravelly. He spoke very slowly and musically.

"Mexico."

"You're from there now, yes. But you're not really from there. You're originally from elsewhere," he smiled. "Where are you actually from?"

That was true enough. I looked again in his eyes. They were remarkably shiny and clear. He smiled at me.

"Before Mexico, I was from the US"

After a silence of a minute, he spoke again. "Do you have someone you're working for? Someone you're working with? A teacher? In Mexico is it? Someone who even now is following and watching over you? Someone who is showing you something about things that can't usually be seen?"

"What do you mean?" I asked. These were surprising, unusual questions. Was he asking me something about the curandero? What else could he mean? I wasn't really doing any work for or with him. We were neighbors, I thought. He had told me he was tracking me and not to get in trouble. But the rest didn't make any real sense. I couldn't answer the question, I said. I just didn't know, I said.

"Do you mind if I look at the palm of your hand? Would that be all right with you?" he asked.

Somehow, this seemed to be a reasonable enough request, so I held out my right hand for him. He stared intently at the palm. He didn't touch my hand. In fact, he didn't touch me at all. He stared intently at my hand.

He made a deep humming sound while he looked. "Oh, I see," he finally said, "I see. That makes sense now. It's definitely in the future. He's definitely following you, watching out for you right now. He's concerned about you. And there's a small marker he's left right there that anybody can see. The rest of it, the teaching, the work, all the rest of it, is coming in the future." He nodded at my hand. I took it back. "He is quite powerful, and he has a lot to show you. You will really enjoy learning what he knows."

This struck me as extremely bizarre. I considered running away from him, but what about my shoes? I couldn't leave. I was not leaving without my shoes. And, after all, maybe there was something more I wanted from him. I sat. I thought. I didn't move. I breathed deeply through my nose. I think my eyes jerked from side to side with my thinking. Then I had a thought, so I thought I'd just say what came into my mind. "I'm sure there's more you can see," I told him. "Can you tell me anything else that you saw just now that might be helpful to me?"

He smiled. "Well, I don't want to go too very far from here," he said. "In my tradition, originally from West Africa, from the original human, from the original community, from the original ones, we don't want to search the many possible strands that can become your possible future, we don't want to disturb them, and if you look at them closely or follow them or rummage around in them to find out what they are or where they will end up, you can disturb or change them in ways you don't really want to. That might not be a good thing to do. We don't ever want to do that by mistake, by just looking, by being curious, by stumbling around, by being nosey. Sometimes we can follow the strands, and even change them, but this isn't really the time or place to do that. And there has to be a good reason to do something like that. And, of course, we have to know what we're looking for and why. Anyway, this isn't when I would do that. That's just not appropriate. So I just looked around very carefully, very gently in the near present. I won't journey to see further into your destiny without a reason. A very good reason. This, as I'm sure you might already have learned, is not something to play around with. This is not for our curiosity. And it's never for entertainment. This is not to be done without first receiving much permission and, of course, much preparation and making many, many offerings.

"But right now, right here, I can see two things I can tell you about. Have they already happened? First is that there is someone, I think somewhere to the west, maybe to the southwest of here, across the Caribbean, I think in Mexico, who is watching out for you, holding you, protecting you. This is very, very good. Excellent. This will be of great help to you. I see that right in the middle of your hand, that he's there. And I see in the very, very beginning of the future, in the seeds that are already germinating and will soon grow to become the present, in the signs pointing the way into the future, that you and he are working on something together. You're learning something from him. Something he knows but you don't know yet. Something he's showing you, teaching you. Is he a teacher of some kind? I don't know what that might be that he's showing you. He knows what it is. Soon you too will know what it is, too. I'm not going to try to go into that now. And whatever it is, it is something you want to know.

"He seems to have selected you, chosen you for this work. He has picked you out from all of the many, many people he knows. From all of the people who have come to him. That seems to be a lot of people. His work is powerful. And for now he has put a very good protection on you while you are traveling, while you are on your journey. He wants to keep you safe, so you're safe. But that doesn't mean that nothing can happen to you. It means that he will make these things more gentle, more mild, more tranquilo, mas calma. Does that answer the question that you asked me?"

"What is the second thing you saw that you mentioned before? You said there were two things you could see."

He frowned. "I almost forgot that. Thank you. I've been forgetting things lately. It's good that you reminded me." He sat quietly for a moment. He closed his eyes. Then with his eyes still closed, he asked, "Who is the woman carrying the ocean creatures in her basket? Who is the woman who is looking at the stars? Who is she? Do you know who she is?"

He looked in my eyes. He smiled. "Do you think you might know who she might be?" he asked.

"I'm not sure. I know who I hope it might be."

He smiled at this and started to laugh. "Well, she too is traveling right now, but she will return. And it looks like when you need her to, she will stop at the side of the road, where you will be standing on your journey. She will carry you to the west, to someplace with ruins. A tall ruin with many steps. And she will hold your head in her hands. That's as far as I can see now. Does that answer the question you asked me?"

Yes, it did. It certainly did. Wow. I hoped he was talking about Mari, that she would return. I didn't have any words for a follow up question. I tried to think of what more I could ask him, but my mind wouldn't come up with anything.

I thanked him for all of the information he had given me. Could I pay him for telling me all of this? No, I could not pay him with money. But, he said, I could instead light a candle during the next few days. Before lighting it, he explained, I should think of and feel the gratitude in my heart for all of those in my life who had offered me protection, my ancestors, my family, my friends, whoever was protecting me now, those who were seen and those who were unseen, those who had already arrived and those who were yet to come. I should then use my breath to blow into the candle all of the thanks and gratitude in my heart for them, thanking all of them for all they have done and will continue to do for me, for making my long journey through life safe and abundant and healthy, thanking them for their protection and for the guidance and inspiration they have offered and continue to offer to me. I would find this gratitude in my heart, he said, and it was from there that I should blow it into the candle before lighting it. Lighting the candle would release all of the gratitude and deliver it to them, wherever they might be, whether they were now living or not.

At that, the shoemaker returned with the shoes. I paid him 2 pesos, about two US dollars. That was all he would accept. I asked the shoemaker's brother whether he too would accept money for helping me out; he declined it. I thanked them all and continued my exploration.

I admit that I then walked all around in the city of Santiago but that I didn't see anything. Instead, I wandered and thought about what had happened. I didn't pay much attention to anything I was seeing. I was walking, yes, but my thinking wasn't in Santiago. Or in Cuba. It was either very far away or very deep inside me. I walked right past the huge Antonio Maceo monument with its gigantic Maceo on horseback and iron girders without really looking at it. Later, when I saw it on a postcard I didn't recognize it. I asked what it might be.

As I walked, I noticed that there was a new warmth in my chest, in my heart, that I had not noticed before. I could make it warmer by inhaling into it. When I thought about it, it seemed that the warmth might be coming from all of the feelings of gratitude I had. I spent the afternoon enjoying the feeling, breathing, making it bigger and bigger. Sometimes it was so strong that it pushed tears from my eyes. Other times, it seemed to fade, to recede, and I would pump it up again by inhaling into it, by breathing into my heart.

I returned to the hotel quite late. The lights on the square in front of the hotel were already on. People sat on benches and talked. The sky was orange and purple and turning darker. The first stars had emerged. There was a soft breeze. The church bells tolled in the distance. Birds were flying to their nests, and the first small bats had appeared.

I didn't tell Ramirez about my encounter. He was not particularly interested in where I had been or what I had done while he was asleep. He was just hungry.

We failed to discover adequate food in Santiago. Great food was a fantasy. We had dinner on the roof of the Casa Granda, overlooking the square in Santiago with its cathedral, and beyond, a harbor unbelievably beautiful but lacking any signs of prosperous commerce.

The next day, we rented a car. Before leaving Santiago, we parked in the same parking spot Fidel had used years before when he unsuccessfully stormed the Moncada Barracks, and we visited the museum in the Barracks, which was a weary homage to Stalinist curatorial devices and overburdened by propaganda. The bullet holes in the building's facade, someone said, were fakes, the real ones had been filled when the building was repaired by Battista's forces immediately after the unsuccessful raid.

Then we left. We were off driving east on the Carretera Central toward Guantanamo and beyond.

Maps in Cuba are works of fiction. There are roads on the map that do not exist on the earth. I asked Ramirez, "Do you want to take the Northern or the Southern road to Guantanamo? Look at this map." There were definitely two roads, definitely two, parallel lines on the map.

He looked at the map. He was driving. "There don't seem to be any signs directing us to either one of them."

We pulled over next to an old, bearded campesino walking slowly at the side of the road in frayed clothing, and I rolled down the window. "Hermano," I called to him, "Where is the route to Guantanamo?"

"Back where you came from, back there about a kilometer," he said pointing.

"But there was no sign."

"You turn left at the tree where the people are waiting for the bus or for a ride. The waiting people will always be your signs."

"Is there some other route to Guantanamo?"

"I never heard of it. That's the only one I know of."

We repeated these inquiries about four times between Santiago and Guantanamo. In truth, it was necessary at every major intersection.

Fortunately, there were few. And at most intersections there were large groups of people waiting for a ride in a car, on a truck, on a bus, on a tractor. Hitchhikers.

There were very few private cars there were on the road. The road was quite empty. Our rented car was a rarity. Most cars we saw had diplomatic or government plates. In the cities old 1950s US cars were still running, and they were joined by horrible Russian sedans and an occasional new car from Japan or Europe owned by a big shot. But most transportation for most people involved standing in line and waiting. Buses, trucks, and camelos, camels, a kind of trailer that could hold a hundred people, were the public transit. And patiently walking long distances.

The Carreterra Central, if that's what it was, eventually deposited us in the City of Guantanamo. After a stop for a beer and some rice and beans, we were off riding the coast road along the South shore of Cuba toward the east. The coast was rocky; the sea was turquoise. It was unbelievably hot and in the distance there were tall, yellow thunder heads. We kept the air conditioning on the highest setting.

"Where are we going?"

"I thought you'd never ask. We're going to Baracoa, on the east coast. That's our ultimate destination. The road we're on, the one that will climb through a pass in the Sierra Maestra mountains and bring us to the far Eastern coast, was first opened in the early 1970s. The Farola Highway was an important project for the Revolution. Before that, for more than 500 years, Baracoa was accessible only by sea."

As we climbed the road, people emerged from the dense forest and appeared on the side of the highway selling fruit and nuts and coconut covered in chocolate. We paused to buy these things and devoured them greedily. And then we drove down the mountain through jungle emerging at long last in Baracoa.

Baracoa must be the Cuban Macondo. It is a centuries old, picturesque, Spanish colonial town on the turquoise sea, with the towering green blanket of El Yunque and Sierra del Purial surrounding and cradling it. The sky is filled with gigantic cumulus clouds. The sea breeze is sweet and gentle. It's a heartbreakingly beautiful, white and pastel town with narrow cobbled streets, and small one and two story houses.

We stayed in an excellent casa particular, the owner of which was away on business in Europe. His daughter and wife would cook for us, dinner and breakfast, and we were free to roam the town.

The Malecon in Baracoa is not as spectacular as the one in Havana. Is anything? But it overlooks a natural, sheltered harbor facing the east, open and facing the Atlantic Ocean. And the harbor is important because when Columbus landed in Cuba, more than 500 years ago, this was where he came ashore. The harbor at Baracoa. Reportedly, Columbus wrote in his journal about October 27, 1492, the day he arrived here on his first voyage, that this place was the most beautiful he had ever seen. Period. This was not an exaggeration then, and it is not one now.

I sat on the roof of the casa particular under a blue, late afternoon sky and watched the glistening sea and the impenetrable, green mountains and the pastel houses, and I watched the people of the town come home from their day. To me it seemed remarkably close to paradise.

In the morning in Baracoa, at breakfast, people of the town drink hot chocolate. Nearby there are cacao farms and there is a processing plant. But like other Cubans they also suffer the consequences of the blockade: lack of toilet paper, bath products, paper towels, chickens with meat on their bones, enough vegetables, the list goes on and on and on. The deficiencies are taken for granted. They are by now facts of life. They are simultaneously measures of the depth of the island's commitment to its revolution and the futility and discomfort of continuing it.

On Saturday night, after we had eaten the most wonderful fish dinner, Ramirez and I sat on the roof for an after dinner rum and a cigar. Fidel was on TV, the show was "Mesa Redonda." In this show, "journalists" ask the Maximum Lider questions, and Fidel answers them. Sometimes the questions themselves are homilies, and the answers are a continuation of their rhetorical excesses. Sometimes the questions go on for minutes and the answer is "Yes." Sometimes the questions are brief and the answer is a full blown polemic. It's boring and it's comforting. If you see Fidel answering questions and not advertisements for McDonald's or Pepsi the Revolution must still be in place. Va bien.

As we sit on the roof, I can hear Fidel explaining something about agricultural production and planned distribution of produce. It is amazing, I think, as Jacobo Timmerman points out in his book, *Cuba*, how Fidel has involved himself in virtually everything, including distribution of the vegetables. And then, all of a sudden, the power goes out. Poof.

The town is black. And silent. Then I hear the voices of the neighbors. An occasional car's headlights illuminate the street. Some people light candles. I notice, and I expect that everyone else does as well, that it is unbelievably hot for night. The air is hot like pepper breath. And still. The earth is hot. The sea is hot. And I am hot. If there is relief, I have no idea what it might be.

I asked Ramirez, "Isn't is unbelievably hot here?"

"I thought it was the rum. And the smoke. It shut Fidel up, though, didn't it."

I had always admired Fidel. Say what you will, he had overthrown Battista and confiscated the property of multinational corporations, he had withstood the blockade, the Bay of Pigs, aircraft overflights from Miami, exploding cigars, the fall of the Soviet Union, a fifty year-long list of catastrophes, natural and man made, and he'd managed to hold off at a distance of a mere 90 miles a far larger, far more powerful adversary.

I didn't want any arguments about Cuba. Or Fidel. It was just too hot. Everywhere in Cuba, if I started a conversation saying how bad things were, Cubans argued that everything was wonderful, the Revolution was vibrant, va bien, it is going well. If I argued that things were wonderful, Cubans countered with how terrible everything was, that even though they had an advanced degree in mechanical engineering, they'd still like to move to Miami and get a job in a parking garage or drying cars at a car wash.

This is what you can expect when a government gives free education and healthcare to a country already brimming with aspiring poets and artists and musicians. This is what you get when people have time on their hands. You get tremendous disputations. About everything. You get arguments about politics and art and poetry and literature and history and even whether Los Industriales are a better baseball team than the Baltimore Orioles. These conversations are usually fueled by rum. And dominoes. And cigars. They are how one spends some of one's time. And there is a lot of time in Cuba. The most important thing the Revolution has brought to Cuba is time.

I asked Ramirez if his family had originally been Cuban.

"It's funny you would ask me this. For years and years while I was growing up in New Jersey, my parents made believe they were from Puerto Rico or the Dominican Republic or something, but, in fact, they emigrated from Cuba a few years before the Revolution. My father got

71

into some kind of problem with the Battista government—I'm not sure what it may have been but he considered it serious—and my family left suddenly for New Jersey in the mid 50's and moved in with relatives who were already in Newark. Nobody in my family ever wanted to talk about the specifics that led to our emigration. They acted like it was not an exile, but instead an economic choice they had made voluntarily. For the betterment of the family, the children."

The stars were brilliant. There was no reflected light. The Milky Way was over our heads, and the moon was reflected on the sea. The sea was a mirror. There were insect sounds, and the sounds of people talking, and an occasional couple would walk up the street talking and holding hands. Ice clinked in our glasses and the tips of our cigars glowed. The owner's daughter smiled at us, asked if we wanted eggs and cheese for breakfast and took away the dishes. Time was suspended. Night in Baracoa was too hot, and at once simply perfect. It evoked sighs.

Eventually, the lights flickered and then returned, and people clapped in the distance. Fidel's show was over by then. It would inevitably return in a week with more questions and disputations.

The next morning at breakfast, Ramirez said he wanted us to go and see "the Cross, the Cross that Columbus planted when he arrived here. When he arrived in Baracoa, Columbus claimed the land not for the King of Spain, mind you, but for Christendom, and he planted a cross in the ground. I'm not sure how many crosses he may have erected here—maybe there were five or six—but they have one of the original ones in the Church."

"How can that be?"

"They even carbon dated it. It's more than 500 years old and it's in the Church and it is one of the very crosses Columbus planted here to claim the Western Hemisphere for Christendom. He did that right here."

I was amazed. And then I was deeply affronted. "So that's when and where everything in this hemisphere went off on the wrong track? This is where the genocide, the slavery, the patriarchy, the class system, the conquest officially began in this hemisphere? This is where the direction of this hemisphere's history was initially determined? This was the initial step toward why things are such a complete disaster now? I have to see this cross with my own eyes."

We walked to the Church. It was locked. We knocked on a back door. There was no answer. There were some men sitting in the square in front of the Church playing dominoes. "We want to see the Cruz de la Parra," we told them. They told us to go over to the parocio, across the street from the Church, and to ask to be let in.

We walked into the parocio. A middle aged woman dressed in the most drab, most modest, most Catholic clothing was behind a counter. "Please, Senora, we'd like to see the Cruz de la Parra."

"Oh," she said, "I'll have to get the key. Please wait just a moment."

She disappeared into the back for a few moments. When she returned she told us to come with her to the church. She opened the back door with the little key and we walked into the nave of the old church. No one else was in the church. The doors were all locked. There is a glass case, with a metal—was it silver?—frame around it, at the left of the pulpit was the Cross. "This is the Cruz," she said, pointing.

"Is that really it?" I asked. It wasn't very big. If it was two feet wide that was a lot. What remained was only about 3 feet tall. The rest of the cruz, I imagine it was originally much larger, was gone, little pieces of it taken by tourists, eaten by termites, rotted, carried off; only the center junction of it remained. I imagined that something this important, something that had such a profound affect on history would be much larger.

"Yes, and it's been carbon dated," she replied proudly. "The wood" she explained, "is from Cuba, not Europe."

There were no armed guards, no soldiers, no lasers, no burglar alarms, no security of any kind. The church's doors didn't even have deadbolts. The windows weren't even locked. To make a long story short, an artifact extremely important to Western Civilization was left completely unguarded in the Baracoa church. Apparently, nobody was concerned in the slightest way about it walking off.

The cross itself was not remarkable. It looked unsurprisingly like a cross of very, very old wood. It was not hard at all to imagine Columbus and his men cutting down trees, making the boards, joining them, erecting a cross in Baracoa and then making speeches in Castillian and saying prayers in Latin. And it was not at all hard to imagine that none of the then residents of this area, the Taino, the original inhabitants of Cuba, knew what Columbus was doing or took umbrage at it.

If they saw the ceremony at all, they may have thought, "It's some kind of ceremony. We do ceremonies frequently. This is their kind of ceremony after a long journey from the East. It seems harmless enough.

These people are dressed in the most hideous and uncomfortable garments, and they have what appear to be their instruments of war. And they have ugly facial hair and they really, really stink. They really need to bathe. But this ceremony appears to have nothing to do with us."

How wrong.

When we were finished looking at the church and the cross, we put a few pesos in the collection box, thanked the woman for letting us see the Cruz. She said I could come back if I wanted to. She would open the door for me if I wanted to return. I thanked her. I said I'd like to come back.

"I need a drink," Ramirez said. We found a small cafe in the hotel that used to belong to "La Rusa," who was a friend of Fidel and Che, and bought a Cristal and a Bucanero beer. It was late morning, and it was getting even hotter. Beer is expensive in Cuba, especially if you try to buy it with moneda nacional. If you're getting paid the equivalent of US$60 a week, spending US$1.50 on a single bottle of beer is a major expenditure. And probably an unwise one. We sat down.

"Well, that's it," Ramirez said.

"What's it?"

"The Cruz. That's it. That's what he wants. The Cruz de la Parra."

"That's completely crazy. Is he nuts? It's not possible," I said. "No way. Cannot be done. Forget it."

We drank our beer silently. My face was getting even hotter. The beer did absolutely nothing to cool us off. Was it making me hotter? We put ice in it. That didn't help either. The beer, and the idea of the cross and of stealing it all soaked me in sweat. We decided to go to the beach and to talk further. It was just too hot to stay in town. It had to be cooler at the beach.

The best beach near Baracoa is Manigual, north of the town. It's less than a half hour drive. There are, of course, no road signs, so we had to ask someone every few kilometers where it was. On the way we passed the cocoa factory, which was emitting a delightful, strong cocoa smell. The beach was much narrower than the Tulum beaches and instead of facing the Caribbean it faced the wide, deep Atlantic Ocean. There was no protective reef. The open sea was deep blue and there were small waves. The beach was populated with Cubans and tourists from Europe, Italians and Spaniards, I think, and large pigs freely wandered and grazed the underbrush. We sat near the surf, away from the pigs. To be frank, Manigual cannot hold a candle to any of Tulum's beaches.

"Well," Ramirez said again, "that's it."

"It cannot be done. It's crazy. It's insane. Look, if it were up to me, I'd take the damn thing and throw it directly into the ocean. As far as I can tell, planting the cross here cursed everything in this hemisphere for the past five hundred years, so removing the charm that holds the curse and depositing it safely and permanently and irretrievably in the bottom of the deep blue sea, I think, would be doing an enormous spiritual service for humanity. But there is no safe way to steal it for your client or anyone else. And removing it from Baracoa seems impossible. There is no way. At least none that I can imagine."

"There's no rush to make a plan, let's spend tomorrow morning checking out the rest of the town, and then we can go. Meanwhile, let's enjoy the beach." He pulled a bottle of 7-year old Havana Club rum and two bottles of non-Coca, non-Pepsi Cola out of his back pack. "How about a Cuba Libre?" It was simply wonderful to be in a country—was it the only left one in the entire world?—where the cola wars could not come ashore because of the bloqueo. We stood waste deep in the Atlantic Ocean and had our drinks. It was cool. And refreshing.

Early the next morning long before breakfast was even an idea for me, I walked back to the Church. To my surprise, the side door was unlocked. Inside a few people were already kneeling in prayer. There was the scent of incense, and a few candles had been lit. I found a new candle and sat with it in a chair near the back of the church. I wasn't at all sure of how to use the candle to honor those who had protected me, so I'd follow the instructions I had received. The rest, I'd just have to make up.

As I sat, I thought about protection and understood that throughout my life, I had clearly received it. It was obvious. I was alive. I was healthy. I was able to take care of myself. I had never gone to prison. Or to war. Even though I committed crimes, I had never been seriously injured or hurt, and I had escaped punishment. I was able to live a simple, more or less happy life. I was able to write and tell my stories. I was able to dream and to enjoy my life. I could sit in my yard and have a siesta. And a beer. It was clear. I had found refuge in Tulum. Tulum had protected me. Tulum had nurtured me even though my writing stories that had lies in them may have created problems for others. And now, too, Don Obdulio was evidently protecting me, and the man wearing white in Santiago could notice that protection and tell me that it was there for me.

And even beyond Tulum, beyond my decades in the ganja trade, even in my early years, even as a child, hadn't I always received comfort and protection? Where was that from? It was initially from my parents and their parents, my ancestors. It was from my teachers. It was from my colleagues. It was also from other gangsters. But all of that, it seemed to me, had miraculously originated from the infinite, the unnameable, Spirit, the one who has a million names but is beyond all naming. My continued existence, my survival, my longevity, all that had happened in my life, all of it was possible because of the enormous grace I had received. It was all protection for me. It was an ocean of blessings and protection for me. It was there in the beginning waiting for me, and it was there now. And evidently it would continue.

As I sat, wave after wave of gratitude broke over me. Again my chest was filled with warmth. Tears came to my eyes and flowed slowly down my face. I took the candle and I blew into it from my heart all of my gratitude for the protection and care I had received throughout my life. Thank you, thank you, thank you, thank you for this grace and protection I have received for so many years. I blew that gratitude from inside my chest, from inside my heart into the candle. When I was finished, I took the candle, put it on the stand. And I lit it. And I who never pray, offered to the unseen and unknowable, great Spirit, my gratitude for all of this, please accept my gratitude and honoring for the protection and comfort I have received throughout my life. Please accept this gratitude from me.

Then I sat quietly in a pew at the back of the church. I don't know how long I was there. I stayed until I felt that I had expressed my gratitude. I stayed until my heart told me it was time to leave.

Then I got up and walked through the side door of the church. A man immediately stepped into the path in front of me, blocking my way. I stopped. "Senor," he said, "Might I have a word with you?" He was a small, very dark man, about 40 years old, wearing a shirt with a collar and khaki pants.

"Well, all right," I said. This is Cuba, I thought, nobody is going to try to sell me a timeshare. It must be some kind of scam, though.

He pointed to a nearby bench. We sat down.

"Senor," he said, "I apologize for interrupting you. I have something I want to give you."

Jeepers, I thought, at last all of those announcements in airports might make sense, the ones about getting things from strangers. But I was skeptical. "How do you know it's for me?" I asked.

"Well, that's a little hard to explain. Let's just say that I can see that it's for you."

Oh, goodness, I thought. Is this how the new scam goes, one I am not aware of? Dubiousness began to stroll across my face like it was out for a Sunday walk.

"I know this is unusual. Let me try to explain it just a bit. I know you're here, I found you, and I'm supposed to give you this." He held out his hand. On his palm was a very small white cloth bag with a red tie-string at the top. He opened the bag, and poured out on his hand a small, round, black stone. The stone was dull but smooth. That's all there was.

"That's all there is," he said. "It's a very special stone, a piece of protection for you. It comes from across the seas, from Africa, it has prayers and protection from the ancestors in Africa and also from those in Cuba in it. It is a very good, very strong protection. It's for you."

When he said the word, "protection," I think I lit up like the crab nebula. I definitely felt my heart decide it should go into pounding overdrive. I am sure my eyes became saucers. And that my mouth was agape. And that I became visibly pale.

"But wait," I gasped, looking at the bag, which was now nicely tied up again with the little stone inside, "Wait a moment. Hold it. Why are you offering me this? I want you to explain it just a bit, as you just said before you would."

It turned out he lived in Baracoa and, in addition to his usual work in the town's public drinking water bureaucracy, he was an apprentice to a shaman. That morning the shaman, whom he referred to as "the Babalao," told him that there was somebody at the church at that very moment who needed to receive some protection, he should take the stone, go down there right now, find the person, and offer the protection stone to him. It was to be a gift.

The apprentice—his name was Sebastian—was initially quite worried that he wouldn't be able to find the right person. But when the Babalao told him to find something or someone, he really meant it, and he was supposed without further ado to find me. No descriptions. No hints. No directions. When I walked through the door of the church he knew immediately that the protection was meant for me. It had to be for me, he said, because among other things I seemed to be radiating a green light from my hands and heart.

Well, ok. I looked at my hands. I didn't see any light, green or otherwise. My hands were definitely sweaty but not green. Ditto my heart. Sweaty, yes. Beating hard, yes. But green?

He extended the bag to me, and I took it. "Part of the protection," he explained, "is to keep the bag a secret from everyone and not to show it to anyone. Ever." And would I mind answering a question for him? Of course not.

"Was I an apprentice to somebody? Somebody powerful?" he wanted to know. And where was that person? He felt the person could not be in Cuba, that he had to be somewhere else.

I told him that in the future I might be an apprentice, that I wasn't at that moment, not yet, and that the person was relatively nearby, just across the Caribbean in Mexico. In a place called Tulum. I told him the person, Don Obdulio, had been tracking me, was somewhat worried about me, and was protecting me. I was, of course, completely surprised that his teacher had sent him with the protection. That was something utterly amazing to me. And I wanted to thank them both very much for their help. He smiled. I put the bag in my pocket.

Sebastian and I sat there for a while grinning at each other and laughing as if we were in junior high school. Both of us were delighted. He was thrilled that, thank goodness, he found me so he could complete the task. He didn't want to have to tell the Babalao that he couldn't do the simple task he was asked to do. And I was very happy to receive the protection. I told Sebastian that I really hoped I wouldn't need it, which was an idea he clearly appreciated as an apprentice, but that it certainly couldn't hurt. And I was also delighted that the protection came to me by such a complicated web of perceptions from so far away. That made it all the better, all the sweeter.

When I returned to the casa particular, Ramirez was getting ready to leave. "What happened?" he asked.

"Nothing."

"You look different."

"Oh." I was certainly not going to tell him anything.

We confirmed that the Cruz didn't need any security it didn't already have. It had all the security it would ever need. There was just no way to leave Baracoa in a hurry with or without the Cruz, and even if there were a way of stealing the cross and hiding it for a while, getting it out of Baracoa, much less out of the country seemed to present insurmountable obstacles. If the cross went missing, the authorities would stop all traffic, search every building, stop every boat until the cruz reappeared. All the foreigners would be detained indefinitely. The government worried about embarrassment, not the so-called human rights of those it might have to detain to prevent its embarrassment. So it seemed utterly impossible.

We began to retrace our drive to Guantanamo and then to Santiago. Outside Baracoa, we picked up an old man who wanted a ride home to Guantanamo. Asked if Fidel had ever come to Baracoa after the Revolution, he responded, "I doubt it. He's very busy. And there's not a lot he needs to do here. He and Che used to come here, to visit La Rusa at her hotel, before the Revolution was over. They were all friends. I don't think he's been here since the Farola Highway opened. There's really no need. He has more important things to think about."

The return drive was beautiful. And monotonous. We had no music. We had run out of small talk. We had exhausted talk about the Cruz. True, the ride was picturesque—the ocean, rocks, dunes, grasses. And repetitious. Ramirez fell silent. The view outside the car windows was the visual equivalent of old, US late night AM radio. An orchestral sleeping potion from a high hotel ballroom overlooking a slumbering city. The soft, slightly muffled songs of long ago. From far away. But I didn't fall asleep. I only closed my eyes. What was Don Obdulio doing? I didn't know. Who was the man in white? Who sent Sebastian? I didn't know. Was the woman with the sea creatures in a basket Mari? What had the man in white seen? Why did it appear that I needed protection? Why was I the last to know about all of this? And, while I was at it, what was "this" anyway? I had no real idea. I fell asleep. I dreamed.

In my dream I was walking quietly through the mangrove just outside Tulum. Although there was water and deep mud all around me, I found places to step that were dry. It was night. I was looking for something. I had no flashlight; the moon was very bright and was reflected on the water around me. I was tired. I had been looking for a while. I found a tree trunk so I could sit down. I closed my eyes.

I heard branches around me move slightly, and when I opened my eyes, there was a large, yellow spotted jaguar sitting directly in front of me. She had yellow eyes. And wonderful, long whiskers. She was quite large. I was shocked, but I didn't scream or move. I just looked at her. At this, she stepped up to me, pushed her face against my face, and began to rub her face on mine. Her face was incredibly soft, and her whiskers were very stiff. I put my hand gently on the top of her head on the bridge between her eyes. She was purring a deep rumbling purr. She was hugging me. And she put a huge paw gently on my left thigh. What an embrace. I moaned, "Oh." And I woke up with a start. I wanted to go back to the dream. Ramirez was driving and smoking a cigar. "I guess you were dreaming," he said. "You were talking, but I couldn't understand what you were saying." I closed my eyes, but I couldn't find my way back to the dream. I tried. I kept my eyes closed, but sleep wouldn't come. The dream jaguar receded. And I could not follow her. I wanted her to hug me some more.

At the Santiago airport, we again joined a long, slow moving line for departure to Havana. Our plan was to fly to Havana and change planes for Cancun without leaving the airport. There was a three hour gap between planes, more than enough time to change terminals and pass through security. As I was standing in line, I saw the first advisory on the television of a hurricane approaching Cuba.

Experience has made Cuba masterful at handling hurricanes. Evacuations are mandatory and well executed. There are adequate shelters. Electricity and gas are turned off to prevent fires. People understand what to do to preserve their homes and lives, and they comply. Officials keep a census of each and every block so they can be sure that everyone has actually left and no one has been left behind.

The storm was at least two days from Havana. Maybe it was farther away. In other words, it presented no problems for us. We would be in Cancun before it ever reached Cuba. It did not appear to be on a course that continued toward Mexico after Cuba. It looked like it was going to the US Gulf Coast or Florida.

We boarded the plane, another flying, thundering, bellowing Russian pachyderm with spraying mist throughout the cabin, and then we waited. And we waited. We sat on the tarmac at the terminal for about an hour. In addition to the boredom of waiting, a boredom partially alleviated by reading *The Harp and The Shadow,* Alejo Carpentier's vivid

1992 indictment of Christopher Columbus on the 500th anniversary of his arrival in the Americas, I noticed that I was becoming worried we might not make our plane to Cancun. We now had two hours in the Havana Airport. That, I told myself, was still plenty of time.

The flight finally took off. It was an hour and a quarter late in departing and there was no explanation of what may have delayed it. In fact, there was no discussion of the delay at all. The flight proceeded uneventfully to Havana, where we slowly taxied past the large plane from Angola that continues to connect Cuba with its African, military adventure, and the plane belonging to the president of Venezuela, who was in town to be schooled by Fidel in toying with the multinationals and the US, to the domestic terminal. We walked to the baggage carousel, and then we waited. And we waited. Nobody knew where the baggage from the flight might be. Everyone on the plane waited and made noises to create a loud buzz of annoyance, frustration, impatience, worry, resignation and exhaustion. About an hour later, and again without any explanation, the baggage miraculously arrived. We grabbed our bags, and we hustled by taxi from the domestic to the international terminal.

We ran into the international terminal, knowing we were late if we had to be there a full two hours before the flight. We looked at the departure board. What we saw was not good: the flight to Cancun was canceled. Not delayed. Not demorado. Canceled. Cancelado.

"How about that?" Ramirez said. "That's not part of our plan."

We sought out an official from Cubana. He summoned us and everyone else who had been ticketed for the flight to stand around him in the middle of the main hall of the international terminal. He stood on a chair. Surrounding him were about 120 people. "The flight," he said in his most authoritative, resonant, bureaucratic voice, "is canceled. We cannot put you on the next flight, tomorrow, because it is sold out. We can put all of you on the flight on Thursday." It was then Monday. Would they put us up in a hotel? No, they would not because the flight was canceled and not delayed. Would they give us a voucher or money for food? No, they would not because the flight was canceled. This produced another extremely loud cacophony of annoyance, frustration, impatience, anger, worry and exhaustion. It was only later that I realized that no reason had been given for the cancellation.

We sought out another official in an office at the rear of the terminal, hoping for better news from someone higher up the organizational ladder. The office was small, filled with two desks, and there were four people seated in it. It had fluorescent tubes across the ceiling. The boss was behind the larger desk on the left; all of the other people were sitting in folding chairs to his right. They were to perform the role of the Greek chorus. The chief, who wore a suit, asked to see Ramirez's passport, saw the blue US passport cover, looked inside, suppressed his smile and said, "I'm sorry. You are not protected here. There is nothing I can do to change this. You can get on the flight on Thursday." No, there was nothing more today, tomorrow, or Wednesday, and no, we could not use our tickets on a flight belonging to a different airline. And no, there were no vouchers or anything else. With each of these announcements, the Greek chorus responded with nodding, supportive murmuring, and no trace of empathy whatsoever, "Si, si, senor."

Why did passengers on another flight just before ours which didn't take off receive hotel vouchers? Because their flight had been delayed and ours was not delayed, it was canceled. Si. Si, Senor. And that was what made the big difference, he said. The Greek chorus punctuated this sentence with "Si, senor" and arms folded across their uniformed chests. "I'm sorry," he said matter-of-factly. There was a slight twinkle of satisfaction in his eye, which he only half heartedly sought to suppress. The Greek chorus mimed recognition of our plight. And even if they wished to help us, which apparently they did not, they were powerless to assist us in any way regardless of their feelings about the matter. After all, El Jefe had spoken to us and told us directly and personally everything that we needed to know. Good day.

Was the boss enjoying our discomfort at being trapped? Was he enjoying explaining something to us that was irrational? I wasn't sure, but it was clearly not what I wanted to hear.

After we left the windowless office, Ramirez turned to me, "We have a larger problem. We have enough cash for some food, but we don't have enough for a hotel or, for that matter, even for a round trip taxi to Havana. This would not have been a problem if we made our connection. As it is, my US credit cards don't work here. I will email someone right now to buy us a ticket out on another airline. Meanwhile, my friend, we're stuck in the airport." He wandered off to the airport's Internet café.

My own money, of which there was precious little at the start, was all gone, too. I had converted it into a few cigars and rum and some souvenirs and some books. How could I have known to hang on to it? And even if I had, my original, few dollars wouldn't accomplish much. First, there was an 80% conversion rate. Then, it was $50 round trip to Havana from the airport by taxi. Then there was the cost of a hotel. Would my dollars have accomplished anything? Doubtful. To be truthful, when I began, I didn't have enough money for a hotel room and the taxi.

There was nothing for me to do but to sit down with my empty wallet and our packed luggage and wait. Around me other people who had been on the flight feverishly made other arrangements: their credit cards from Venezuela and Europe and Mexico, of course, worked. They got cash from the ATM. They made hotel reservations. Their cell phones worked. They left. They were not going to let Cubana ruin their day or even a precious minute of it. They would deal with the dictatorship of the proletariat the only way they could, with the tools of capitalism. They'd just extend their vacations or easily make other arrangements.

Left behind, in addition to us, was a young American hippie couple with their baby and packages they were trying to bring to Mexico. By then it was late, there were no more flights to Mexico, and there was nothing to do but try to sleep until the morning on the blue plastic seats near the terminal's front windows. This seating was not designed for prolonged sitting, let alone sleeping.

During the evening, a passenger on a late night flight to Spain took pity on us and gave us half a bottle of rum. We spent our last pesos on sandwiches, reserving just enough for Internet minutes and exit tax.

The night passed painfully. And slowly. The rum did not help. It did not allow us to pass out. It did not even numb us. Or distract us from our waiting. The lights in the terminal dimmed slightly, but it was essentially like sleeping in an ill equipped jail. While we slept, workers swept the terminal and mopped it. The seats were brutal to my back. And my neck. I couldn't turn to lie on my side or chest. I woke up sticky and aching and annoyed. My eyes and face were puffy. My feet were swollen. I wanted to change my clothes.

After brushing my teeth in the bathroom, there was nothing to do but to sit or wander the floor and wait for an email telling us what flight we might have tickets on. There was only the simple boredom of basic, civil confinement. There was virtually nothing to distract us.

There was no reading material to buy in the terminal, even if we had money for it.

In the meanwhile, the television news reported that Hurricane Leo, as it was now called, had apparently accelerated. It was still churning through the Caribbean toward Havana and was about 36 hours away. Shortly, the news reported, the airport would close and evacuations would begin in earnest in Havana. All flights to the east had already been canceled. The storm was being tracked, and the Government, unlike the US barbarians who committed genocide and let their citizens be drowned and injured in places like New Orleans, was quite ready for it, as your Government always is ready to safeguard the Cuban people and their lives from danger, whether it is man made or natural. Viva la revolucion!

This broadcast put some spring into the step of those then boarding flights for the South and the West, who were apparently leaving just before Leo arrived. Those who had been planning to fly to Europe returned dejectedly and with worried faces to their hotels. At least they had hotels. Ramirez and I continued to sit on the blue seats in the terminal near the window. I found the small bag and its stone in my pocket. I held on to it.

"Want a café con leche?" I asked. "I have a little left in coins."

"Our luck," he said. "Maybe I shouldn't say it, but I am not optimistic that we are going to get out of here before this storm closes the airport." He frowned. "I agree the job does not seem possible for us. But I feel like the Fates are now toying with us, playing with us, testing us."

"Look," he continued. "It's being just one enormous obstacle after another. And we need to have a reply to my email pretty soon. I'll go and check on it." He walked across the terminal. He seemed disturbed, or perhaps angry. I was sure that I personally had done nothing to cause our many problems.

Or had I? Don Obdulio told me not to do bad things. Was casing a church in Baracoa for a burglary a bad thing? Probably. Was discussing whether the burglary could be done a bad thing? Probably. Was planning a crime a bad thing? Probably. What exactly was the line connecting these acts and their consequences? Well, the Buddha taught that from interdependent causes all things arise and fade away. Maybe my deciding despite Don Obdulio's warning to go to Cuba was making a problem. Maybe. But at the same time, Don Obdulio was obviously protecting me, he had done something to put a mark of protection on me, and he somehow had arranged for Sebastian to give me the stone. If he were making these problems happen, why was he also trying to protect me from the consequences? How would I know? How could I tell why these things were happening? Did I cause this? Did somebody else cause this? Did Don Obdulio cause it? I had no idea.

Ramirez returned a few moments later smiling and waving a small, yellow piece of paper. We had paid reservations on a Mexicana flight to Mexico City that left in two hours. I was relieved. We were at last going to leave. Once we got to Mexico all of his plastic would work. We'd be fine. In fact, everything would be wonderful. I'd lay aside for the time being my worrisome speculation about the extent of my responsibility for all of the inconvenience.

We checked into the flight, proceeded through security, and waited at the departure gate. Around the gate were better stores and several restaurants, but of course, we had virtually nothing to spend. It seemed reckless to pay our last few pesos for anything. We'd have to be content just sitting and waiting and being grateful that we were finally leaving.

"I think," Ramirez said, "that the job can be done. I was thinking about it last night. It requires local participation. You have to take the cross at night and you have to have a place to hide it, in Baracoa, where it can be safe, for several months, despite repeated searches. I'm sure there has to be such a place. After six or seven months, when things have cooled off, you put it on a fishing boat or a cruise ship that is going to a port outside the country. That's the general outline."

"You're just trading one kind of problem for another. Even if you had local help, you'd have to pay them most of the money up front, and you'd have to worry that they'd do the job themselves and sell it to somebody else or even sell you out to the government and keep the money. I don't think it can be done. It's too complicated and far away. And, let's face it, we don't belong in Baracoa and we stick out badly. It's obvious that we're tourists. And gringos."

I looked up at the departure schedule and saw, next to our flight, the blinking, red notation, "Demorado." It could as easily have said, "Don't talk any more about doing burglaries." The flight to Mexico City, our flight to Mexico City, was now officially delayed. I again reached into my pocket and held onto the small white bag.

I pointed at the screen. Ramirez looked at it, too, and frowned. "If it wasn't for real bad luck, I wouldn't have no luck at all." He shook his head.

We sat and waited. All of the other flights began to blink "Demorado" also. So we weren't going to leave after all, and neither was anyone else.

We spent an additional 24 hours in the departure lounge of the terminal accompanied by everyone else who had cleared security and was trying to fly to the west or the south. When all of the flights on the screen were stopped, officials appeared and explained that because of the storm, we could not leave the terminal, that we were safe where we were, that all of the airport was entirely safe, that the airlines would make food available for their passengers including us, and that we would be on the first flights to leave as soon as the airport reopened, after the storm passed.

"Great," Ramirez sighed. "Everything is going wrong, but at least we won't starve. This is really a first for me. Nothing I ever do gets this messed up, gets so completely undermined, so totally subverted. And I'm sure, amigo, that I myself didn't cause this." He looked directly at me.

"Maybe it's me, then," I said. "Maybe I have some kind of deep, karmic curse on me. Maybe I have the bad juju. You have to admit that almost everything that's happened on this trip has gone wrong. I'm wondering whether that has something to do with me. Maybe I have a curse. Maybe it's me who's causing all of these problems. They are gigantic problems, right?" As I was saying this, my right hand was cradling the white sack and its small black stone.

Ramirez laughed at this. I wasn't so sure it was funny. I began to wonder whether Don Obdulio had something to do with creating all of these calamities. Was he capable of doing that? I had no real idea. Was he playing with us? With me? Was someone? Why, I wondered, did I think it had to do with him, that he was the one causing these problems? Or was this just what he saw in his tracking, that he knew what was going to happen, that he had tried to warn me about it, and that he had even tried to give me protection from it? Maybe it would be even worse if he weren't protecting me. One thing seemed obvious to me: it couldn't just be bad luck. There had to be more to it than that. And, though I hated to admit it, it sure did seem to have something to do with me. In some way it was personal. In some way, in a way I didn't like, it was about me.

I didn't want to take the situation personally. Really. I tried not to. And maybe it was a failure of my imagination, but I couldn't believe that all of this had nothing to do with me. How else could it happen? Could it purely be coincidence? I didn't believe that.

We sat looking out at the runway as the sky turned black and the wind picked up. Things that were not tied down, chairs, carts for baggage, garbage cans, plastic cones, all flew away or were trapped and piled up in corners of the building. The rain was torrential and blew sideways. Water slid under every door, through cracks in the roof, down windows. The storm made a deep rumbling sound like the full throated gurgling of a large diesel engine. Everything vibrated. The floor became incredibly slippery, as if it were an ice skating rink. And then the power went out. The terminal was in complete darkness.

There was nothing to do but sit and wait. The darkness continued; there were no emergency lights. The storm's intensity continued unabated. The building shook and moaned. The winds whistled and growled. Things that were not tied down flew around and smashed into things that were stationary. Things that were stationery bent over or became detached and started flying around. The storm's roaring was punctuated by things crashing into each other and breaking. I sat with my hand in my pocket, cradling the white bag.

In the midst of this, my nose detected the faintest whiff of what I thought was marijuana. Maybe something was on fire. Maybe something was burning. I turned to Ramirez, "Do you smell that? It smells like grass, but that's impossible. It cannot be weed. Is something on fire?" He responded, "Well, it's not me smoking it, if that's what you're asking. It smells like grass. Maybe it's just a fire."

"I'm going to see if I can find it, I'll be back."

In Cuba nice, legal distinctions between marijuana and other illegal drugs don't exist. There is no legal difference between heroin and pot. Nobody wants to be caught with anything. Ever. The Government takes the matter quite seriously. The result can be prison. For a long time. There are no technicalities about this. There is no such thing as an illegal search. And so, whoever might have been smoking in the airport was at best reckless. Or ignorant. I wondered who it might be.

I shuffled around the terminal trying not to slip and fall down on the slick floor. I found people smoking cigars and cigarettes, but I'm apparently not much of bloodhound. I could not follow the scent at all. After about fifteen minutes of skating and shuffling and holding on to things, I returned to my seat empty handed.

"I found it," Ramirez whispered when I returned. He pointed to the silhouette of a couple sitting at the end of the row of seats facing us. "They're headed to Caracas. They say they made a mistake bringing it to the airport, they meant to get rid of it before coming here, but they didn't. Apparently partied too hard before coming here and forgot to dump it. Anyway, they somehow got it past security, which in itself is remarkable, and they now need to get rid of it before they arrive and go through yet another inspection. We're going to help them with this project. It's not much." He pulled out a small joint.

"Why don't they just throw it away?"

"Are you kidding me? Nobody ever does that. Tell me, if you can, of a single time when anybody you knew or even knew of threw anything away. Ever. Here." He handed it to me. I once threw an entire truck full of pot away, but I didn't say anything about that.

I spent the rest of the evening intermittently trying to sleep on yet another row of uncomfortable chairs and talking to the other passengers who were awake. Being stoned made the time pass even more slowly, but at least I was entertained by conversations I would otherwise have found uninteresting or aggravating. I said a lot of stupid things, and I heard many even stupider ones. I may have dozed off. I don't think I dreamed. I think I was too exhausted to.

At about 4 am the lights came on in the terminal and large crews of cleaners appeared and began to mop the floors. Soon, the sun rose and the monitors came to life announcing departure times for all of the flights. Ours was to leave in 3 hours.

I brushed my teeth and shaved in the men's room. Again. There was no hot water. The razor seemed to be pulling out as many whiskers as it was cutting, but eventually my face was more or less smooth. I washed my face in cold water. I wet my hair so I could brush it. And I then had breakfast courtesy of Mexicana. Breakfast was a miracle. Despite everything, life suddenly appeared to be remarkably good. Much better. I was optimistic. I was being rescued. I was returning to the First World. To civilization. I was saved. I patted the small bag in my pocket, I said to it, "Thanks."

In contrast to Havana, the airport in Mexico City seemed to me to be unbelievably beautiful and 100% clean to the most demanding, advanced, First World hygienic and sanitation standards. It was so very spotless and shiny. The carpeting on the floor was so beautiful.

The paint on the walls was so new. There were dozens of restaurants. The place was jammed with well dressed travelers. Had I been reborn? Was this heaven? It was so very comfortable. It was so wonderfully air conditioned. It was so quiet. It seemed like paradise. I inhaled the comfort and richness of it.

Ramirez would not be returning to Cancun with me; he had a flight to somewhere in the Caribbean, Barbados, I think. He handed me a coach ticket to Cancun and a 500 peso bill, and said he'd be in touch, buen viaje. I wandered to the domestic Mexicana flight and decided I would stop and have a steak at the restaurant nearest the gate. And a beer. And a salad. And French fries. And a second beer. By the time I got on the plane, I felt restored and ever so slightly, pleasingly drunk. My sense of well-being had returned. I slept throughout the flight. When I awoke on landing in Cancun, I realized I hadn't been paid for the trip. Not one cent. Not one peso moneda nacional. The 500 pesos didn't count. In comparison with the cigars I had in my bag, the most expensive cigars at Super Mar del Caribe would have been a wonderful bargain.

My intention when I reached Tulum was to rest from the trip. And to take up where I left off: sitting in the yard, taking a nap in the white plastic chair, reading, dreaming, writing. I would see what stories floated by and try to catch them in my net. I wanted to write more about Tulum, and how it mixed the ancient with the modern, how it mixed Mayan ruins from centuries ago with a pueblo in which the oldest present business was founded in the '90's. I wanted to explore how it is changing, constantly changing, constantly remaking itself, always under construction. I wanted to point out that the Tulum I'm telling you about will very soon be in the past, just a memory, and that a new, different Tulum will have grown up here in its place. The new Tulum will be built over the old Tulum, just as 500 years ago churches were built over Mayan sacred sites.

Unfortunately, when I finally dragged myself into my yard, my chair was already occupied by the curandero. He had a bottle of beer in his hand and was looking at the sky. "Todo bien?" he smiled. Is everything ok?

"Not really. No. Are you joking?"

"Are you surprised? Listen, didn't I tell you? Didn't I warn you? Didn't I? Do you remember what I told you? I know you must remember what I told you."

He had a point. I did remember exactly what he told me. In fact, it was troubling me. "You have no idea. OK. Maybe you have some idea. The trip had some problems. Some very major problems. Like missing a flight. Like being stuck in the airport for the hurricane. Like sleeping in the airport for a couple of nights. Like not making flights. Like being stuck. Like running out of money. I imagine you know all about all of that already, right?"

He laughed. A deep, long, wheezing and snorting laugh. "I bet it did have problems. I bet it did. There's no need to be angry with me. No need to be hostile or upset. You're ok. You're completely fine. You survived it. All of it. Now you're here again." He offered me a beer. "Tomorrow, we can talk about it, if you want to. For now, drink the beer, sit in your chair here, relax, enjoy yourself. Do what you always do." He got up, shook his head, smiled, said, "Welcome back," and wandered out of the yard. He turned and waved before disappearing around the corner of the house.

I settled into the chair. I took off my shoes. As I finished the beer, I fell into a deep sleep with my arms crossed on my chest. I could hear the birds singing and the coco tree branches softly chattering while I slept. Tulum's humidity wrapped me in gauze, and all was again perfect and restful in the world.

When I awoke, it was starting to get dark. And to my dismay, Federales were in my yard standing over me. Three of them. Their Dodge Hemi Federale mobile was parked in front of my house with all its blue and red and strobe lights flashing. The neighbors were standing back on the sidelines, in the shadows, watching the show. The Federales' guns remained in their holsters, they had flashlights in their hands. They wanted to know whether I have any visitors now. I don't. Would they like to look around inside? No, they wouldn't. Do I know Sr. Ramirez? Of course, I do. Doesn't everybody in town know at least one Sr. Ramirez? They evidently didn't think this was very funny. They showed their lack of good humor by saying from behind their utterly unnecessary, reflector sunglasses that if he, my Sr. Ramirez, the very Sr. Ramirez in whom they were interested and thought I might know where he was, came back they expected me to call them. Right away. Do I understand what they are telling me? My mouth overflowed with submission, "Yes, of course, most definitely, certainly. Cierto. Segurro. Yes, sirs." They strutted away.

Oh, this was more bad news. This was not the kind of wake up I liked. This was the kind of wake up I had been successfully avoiding since I arrived in Tulum. My surprise was gigantic and was equaled only by my annoyance. I had done absolutely nothing to deserve to have these officers of federal law enforcement arrive on my doorstep. I do not like it when policemen seek me out and talk to me. And I like it far less when it's not just the routine. I do not like it when they ask questions and demand phone calls from me and eyeball me and stand over me with their arms folded across their chests. I do not like that at all.

There are apparently two dominant law enforcement strategies in this hemisphere. One is the US model. When a crime occurs, the police hurry and try to find out who did it. The second is the Mexican model. By showing their presence and their willingness without provocation to use physical force, the police think they actually prevent crimes. That is why every single Federale mobile on Highway 307 has all of its lights on all of the time. That is why occasionally, the Federales lay on the siren for no reason. That is why all encounters with the Federales are to be scrupulously avoided, lest one become an example for something. Is the Mexican strategy effective? I know nobody who acts up when they know the police are nearby, whether they're watching or not. And nobody ever wants a personal visit from these officials of national law enforcement because nobody wants them to demonstrate their touted, well publicized ability persuasively to deter crime.

The arrival of the Federales and their inquiry about Ramirez sent me into pacing the yard and an attempt to figure out what he or I may have done in Mexico that the Federales might now be interested in. I was certain that they didn't care about our trip to Cuba. Not at all. That was completely unimportant to them. I couldn't come up with anything. Not a single thing. I kept getting stuck on thinking about Mari Estrella and thinking that the Federales were a sure sign that I'm never going to hear from her or from Ramirez again. Forget about ever being paid. Now the Federales thought I knew someone. Or something that interested them in some regard known only to them. I definitely didn't want them to think of me in that way at all. I wanted them immediately to forget about my existence and to move on to someone or something else they would find far more interesting, more compelling, a more intriguing subject with which to occupy all of their ample time and attention. I wanted again to become invisible to them, someone utterly unworthy of even the smallest particle of their scrutiny.

I decided to take a long walk to El Point for the Internet. I could think while I was walking. I could calm down, maybe. I would breathe deeply. Maybe I could perceive what I had done that was worthy of such intense Federale interest. Truth be told, I had done nothing. Zip. Nada. Nothing at all to merit police contact.

El Point is at the northern end of Tulum in the small strip mall at the light. The mall has a car rental, a realtor, an ATM and San Francisco de Assis, a large supermarket. The supermarket and El Point have been open only for a few years.

Each of the computers at El Point is named for a sports figure; there is some sports memorabilia on the wall. El Point at one time was the newest, most air conditioned, most upscale of Internet stores. It was in a different league from the others in town, most of which were open to the street and were not air conditioned. And El Point had speedier Internet. Nobody knows if the speed was actually quicker, or if air conditioning made the waiting for connection more bearable. El Point was cool and fast; the others, hot and slow. At first I was going to use the computer named "Maradona," but I decided that was not a good idea because of well known allegations about his drug use. I didn't want a criminal computer or one associated in any way with crime, however tangentially. Then I was going to use "Muhammad Ali," but I decided that this too was a poor choice because his case went to the Supreme Court before he finally won. And then it was too late for his boxing career. That computer probably wouldn't make things happen quickly enough for me. No, the perfect computer was "Ferrari." It promised to be fast, mechanical and hopefully very impersonal. A machine. So I sent Ramirez an email using Ferrari. It was simple and in English and to the point, "The Federales are looking for you. I'm looking for some money." I was thinking of witty things I could add about Mari, the tortugas, and a long discourse with ceremonial hand wringing about how on earth could he succeed in immediately getting me into such a jam with the cops, one that I had successfully avoided for more than a decade. Instead, I decided to send just the simplest message and immediately to leave. No, I was not worried that the police would search my email account, or that they would intercept Ramirez's. The Mexican police model is not that big on that kind of surveillance. If they wanted Ramirez's email address, they would have asked me for it. I had no idea whether I would receive a response, let alone an explanation. I would check my email the next day or so.

I spent the rest of the afternoon sitting in my chair, smoking my new, Cuban cigars and reading Ricardo Piglia. Although I was sitting in Tulum, my attention was in Montevideo with a few desperate robbers holed up in a house with their loot trying to hold off an enormous assault by an army of Uruguayan and Argentinian cops. It seemed a perfect story for me. Of course, I, and probably every other reader identifies solely with the robbers. The story provided a further example, as if one were needed, of why I wanted nothing at all to do with the police, Uruguayan, Argentinian, Mexican, whatever kind. It didn't matter where they were from; I would thrive beautifully without any of their police attention. I would thrive wonderfully on being overlooked. And ignored. The last thing I wanted was for the police to know my name or where I lived and to think they should pay me a visit. Or worse, ask me questions.

In the middle of my reading, yet another surprise. A visit from the dog police. Do I have a dog? No. Well, here's a notice anyway. The notice, citing chapter and verse of the Mexican dog law, says that all dogs are supposed to be wearing a collar and walking on a leash and that if they're not the dog police will come back tomorrow and round them up, kidnap (or is it dognap?) and kill any offending dogs. It actually says "kill" in plain Spanish. One guy has the job of handing out the notices; three other guys, some kind of canine lethal injection team, stand around solemnly with folded arms, frowning sadly, making it clear by their presence that they mean business. I think that the bribe, la mordida, must work on this if your dog is arrested, but I'm not sure who gets the ransom, who gets to save the innocent dog, the four legged Jean Valjean, for good. Probably one of the frowning members of the execution team. At any rate, it's not time for that. Not yet. That time will doubtless arrive when they make their promised, advertised return tomorrow to seize any local dogs they can find.

I'm amazed at this affront to the usual order of things. Of course, every owner of every dog decides instantly to go and find the pooch loosely affiliated with the household and to tie or pen it up for at least 24 hours. This includes dogs that have never in their lives worn a collar or been tied to anything. Dogs that spend their afternoons sleeping at my feet snoring. Dogs I know but don't know whether they have owners in any usual, common sense of that word. Dogs who have no owners are, of course, taken in by the owners of dogs they have befriended. Luna gets tied to a tree with Cuquis. Chubi gets locked in the bodega with Chappo. Woofie, a proper dog name that is common throughout the entire Southern Hemisphere, gets dragged into the kitchen and tied to the very table he has been told for months to stay away from. This is probably confusing and probably will result later on in a rain of kicks or blows. But for now, the dog is safe.

Dogs in Tulum have a very unusual, intricate, canine society. Most have remarkable freedom to roam with their companions. They seem to share the bounty of food and shelter and companionship, human and canine. They tend to play quite rough with each other. Occasionally, their roughhousing requires serious veterinary care, but in general, the dogs seem to work out their issues without human assistance and without maiming each other. There are, of course, some scars and injuries, some ripped ears, nobody can deny that. But that is infrequent. Surely, the dog police know all this, they've lived here themselves, but in response to a complaint from somebody, they are directed to show up, to present notices, and to pay an extended visit to particular neighborhoods in Tulum with allegedly problem dogs. This ultimately will lead to the seizure and summary execution of the most aggressive, homeless, friendless, threatening dog, who will be found wandering the streets despite the written warning and the cyclone of word of mouth warnings the written notice provokes. This condemned dog will be either the one that decides to volunteer for martyrdom or the one that absolutely no one in the community is willing to shelter, usually for good reason. The dog police seize this dog and then they go back to City Hall or wherever they answer their dog complaint telephone line, and the other dogs in town are gradually freed again, to resume their lives, until the next occasion when a complaint is made and the dog police again have to issue their warnings and the cycle of policing begins again. All of the dog owners are, of course, unhappy that someone has made a complaint. But the complainer remains anonymous so that human retribution will be forestalled.

In the morning when I go out, the streets of Tulum are strangely silent. There appears to be more birdsong. There is much less barking. Dogs that usually greet me or walk with me toward the main drag or beg food from me are nowhere to be seen. It's as if the dogs have gone to the mattresses, gone into hiding. When I round the corner, there is a gigantic iguana sitting on top of a pile of cement blocks. It, of course, is unafraid of humans. It is afraid of dogs. It stares at me and flicks its tongue. It, too, realizes that there are no dogs this morning, no reason to limit its hauteur, no reason to move. It stares insolently. It has no intention of moving. No matter what.

My long walk back to El Point is solitary. And bright. There is no email from Ramirez. That is not a surprise. I begin to wonder whether he could still be involved in some aspect of the drug trade. Drug trafficking in Mexico now is a far cry from our former business. Mexican drug gangs are extremely violent, both to their rivals, whom they sometimes behead and then throw the severed heads into saloons or hang from bridges, and to the police and army, whom then often ambush or shoot or kidnap. Some of the people they kill in rival gangs, it is said, are fed to their dogs. I doubted Ramirez could be involved with such people. They seem far too driven and violent and crazy for his taste.

There was a time in the not so distant past when the coast of Quintana Roo, and particularly the small, sheltered bays near Tulum, was a locale heavily involved in drug trafficking. Packages containing drugs were thrown off of boats on the inside the barrier reef so they could float toward shore, where they would be retrieved. There were occasional meetings of boats in the middle of the night. And people walking the beach at first light, at 5 am, looking for the package. But also, packages were rumored to be retrieved sometimes by people for whom they were not intended. This could be a curse, if the traffickers successfully searched out the recipient, or an opportunity, if they failed to find the person who had retrieved the package, and the recipient had a plan. There is a local legend about how the mayor of a small village on the coast south of Tulum found such a package on the beach one morning. He apparently had a plan in place in the event that he should ever be so lucky. A month later he and about 12 other villagers were living in Spain. In Madrid. Is this oft repeated story true? Nobody knows, although some people claim to know the name of the mayor and of the town.

These narco-trafficking activities, however, seem recently to have been curtailed. Federales and soldiers in uniform occasionally patrol the beaches. Road blocks are sometimes set up on small, rural roads south of Tulum. And, it appears, the cartels have decided that the West coast of Mexico, far from here, and the states on the US border are a far more fertile area for their activities. It seems unlikely to me that Ramirez might be involved, but it is not completely out of the question. Why else, I ask, had the Federales come to my house? What did they want? What do I have to do to get them never, ever to come back and totally to forget that I even exist?

After a week without an email response I was beginning to try to reconcile myself to a life without the money and without further contact from Ramirez. This, I was beginning to think, was not such a bad prospect. The Federales had not returned. Thank goodness. Things could slowly go back to how they were before, and my life would not take on any new, possibly dangerous aspects. I would return to appearing to be an anonymous, common lizard. One who liked stories. I would sit in my chair and dream. I would get out my net, see what stories I could capture, scribble them down in spiral notebooks and on the backs of envelopes. Tulum would continue around me. I would be almost invisible again. My routine would continue. What could be better?

I'll tell you instead what could be worse. I could've gone into a reptilian rage about the money and started making plans for the unceremonious gangland style execution of Ramirez. But I didn't. No, I was more civilized and was heavily into rationalizing my seemingly passive response, my lack of homicidal wishes. Basically, repressing my desire for money, and failing that, revenge.

Except that I was nevertheless angry at being ripped off. Yes, I enjoyed the trip to Cuba. Yes, the cigars I now had were far, far better than what I had before. You have no idea how wonderful a real Romeo y Julieta Churchill can be. Yes, it had been an adventure, an exploration. But, alas, I wanted the promised money, and I wasn't ready to drop the subject. Not by a long shot. I wanted to be paid. In full. And, after all, the police had visited me. At the very least, I should be compensated for the lingering and intrusive inconvenience Ramirez had so recklessly, so thoughtlessly brought into my life. And for my reasonable apprehension that the cops might at any moment return. And ask more questions, and glare at me, and write down more things about me.

It was obvious to me. I had to be paid. But how? I had no idea where Ramirez was, and I had no idea of how to get in touch with him. Except his email, which is the world's weakest, most easily evaded form of contact imaginable. Did you get my email? Even the question itself invites evasion. And the idea of a "read receipt" is laughable. Does anybody ever click "yes" about an email, the content of which they'd like to avoid?

On a Thursday morning—I remember that dog life had resumed as it was before the visit of the dreaded dog police—I was out for a walk around the neighborhood. I like my morning walks, before it gets incredibly hot. It's a chance to breathe deeply, see the sights, ruminate about whatever needs digesting, talk to myself, hash out whatever might be in need of vigorous hashing. On the corner of the main street, across from the town hall, I ran into El Kid, the kid who worked for the curandero. How was he doing? Fine, OK, thanks. At this, the curandero came out of the fruteria with a big bunch of herbs, which he handed to El Kid. I said hello. He nodded Buenas. After the usual pleasantries, and taking into consideration my gnawing need for money, I thought I'd ask him directly for some help.

"You remember when you were telling me about tracking me?" I asked.

He made a sound, "Mummum," and he nodded.

"Do you think you could find somebody, if I didn't know where he might be? I mean, could you track him down if I don't know where he is? Is that something you could do? Could you find this guy for me? Tell me where to find him?"

"Mummum."

Taking "Mummum" as an affirmative response, I began, "Well, I." I wanted to explain how all I had was his email address, what I wanted him to do, whom I wanted him to find. I thought I should provide some helpful details, some speculation, some ideas that might be needed to start a productive search. Maybe a description of who I was looking for might help. Maybe his name. Maybe I should even tell Don Obdulio the whole story, beginning way back with my deliveries in Newark. In my mind he needed some information to think about where Ramirez might be. In his world, evidently, thinking isn't all that vital, so the facts that might be plumbed by thinking are, well, virtually irrelevant.

He interrupted me at my "I". He held up his hand, as if to stop all traffic, immediately stopping my narration. "Ah," he said. "You should look in Playa del Carmen." Evidently he didn't want to hear my story at all. He didn't need the story. He didn't want to hear the facts. He wasn't going to distill the events leading to my request. Did he have enough details just from seeing me? Whatever he was observing to get an answer, it seemed that he didn't want me to tell him anything about what I wanted.

"Where in the city?" I asked, ignoring obvious questions about when I should look. It is, after all, a large place to search for somebody. He again held up his hand to stop me. Evidently, he wasn't going to engage in any discussions with me about my request. No. He was just going to cut to the quick.

"Listen," he said softly and matter of factly, "Just go to Playa del Carmen and look around, ok? That's where he is. When you look around, you'll find him." It was as if he were telling me how to find a nearby address just across the street from where we then were standing, just go around the corner, and you'll see it immediately, it's there on your right.

"Is it that simple? All I have to do is go there and, poof, I will find him?"

"He'll be there when you are. You just have to look out for him. That's what I'm telling you to do. I have tracked him. And you. To the point where you meet him in Playa del Carmen. You can definitely rely on this. It's a sure thing. You meet him in Playa del Carmen."

"Do you mind telling me how you do this?"

"I wouldn't mind telling you, if I could, but I cannot. It's not like that. It isn't easily explained. And what good would it do you to know how I do it if you don't know how to do it on your own? Let's not worry about how. Or what I do to find him or anyone else or anything I might be looking for. If you want to find him, and I assume you do, you should just go there to Playa del Carmen and find him. If you actually want to find him." He made it seem like it was no big deal at all to pluck someone's location out of the ethers as if Don Obdulio were a GPS and the person he was looking for was wearing a beeping aircraft beacon. All he had to do was tune in and, presto! there he was beeping away. And to know who I was looking for without ever asking me was apparently not a very big deal for him either. The facts, the details, the history of events were all apparently utterly irrelevant.

And if all of that was irrelevant, what was relevant? I have no idea. I have no idea what Don Obdulio was scanning. Or what he was doing to get this answer. It seemed unfathomable.

I thanked him for this information. I made a mental note that if this information were correct, and I was beginning to think that in all likelihood it would be—didn't it have to be?—I'd have to bring him a really good reward, maybe some better tequila. Maybe I'd also have to give him one of my precious Cuban cigars, especially if Ramirez actually paid me. I know for a certainty that the curandero has never smoked one of these. And I knew that he would truly enjoy one. Even if my giving it to him probably wouldn't come as a surprise to him. Could he be surprised? By anything?

There is something fascinating to me about the guy's claimed ability to find people, to see into the future. But it's not theatrical in any way. He's not claiming he has special powers. He's not involved in the pretenses that underlay so very many theatrical illusionists who claim to be able to predict the future. Not at all. He treats his answers to my questions about Ramirez as if they were the most natural, most basic thing in the world, like involuntary respiration. Or gravity. Or oxidation.

My next door neighbor, Miguel, the proud owner of a 9-year old, tan Nissan Tsuru, the former taxi cab of choice in these parts, agreed to drive me to Playa del Carmen, about 40 minutes away, if in exchange I'd buy him lunch afterwards. He wanted me, as a fee for his being the chofer, to pay for the gas and to take him out to lunch at El Oasis or La Floresta, small outdoor restaurants on the access road for the main highway, nestled next to the electric transformer station, in Playa del Carmen. The specialty of both was shrimp or fish tacos. The hot sauce at both is extremely picante. The beer is very cold. These places have been discovered by a few tourists, but mostly they cater to the locals. The total cost of the adventure would be a half tank of gas for the car and an inexpensive meal for its driver and me at El Oasis, my choice as the better of the two. An unexpectedly good and complete bargain for all concerned.

The car had seen better days. It was a lot like traveling inside a dented, vibrating, half crushed beer can. Don't get me wrong. I have no real complaints about this. It was transportation. The air conditioning had been broken for about a decade, and I had some serious questions about the tires and brakes and our ability to stop the car if we ever had to. The seats were worn out, and pieces of yellow, decayed foam stuffing were sticking out of them. Couldn't he at least put a cover on them? A blanket? Once we hit the 4-lane, the vibrations diminished and the time passed uneventfully. The ride wasn't uncomfortable. The

Tsuru did exactly what it was supposed to do: transport me to Playa del Carmen without any real hassles.

We parked on 30th Avenue near the corner of 14th Street in Playa del Carmen. We agreed to meet up at the car in two hours, which left me with the lingering question of where in Playa del Carmen to look for Ramirez. I had no definite ideas. Don Obdulio hadn't told me where to start or where to look. And of course the time for looking remained a primary mystery. All of this didn't matter. At all.

Playa del Carmen is large; Ramirez was not a native. I could eliminate, I thought, huge swaths of the city, the parts that are primarily occupied by Mexicans and are never visited by tourists. It would be unlikely, if not odd indeed for Ramirez to turn up in one of these neighborhoods. So I figured I would have to look in one of the more popular tourist areas. Probably upper Quinta Avenida, a major pedestrian street with the best shops, was a good place to begin. I imagined that Ramirez would like the boutiques and restaurants more than the more honky tonk tourist traps further toward Playacar, at the older, south end of the street. He would probably avoid the gated Playacar community, which seemed too insulated and far too gringo for his taste. Also, I just couldn't imagine him going there. If I didn't turn him up on the north end of Quinta Avenida, I'd have to just wander around for the rest of my time and hope for good luck, if he were even in Playa del Carmen in the first place.

I thought I would start at Constituentes and walk south toward Juarez on Quinta Avenida. I stopped first at Ah Cacao on Constituentes to buy an extremely rich, somewhat expensive, 72% cacao chocolate bar. Ah Cacao is a small shop in what amounts to a foyer. It sells chocolate and chocolate mousse and chocolate ice cream and chocolate everything else. Even if I couldn't find Ramirez, at least I'd have something to reward myself for my willingness to wander around and try to ferret him out. Then I wandered slowly down Quinta Avenida, looking carefully at the people on the street, in the shops, on the side streets, on balconies. I didn't want to find out later that somehow I had missed him, that he was actually there but that I wasn't paying the right kind of attention to find him. I wanted to be observant. Vigilant. Thorough. I wandered cautiously. Slowly. I don't usually walk around in this state of mind, panning left and right and back and forth, looking, looking, staring. Usually, I just wander around. And I don't pay much attention. Usually, I'm not really observant.

Near the corner of Calle Corazon, there is a shop that has a "book trade" at the curb. The shop sells towels and tee shirts and cloth purses from Chiapas. Not books. The "book trade" might not even have anything to do with the shop. The books stand, facing the street, leaning against a long, rounded, pink cement step, just above the curb. A person leaves a book so others can read it, or exchanges it for a used one someone else has already traded in. There are some dreadful books on this Thursday morning, including some romance novels in German and Italian and some horror novels in English. But not all of the books are terrible. In fact, there is one small gem. At the very end of the line is a shiny, blue, one volume paperback of Juan Rulfo's *Pedro Paramo* and *Llanas En Llamas* in Spanish. Two wonderful novellas in one sparkling, crisp book. The entire oeuvre of an extremely influential author. There is no doubt, this is clearly the pick of the litter.

How much of a prize pup is this book? Garcia Marquez reportedly loved it so much he could recite long stretches of it, if not all of it from memory. The book has an astronomical literary value. And it is obvious to me that I want to take this book home with me. There's a small problem, though. I have nothing to trade, but, I think, no matter, this book deserves an appropriate home anyway, namely, mine. It cannot remain on this street, subject to the vicissitudes of chance. And besides I can always return with another book to trade for it at some time in the future. When I return to Playa del Carmen in the future. Or maybe I can just buy it? No. There's nobody to buy it from. I look and find no one who is in charge.

There's something deeply disturbing about the 1 to 1 exchange of books in this book trade. The trade treats the books as if they were all fungible. As if they were equivalent, each worth exactly the same thing. Vargas Llosa's *The Green House* in this exchange is the same as a book by Danielle Steel. Chekhov's plays are the same as Tom Clancy. *One Hundred Years of Solitude* is the same as Clive Cussler. Or a Dutch bodice ripper. Jeepers. They really aren't equivalent. But strangely, it all still works out: those who want to read what I consider garbage, leave garbage. Those who want something a little belletristic, as I do, leave other masterpieces in their wake. Put simply, almost nobody puts down Danielle Steel and picks up Roberto Arlt. If that were to happen, the book trade would crash in entropy, in chaos. It would contain only the least common denominator of written words.

To me, however, skipping this analysis, it's completely obvious. And simple. I really want Juan Rulfo. I envision the delight of opening the novellas up in Spanish and comparing the original text with a battered, dog eared English translation I have had for a decade. This seems like a wonderful, enjoyable way to spend some time. I am looking forward to this adventure. I wonder what I will find when I put the two books side by side.

As I contemplate this small, bibliotheft of Juan Rulfo's only two masterpieces, and start to justify it on literary, historical and critical grounds, by recalling how in Roberto Bolano's *Savage Detectives* the protagonists consistently stole books of poetry from various Mexico City bookstores, a much more serious larceny than the very small, very insignificant one I was contemplating, somebody bent over to pick up the very book I wanted to steal. I couldn't believe it. Somebody was going to take the book I wanted before I myself could steal it. What an outrage. Who does this person think he is?

I looked at the person whose fat hands were now pawing my intended, pristine book. It was Ramirez. This time he was wearing a blue and yellow Boca Juniors baseball cap. I stood silently watching him and staring, my mouth agape. My eyes were afire. Their flames should have ignited his hands. And the book he clutched with them. My top lip vibrated, as if it was receiving a small, sustained electric shock. He was shuffling the pages of the book. My book. My heart was pounding. Hard. Is this what Ahab felt when he finally encountered the great, white whale in the midst of a vast ocean? More important, is this what Juan Preciado would feel if he had actually found Pedro Paramo alive in Comala? I was stunned. My arms and legs were shaky. My eyes were ablaze. I was electrified.

I walked slowly over to Ramirez and quietly whispered in his ear, "Hey, remember me?"

He turned, looked up, recognized me, smiled, gave me a hug and a pat on the back. "How great to find you," he said. Actually, I found him, he didn't find me, but I didn't say so. I didn't want an argument, I wanted my money. And I really hoped he had the money I wanted. "I have something for you. This is great. I just got in to Playa today."

"Did you get my email?"

"I didn't see one. Nope. Did you write to ask about your money?" he smiled. "I bet you did. Ah ye of little faith," he shook his head slowly. He sucked his teeth. He continued to smile at me.

Was he lying to me? I bet he was. How many "l's" are there in "gullible?"

"Yes, I did ask about the money, but also there's this other, small problem. The Federales were looking for you. And they came to my house, three of them, in their Batmobile. I told them, truthfully, that you weren't with me. That I didn't know where you were. I didn't know when you'd be back, and so on and so forth, et cetera. I didn't even tell them that I had your email address."

"I bet you think I'm in trouble, right?" He continued to smile. "You think I did it again, that I'm in trouble with the Mexican law. Or maybe even Interpol. Or the FBI. Or the CIA. Some other agency with initials. Eh? I bet you think you're in trouble, too, right? By association with me. That somehow I got both of us in trouble. But right now, you don't even know what you might be in trouble for. Not yet, you don't. I bet you're starting to get really scared." The jerk. He started to laugh. It was a deep, unrestrained, delighted chuckle. The bastard. "Don't worry. You're wrong about this. You are completely wrong. Everything is fine. Come on. I'll buy you a morning beer and explain it. And I'll give you the money I promised you, too. Come on," he said, "Everything is really OK. Come on." I, of course, didn't believe him. How could I? He put his hand on my shoulder, patting me on the back.

It all turned out to be surprisingly simple. Somebody had stolen his laptop when he was in Tulum. This is something that happens when computers, iPods, and watches are left unattended. It happens all over the world. These small, valuable items tend very quietly and quite suddenly to walk off, mysteriously to disappear, to find themselves new owners. He had reported it, probably because he needed a police report for an insurance claim, which I'm sure he would then grotesquely exaggerate. I'm sure he didn't expect the police ever to find the computer. How could they? Miracle of miracles, the police had actually recovered it when they busted a warehouse full of stolen property in Cancun.

They were looking for him, of all things, for a good reason: to return the laptop to him. It was at that very moment already in his hotel room none the worse for wear, recharging its depleted batteries and enjoying the luxurious air conditioning. He had picked it up that morning from the Federales. He was, he insisted, on his way to pay me a surprise visit, to deliver a payment to me. How lucky he had found me, now he wouldn't have to go all the way to Tulum. He'd go back to Cancun where he had other business to attend to.

I don't know how much of this I believed. I wasn't sure about the long chain of so many obvious coincidences. In fact, the coincidences seemed overwhelmingly fishy. None of it made any real sense. Most of it seemed to me to be frightening. And not the least of the scary part, was how I had found him. That was something I would definitely have to keep very close to my vest. Evidently, somebody had attached a secret homing device to him when he wasn't looking and Don Obdulio was the only person on earth who could locate it, the only one who could hear its beeping.

I had no intention of asking him about his "other business" either. I didn't want to know anything about it. I had had enough of the excitement of my semi-retirement. Unless, of course, it had something to do with ecology, with the turtles, then I might be somewhat interested in just one aspect of it. I found myself wondering about Senorita Mari Estrella and how, now that I had been paid and there was nothing further to do with Ramirez, I would ever see her again.

"And your traveling companion?" I asked. I could've kicked myself. That was so uncool. It was definitely too quick. Coolness requires, I think, expressing both interest and ambivalence simultaneously. It requires nonchalance. I obviously couldn't get to that, I couldn't stop myself. Or didn't. "Is she with you?"

"You wish. I know you're, shall we say, a very big fan of hers, but no, I'm here all alone. Without her. She's still on the island. I think she's writing an article or something about the turtles. I'm here mostly for the guy with the cross, something about other artifacts. This time, old Mayan and Aztec artifacts, small golden items more than ten centuries old."

"Don't tell me," I interrupted. "Please don't tell me. Really. Please don't talk about that. I think the curandero has put some kind of a spell on me. Maybe a small curse. Whenever I think about or hear about or even consider certain kinds of illegal or questionable activities, there are immediately serious problems for me. Like our trip to Cuba. All of those problems were an example. I don't know whether he's the one who's making the problems or whether he's just predicting them accurately, but either way, it's not in your best interest or mine, definitely not in mine, for me to know about anything more about any of these kinds of activities. Really. It's like I have some bad juju on me. It's like a curse. I know this must seem really strange to you, but it seems it's really a problem for me to know about or get involved in anything at all while this is going on with me. Please don't tell me anything at all about it. Nothing. Nothing at all."

He was smiling, looking at me as if I were a loon. "You're kidding, right? Who is this you're talking about, the curandero? I thought that stuff was long over, that nobody did that anymore, only the old people around here still believe in this strange kind of magic, these old superstitions. Sorcery, if that's what it is. Black magic. Are you making this story up? And do you yourself believe in this stuff now?"

No, I wasn't kidding. I didn't really want to talk about Don Obdulio. I didn't want to discuss any of this with Ramirez. If he could find Ramirez so easily, I thought, he probably would know exactly what I said about him to Ramirez, right? No, I wasn't going to talk about it, or him, and I'd let Ramirez know if things changed. Really I would. I was convinced, though, that things wouldn't change. Not about this. Not for a while. I didn't want to answer any more questions about anything. Instead, I wanted to beat a hasty, awkward retreat. I wanted to run away. I thanked him for the beer, and for the money, more than US$6,500.00 mostly in crisp, 500 peso notes, wished him the best of good luck, and left him with the bar bill. Sure, we'd be in touch. Certainly. Right. The prospect wasn't something I would be eagerly looking forward to. In fact, I couldn't get away from him fast enough.

When I returned to the car still looking over my shoulder, my neighbor was standing on the curb frowning and pointing to where the front license place used to be.

"Damn it," he said, waiving a white, cardboard parking ticket at me. "They say we were parked too close to this corner. I don't think we are. In fact, I'm sure we aren't. Look. We aren't. I didn't move the car. It's not even that close. How close are you allowed to be anyway?" I knew instantly that this was another gift from the curandero, another warning, if you will, a small one, but one nonetheless.

In the gringo world, when you get a parking ticket, they put the ticket under your windshield wiper blade and they assume that you'll eventually pay it. The cost increases steadily over time. If the ticket doesn't get paid, they eventually will find your car when it's parked on the street and put a boot on your wheel to immobilize it until you pay, or tow your car to an impound lot and demand massive amounts of money in cash as a ransom for the car. No extortionate payment, no return of car.

This is not how things are handled in Playa del Carmen. It would be bad governance in Mexico to let things be eventually resolved. Eventually, like the word "manana," might mean decades of delay. Or longer. Or not at all. Never would always be a possibility. In Playa del Carmen, the parking police writes a ticket, puts it on the car, and takes off the front license plate, which is then delivered to the Transito Departmento. The parking police are all armed with a collection of screwdrivers and wrenches, in sufficient numbers that no plate can be permanently affixed to any car. Want to re-register your car? You have to have both license plates, front and back. You have to pay whatever the fine is to get back the plate. Got two pending tickets? No plates at all on the car. This, too, is common. There are dozens of cars on Quintana Roo's roads with no license plates at all, but they all have a decal registration sticker in the rear window. The parking tickets are the proof that the driver once had a plate. Or two. If you get stopped for some other infraction and are asked where your license plates might be, you show the cop your parking tickets as proof you once used to have them.

My neighbor and I went to the Transito Departmento, which is located far to the west side of the highway after blocks and blocks of brand new apartments. There I, newly solvent, magnanimously paid the parking ticket. The ticket was US$40, but because it was paid within a week, there was a 50% discount. Then we took the receipt to the window across the hall and got in a long line. There, in the room with three attendants are the many seized license plates. All of them. Thousands of them. Sorted by country, state, letter, number. And standing in the line is a broad cross section of the now unplated driving public, including tourists with rental cars they cannot return with just one plate, four taxi drivers who are commiserating with each other about the particular hazard of their occupation involved in ever parking the cab to use the bathroom or get a bite to eat, and us. Eventually, my neighbor receives the placa, which we replace in the sweltering parking lot with its original bent screws and original rusted nuts using a 2 peso coin as a screwdriver, and we are finally off to El Oasis, for the promised lunch and beer. The beer was getting to be a better and better idea as the day went along.

What a miracle Don Obdulio delivered. I had found Ramirez, he paid me well, and even though he started to bring up activities that Don Obdulio told me not to be engaged in, I managed not to get involved and I was able to escape with only a $20 parking ticket. A minor penalty, considering the wide range of possibilities. I could only imagine what would have happened had I decided to find out some of the details of whatever larcenous activities Ramierez's client wanted him to get involved in, or, even worse, if I agreed to participate even in a very minor capacity in one of them. Would I now be in jail? Would I be in the hospital? Would I be dead? All of the possibilities were quite scary. None was promising.

In some ways, it felt as if I were on probation or parole and Don Obdulio was supervising me, that he was the probation officer. He didn't seem to have to rely on visiting me unannounced, searching my house, interrogating me, asking me to submit to urine testing to see whether I was following the rules. None of that. His information was coming from somewhere else entirely. And all of it seemed to be frighteningly reliable.

Remarkably, it had suddenly become very risky just being me. It hadn't been at all like that before I first went to the curandero with my rash. Back then, I was just a seeming lizard who loved stories, and dreaming, and being a reptile, I got lots and lots of the kind of slack afforded to iguanas. I was just another lizard. If I contemplated murder or larceny or assault, that was just fine. These were lizard thoughts. Lizards have lizard thoughts. Nothing at all happened. There appeared to be no consequences for any of these fantasies, even if they started to transform over time into the incipient phases of planning or committing crimes. They were just my reptile thoughts, and you have to expect reptiles to think these kinds of mean things. That's just how they are. Being a reptile, I'd eventually forget about each of these ideas. Probably before I could carry it out. Or I'd get distracted and go on to think about something else. Before, it didn't matter what I had thought about, or how bad it might have turned out if I had followed through or how tightly I held onto it before I forgot it. I didn't actually do anything about bringing these thoughts into physical reality. But I definitely had lots of dark thoughts, most of which I wrote down and expanded upon and enjoyed. And later turned into stories.

Jung called it "the Shadow." There were lots of occasions when I had the clear, reptilian thought, "I'm going to kill that guy. I'm going to shoot him seven times through his head. Then I'm going to run over him with a truck and crush his heart. And his head." This is not an enlightened thing to think. It is not evolved, really. But it's what I thought. It didn't matter that I didn't have a gun. Or a truck. It's the thought that counts. And, of course, I wouldn't tell it to anyone. That would be shameful, disgraceful, cause me to be held in a very bad light. Anyway, eventually, I'd forget it. I'd go on to something else. I might scan the Internet to see where I could get a gun, or ask the neighbors on the down low. I might think about whose big, heavy truck I could borrow, but eventually, always, I'd drop it and go on to something else. On my own. These thoughts of revenge and murder and mayhem weren't things I talked about to others. It pains me slightly to disclose them here. But the point is that eventually they'd disperse, and be gone. And nothing would happen. To anyone. Or unfortunately, to someone who really in a just world deserved to be shot. Or to me.

When I sat down at El Oasis, in yet another white plastic chair with a beer logo on the back, I was shocked to notice that there was something hard in my rear pocket. It was the book. I had stolen Juan Rulfo. He and his two stories had stowed away in my rear pocket. Now, at the very least, I'd probably have to bring a book to Playa del Carmen on my next trip to replace this one. To make things right. Maybe I would. Maybe I wouldn't. It wasn't such a big deal either way. I was somewhat relieved; the parking ticket, it turned out, really covered not one, but two minor infractions. It was even more of a bargain than I initially thought. Put another way, in my mind, and I admit this is another example of my reptilian laziness, the parking ticket might also include the necessary payment for the book. Do you wonder why I said I had lizard thoughts?

Tulum has been growing very rapidly for the past few years. I am told the town will eventually expand through the mangroves all the way to the Caribbean beaches. If Playa del Carmen's growth in the past decade is an indication of what is now happening here, Tulum will eventually mushroom into a newer, shinier, even more globalized Playa del Carmen. It will no longer resemble its past or even its present. It will be as far away from what it is now as Playa del Carmen is from being a small, dusty, sleepy fishing village.

Evidence of the changes is everywhere. On my walk one morning, I found a paper cup from Starbucks in the gutter. The nearest Starbucks is in Playa del Carmen; there are others in Cancun. There are none to the South. Tulum, however, has so far only sprouted one new 7-11 (Siete Once? Siete Eleven? Seven Once?) and a Subway. But make no mistake, the tide of globalization is lapping on Tulum's shore. Who knows what will be next?

Meanwhile, Flor de Jasmin, a wonderful, simple tortilleria that sat a block west of the main street for a decade or more, has closed, only to be unceremoniously replaced, ironically, by a tornilleria, an auto parts shop. And the hole in the wall, extremely picturesque hardware store on the main street, a fixture in the town for decades, crammed inside and piled high with items and with its sinks and tools and griddles spread out on the sidewalk also in piles, remains, impervious for now, defiant of the invasion of Home Depot, Boxito, Cocopeza and a dozen other purveyors of screws. The town hasn't yet turned into some kind of sanitary strip mall. But there is pressure toward that. Intense, persistent, global pressure.

What is coming here? Is it a homogenized, uniform, shiny, trendy Tulum that is dreaming itself into existence? Will I and my neighbors still be here when Tulum awakens from its slumbers? Will we survive that? Will everything that is rusted or scruffy or wearing out be removed? Including us? Will we too be displaced? Where will we go? And what and who will take our places?

Oddly, in Pool's fruit store on Satelite Sur and in the San Francisco de Assis supermarket, NAFTA has now brought to Tulum, of all things, US apples, both red and yellow, from Washington State. And Borden's milk products. Apples are not really a part of local Mexican cuisine. Who is supposed to buy all of these imported apples with their silly, universal price stickers? Not I. Certainly not my current neighbors. What does the presence of the piles of apples signify? Frightened, I ask, "Does it mean that huge masses of gringo apple eaters are about to descend on Tulum with all of their money and rapaciousness and noise? Is the next step Walt Disney Tulum? Or worse. Is it gated communities and yacht clubs?"

From my plastic chair in my backyard, I can feel a distant, tectonic rumbling foreshadowing the oncoming changes. At the moment, the coming changes have not directly affected me. Nobody has showed up and offered me a ton of money for my house. Nobody has come to discuss the implications of these changes with me. I feel what's happening, but, like my neighbors, I'm not directly participating in any of it. I'm not planning and developing the "New Tulum." These proposed changes are not really doing anything for us. Not now. Later, however, they might do something to us. I hope against hope that will not happen. Is it impossibly romantic to hope that the global tide will pause, will magically ebb before it overwhelms and floods Tulum? Is it just wishful thinking to want Tulum to be spared a global facelift? Is my Tulum in danger of being be destroyed by a tsunami of development? Is "urban planning" going to remove everything that Tulum is now?

Carrying a beautiful Romeo y Julieta Churchill cigar and a very costly bottle of Don Julio Tequila Blanca, thinking about these impending changes in Tulum, I went looking for Don Obdulio. I wanted to thank him for helping me find Ramirez and for getting me paid, and also for letting the parking ticket suffice. I wanted to tell him that I understood what he had told me. That I really was paying attention. I also wanted to see whether he'd be so kind as to stop, or at the very least, let up, give me a small break, or just pause for a while, while I caught my breath and got used to my new, high stakes life of thought crimes and quick retribution. A little gradualism would be good, I thought. Truthfully, I thought he was making things happen to me, not just predicting the bumpy events.

I am not proud of my reptilian, dualistic analysis of the recent events in my life. But it's what I thought. Yes, I could have thought that the missed flights, the sleeping in airports, the parking tickets, were just coincidences that happen in a complex, developed world. But I didn't. I thought that Don Obdulio either was causing calamities for me, or at the very least, as a fall back position, he was accurately predicting them. The former had an awful lot of appeal. Yes, it's quite paranoid. And lizardlike. But it had a certain kind of sense. After all, I wasn't having things like that happen before I went to Don Obdulo with my sarpudilla. And now I was. So it must have had something to do with him, right?

It had just turned dark when I went to find him. Thunder was rumbling in the distance, and the clouds over the sea were lit from the inside by bright flashes of lightning. There was very little breeze. The humidity bristled with legions of foraging mosquitos. Every once in a while a coconut would fall from a tree and smash itself on the ground, or a car, or a sidewalk. Tulum seemed especially quiet. It seemed to be breathing shallowly, half asleep, falling slowly into its deepest dreams, still, slumbering, tranquil, wrapped in the softest of thin cotton blankets. At peace. Resting. Restoring itself. A gently sleeping city.

Two blocks away, on the main street, I saw a "party bus" go by. I couldn't believe it. It was lit with bright, flashing, strobing lights, and it played loud, thumping, hissing, percussive music. A few tourists sat on the roof and inside it, apparently drinking. People standing on the side streets pointed at it. What a horror. Maybe, I thought, Tulum is going to transform itself before my eyes into the dreaded hotel zone of Cancun sooner than I anticipated. Then it could be filled with drunken spring breakers peeing in the gutters and vomiting in alleys. And high priced convenience stores. And many franchised shops. It like Cancun would resemble a slightly more chaste, slightly more Mexican Las Vegas. If that was where Tulum was headed, turning Tulum into Playa del Carmen wouldn't be nearly as pernicious, as offensive. To be sure, both possibilities felt dreadful. It was like asking whether Tulum needed a chronic tooth ache or a perpetual stomach ache. Both were gigantic possible mistakes in the making, evolutionary errors that might ultimately reap morbidity.

Don Obdulio was sitting on a crate in an open garage. A candle for the Seven Archangels was burning nearby on the floor, and he was wrapped in a thin, red, striped blanket. In his hand was a glass of water. He started to cough. He looked ill.

"Not feeling well?" I asked.

"It's not much. Just coughing a little. A little fever. I just took some aspirins. Nothing much. Soon I'll be fine." He coughed again.

"I won't stay long. I came to thank you for tracking down my friend in Playa del Carmen and for helping me get paid. And also for the parking ticket."

"A parking ticket? I didn't know you had a car. What do you mean by that?"

"That wasn't from you? They ticketed the car for parking too near the corner. I thought it was a coded message you had sent to me."

He looked at me like I was crazy. He shook his head. "A message in code? How could that be from me?" he asked. "What are you saying about me? That I gave you a ticket? I didn't. I'm not a cop. I never left here. What are you talking about? A ticket from me? What are you saying about me, are you accusing me doing something bad?"

"Didn't you give it to me? I thought you did. You told me to be careful, that you had tracked me, that I shouldn't do anything that was bad. And you apparently knew what I was doing and about all the disasters during my trip. What about those? The parking ticket is tiny, it's really nothing compared with all of that."

"You think I had something to do with those, too?" He started to laugh. And to cough. It was a rattling, wet cough and it thwarted any laughter. And it stopped him briefly from talking. He spat something heavy on the ground. He looked at it and frowned, then he stared into my eyes. "You're crazy. Completely crazy." He laughed weakly. He waved his hand at me, as if to say, "Go away." Then he smiled at me, and he shook his head. "That's a good one. That's really a good one. You're definitely cheering me up. Please don't stop. Tell me more."

"Seriously," I said. "You're kidding around with me now. Come on. Admit it. I think you had something to do with all of the hard things that happened in Cuba and then yesterday the things that happened in Playa del Carmen. You did, didn't you? I think you did. Come on and admit it."

"Oh, please, stop," he interrupted me. "I cannot do those things. Nobody can do those kinds of things. I'm not a wizard or a magician or a sorcerer. I don't do sorcery or magic, those kinds of things, getting involved in other people's lives, doing things to them, doing things without getting permission from them first. Even if I could do those things, which I cannot, I would never do such things to somebody. Especially to you. Do you actually think I can do things like that?" He started coughing again.

"Actually," I said. "I do. I really do. I'm not superstitious, I just think you did things to me on my trip to Cuba because you knew, somehow, that I was involved in bad things when I went there, and I think you did more things to me yesterday on my visit to Playa del Carmen because I almost heard about some new, bad things, some new crimes, and I even stole a book while I was there. Though stealing the book was actually an accident. Really it was an accident."

He started laughing again. "No, no, no. You don't understand. I didn't do any of the things you're accusing me of. Not a single one of them. You're giving me entirely too much credit for things I didn't ever do. Let me assure you right here and right now that I didn't do any of those things you're thinking I did. Actually, I cannot do them. As far as I know, nobody can actually do such things. Did you ever know anybody who can do things like that?"

I had to admit I didn't know anyone who could do what I was accusing him of, well, except him. "But look," I said. "You know about all of the things I'm talking about, right? All of the things in Cuba?"

"Definitely. Of course. I know exactly what you're talking about. I know about all the things that happened."

"And you know all of the things I'm talking about from my trip to Playa del Carmen also?"

"Certainly. You just told me you got a ticket and you stole a book. And you got paid. That was it, right?"

"But you say you didn't do it?"

"Certainly not. No." He shook his head. "I didn't do it. I didn't do it at all. None of it. None of the things you accuse me of. I didn't do any of them, not a one. I have nothing to do with any of that. I'm entirely and completely innocent of all of this. Such accusations. It's amazing to me what you accuse me of." He started coughing again. This time he was turning red. "I'm not like that, not at all. I can tell you what's happening, and what will happen, but I don't make things happen. I never do that. I am not doing things to you. Never. Not now. Not before."

I didn't believe him. Not one bit, not even for a tenth of a second. I was sure he was the one who was creating all of these problems for me, all of this drama, that he was meddling in my life, that he had put a curse or a spell or something of some kind on me. I was sure of all of this. There was no doubt about it in my mind. How else could it happen? He was definitely messing with me and then he was lying to me about it. There was no way I was going to accept any of his fervent denials.

Nevertheless, I happily gave him the great bottle of Don Julio and the wonderful Cuban cigar, and I sincerely thanked him for helping me to find Ramirez. I told him I hoped he would feel better soon, that we could talk about all of this later on when he was feeling better, and maybe we could have a drink then, but that I wanted to give him these gifts now because of how very much he had helped me out. I greatly appreciated it, and I thanked him for all of his help. I then left to go home.

On the street, the thunder continued to roll and crash, and the first few heavy drops of rain, drops like shiny ball bearings were beginning to bounce on the ground. The air was filled with the lovely, sweet, dusty scent of fresh, tropical rain. El Kid was standing on the sidewalk under one of the few street lamps apparently trying to teach himself how to juggle some tennis balls. We mumbled Buenas and I got home just before the rain began in earnest. Unfortunately, the thunder and lightning and rain instantly knocked out the power, it frequently does that, so my neighbors and I found ourselves sweltering in our houses or huddled under overhanging, dripping roofs getting wet in the dark. I could hear one of my neighbors playing a guitar and singing a corrida about a hungry farmer who was going to flee to the US so he could get a job and send money to his wife and six children, all because the corn would not grow without much needed rain. All of us who heard the song sympathized with the pain of forced departures, unwanted farewells, despedidas. It seemed far too common a shared feeling. I wondered whether anybody cared that the woman in the song was about to become the single parent of six kids for the foreseeable future.

I awoke early the next morning. When I walked down the street, all of the many deep potholes, all of the potential puddles were filled to their brims, making vast grey lakes in the monochromatic, wet street. The rain had hatched out ten zillion small, black, flightless, roach-like bugs, the size of watermelon seeds. They scurried away from me as I walked down the dry part of street where they were congregating and swarming. Some of the bugs ran before me, running away from me, others ended up running into the grey water and struggling not to drown. Still others ran around my steps and circled behind me. I didn't want to stand still among the bugs. I didn't want to continue walking. I didn't want to turn around and go home. I settled on walking even slower than usual to allow the insects to flee from my slow, but inevitable, predictable but deadly steps. I lifted my feet and put them down very slowly. Very carefully. I couldn't wait to reach the main street, so I could finally walk on the sidewalk and escape the bugs. "What," I wondered, "is the purpose these insects serve? What hidden things do they contribute to the web of life? In how many ways would the world be different if these creatures weren't here?" It was simply horrible to drive them away with my footsteps, stepping on and crushing ones that didn't flee or were too slow or in their panic turned from successful escapes to run under my feet even though they were safe before they ran. It was like some feverish dream Jose Lezama Lima had invented: something small and totally horrific and unavoidable and utterly disturbing. I hoped, I prayed that by the time of my return to home, which I would delay as long as possible, the insects would go back to wherever they had been before and that they would just stay away so I didn't have to see them or kill any more of them.

When I finally reached the main street and the sanctuary of a sidewalk and paved, bugless roads, it was clear to me that I would need to spend at the very least an hour before going home. I decided to stop at Café Gaudi, a small, shiny coffee house on the main street for a cappuccino and something to eat. I hardly ever stop there. Café Gaudi, I discovered, used apples in their fruit plate. I immediately felt extremely prosperous and very First World. Very hip and European also. Can you tell you're in the First World because of shining stainless steel display cases? Or is it the apples, or the steamed milk? Or the high prices? Or the well dressed, prosperous tourist clientele?

I wasn't really hungry, I just wanted time to pass so the bugs would leave, so I could walk without creating more anguish and misery and an avoidable drama of pervasive and incomprehensible insect suffering and death.

As I sat at a small round table near the entrance above the sidewalk, I found myself eavesdropping on two women from the US who sat at the table directly behind me. They were both in their early 40's. They were attending a yoga retreat and apparently didn't know each other before this trip. They talked about their practice of yoga, their lives in the States, their work, their relationships, their families. To my absolute delight, they said nothing, nothing at all about any curanderos. I heard their entire conversation. Every word. I was relieved that Don Obdullio didn't come up, nor did anything about indigenous energy medicine, or shamanism, or anything else Mayan. Nothing was said that could lead ultimately to him or to anything or anyone indigenous. They wanted to buy silver earrings with turquoise stones. They didn't seek to enroll in finding Don Obdullio, whom they thankfully may never have heard of. Thank goodness.

Fortunately, when I returned to the street, the bugs had all but vanished. Except the many dead ones. And I took it as an extremely good omen that my neighbor and his powers had not been mentioned in the conversation I overheard. Maybe, I thought, I might be wrong about Don Obdulio. Maybe, but I still doubted it. No. I'm sorry. Truth be told, I knew it, he was playing games with me. I knew he was. I couldn't prove it, but so what. I was certain of it. How else could these things suddenly be happening to me?

While I walked home, I ended up talking to myself. It might have been aloud. In English. Could I just go back to how things were? Could I just be an unremarkable lizard again? Could I just sit in my yard? Could I write some short stories or articles and get them published and get paid? Could I just fall asleep in my chair? Could I resume my life without the constant fear that at any second, because of something I had said or thought or done, I'd be involved in yet another dangerous drama? I shook my head from side to side. It just wasn't right, I complained, after all of my intentionally quiet time in Tulum to have so many calamities occur so suddenly in such a short period of time. Somebody or something new must be making that happen. It sure didn't happen before.

It was truly exhausting. It felt like being under a microscope. It felt like being a plaything. I went into the yard, sat in my white plastic chair and immediately fell asleep. I had a very long, very strange dream, one which I recall perfectly.

In my dream I was again walking home from the Café I had just left. When I got to the door of my house, there was an envelope wedged between the door and the door frame. I thought it might be a bill for something, or an advertisement of some sort, or yet another notice from the dreaded dog police. The neighbor's dog was lying on his back, stretched out and snoring near the curb, so it wasn't from the dog police. It was a plain envelope. I opened it. Inside was a handwritten note, "You left your notebook at the café."

I don't have a notebook. I didn't leave anything at the café. I'd have to return and tell them that it wasn't mine, that it must have belonged to somebody else. After all, I didn't have anything I had to do that couldn't wait, and maybe if I told them soon that it wasn't mine, they would be able to find the true owner who had probably been at the café at about the same time I was.

When I arrived at the Café, a very thin man in his late 40's or early 50's with disheveled, curly hair, round framed glasses and a cigarette in his hand, sitting at a corner table stood up and waved at me with a black Moleskin notebook. He needed a shave. He was too skinny. And gaunt. He didn't look healthy. His skin was slightly yellow. "I think this is yours."

I looked at it. "Actually, it isn't. I don't have one like that. I like those very much, they're great, but it's not mine."

"No, this is definitely yours. Please sit down." He waved at the chair with the notebook and the cigarette. He seemed too thin, too yellow, quite drawn, frail. In a word, unhealthy. Was he some kind of junkie? Did he have some kind of chronic illness? Aids? Chronic Stress? Crones?

"Really," I said, "I don't have one like that. It's very nice, but it just isn't mine. It must belong to someone else."

"Do you know Don Obdullio?" he asked. I was really surprised. I may have gasped or startled. I immediately began to pay rapt attention. I sat down. I squinted at him. I leaned toward him, "You know Don Obdullio?" I whispered incredulously. He smiled. "He said I should meet you. I know it's not your notebook. Not yet. But you can have it. It's a gift from me. I'm Roberto Bolano."

"No, no, no you're not," I said. "You couldn't be him. You died about six, seven years ago, didn't you? You had liver problems. Heroin, they say, ruined your liver, but I don't know if that's so. I do think the papers reported you had died." That should have stopped the conversation, but it didn't. It didn't wake me up. To my amazement, I continued, "I've really enjoyed reading your work. I particularly loved the stories about the sky writer. That was really brilliant. You're really inventive, really clever. I always wanted to meet you, though I find this particular meeting quite odd, seeing as how I thought you had, well, passed on, and here I am in Café Gaudi in Tulum, Quintana Roo, Mexico talking to you, and more peculiar, you're in Tulum, not wherever I thought you might be. May I ask you a serious but unusual question? Am I dreaming you up? Am I hallucinating you? Am I drugged? Am I dead, too? Have I been poisoned or something like that?"

"No, no, no," he said calmly, smiling. "You're just fine. Really. Everything is perfectly OK." He then handed me the notebook. "This is for you. It will be helpful to you. You can write in it. I think you need a good notebook. Like this one. For your stories. For the ones that fall on your skin, and the ones that are found in the ocean. And this, as you can plainly see, is a very good notebook. Made of really good paper, not like so much of the miserable paper in this country, which is far too thin, and rips too easily, and is far too porous and is like a blotter, so it allows your writing to smear and blur and makes what you wrote seconds before completely blurred and unreadable."

"Thanks," I said, taking the notebook from his hand. He was entirely right about Mexican paper. Then we sat quietly.

"You know," I said eventually, "I don't understand why you took part of one work and put it out in another work. Why did you do that?"

"Oh," he frowned. "I guess you didn't like that."

"Well, it's not dislike, it's just that you already told that story in another book, so in the other book you . . . ."

The sentence just drifted away like a helium balloon. It never got completed. It evaporated into a strange, full silence, into a silent void. All of a sudden other things seemed to get louder: you could hear the milk steaming, and people talking, and the chattering of the baristas. But Bolano was silent. And so was I. I didn't know what else to say. My brain too had stopped functioning. I couldn't say anything more; he didn't speak. I was just completely silent. I couldn't think of anything more to say to him. If I had been on a television interview show, I would have gone on to something else from my notes. Or made something up. But I didn't have anything else to go on to. I couldn't get my brain out of neutral. It was stuck. It had frozen. I began to feel quite awkward, uncomfortable, like I should make conversation or ask more questions or comment or something. There was a harsh stiffness in my shoulders. I just couldn't find anything at all to say, my brain couldn't find anything. I smiled stupidly at him as if I had been lobotomized. It was as if a gas had been pumped into my lungs and had stopped my mind from producing any thoughts. Yes, my brain was still there, but it was stalled. Or flooded. It was on tilt. It would not run.

"I wish I knew what to say to you. I'm not able to think of what to say right now, that's really embarrassing, how my brain has become stuck. I hope you'll forgive me. This feels really stupid. I think this might be a dream I'm having, and it seems that in the dream my brain has now been paused. It's on standby."

He didn't say anything either. After a while, he said, "Well, it was very nice to have met you. Hasta pronto." He then got up and walked slowly out the door. I lost sight of him as he rounded the corner and turned right into the first side street.

I must be asleep, I thought. I have got to be dreaming. Either that or somebody has fed me a ton of LSD. Didn't I tell him that this might be a dream? Well, this has to be a dream of some bizarre kind. If I order a cup of coffee, and I can't drink it, I'll know I'm asleep and that this is a dream.

When the coffee arrived, I put cream and sugar in it and promptly plunged my right thumb in it. I couldn't feel anything. I was dreaming. Dammit. It was definitely a dream. I woke myself up. Floods of disappointment and disorientation flowed over me. Where was I? I had forgotten where I was. I had to look around and see whether I could recognize where I was.

I was still in my plastic chair in the yard. I focused on remembering the dream. I had fallen asleep, and I had definitely been dreaming. But in the sand at my feet there was a notebook. All the notebook's pages were blank. It had squares instead of lines on the pages. It was just like the one Roberto Bolano had offered me in the dream. My favorite kind. A medium sized Moleskin. As I put the notebook in my pocket, I scanned the yard to see whether anybody was there. There was no one. And I saw no footprints near my chair, not that that meant anything.

I decided to go directly back to Don Obdullio's house to tell him that he was scaring me badly and to ask him please, please to stop playing tricks on me. The "please" part of my message to him was becoming extremely necessary and quite urgent. I would beseech, if not beg him, please to stop.

When I got to the street, I was still wondering why the silent part of the dream seemed so awkward, so uncomfortable. It was, it occurred to me, because in some sense I had blown it. Don Obdullio, I thought, had somehow sent me Roberto Bolano in my dream, and a new notebook in which I could dream up and write down a bunch of new stories, but I didn't really talk to Bolano about all of the many things we could have and should have talked about. I tried yes. But my brain wouldn't work. Even if it was a dream or a hallucination, I thought, I didn't really get to take advantage of the unusual opportunity that had arisen. I had squandered a wonderful chance. Was it because I was surprised? shocked? I wasn't drugged. Nobody stopped the flow of electricity in my brain. Yes, the void sucked away what Bolano was saying, but so what? Why didn't I regain my stability? What happened to my desire to communicate with him? Where was my audacity? Didn't I have any? Why wouldn't my thinking work? Was I under a spell? Why did I fold and crumble and stop, rather than press on? Why didn't I force myself to ask him something more? What a complete and utter waste. What a dummy I am. Why, I could have asked about the visceral realists, or *2666*, or more about the sky writer, or *Nazi Literature in the Americas*. It's not like I don't know his work. What a dolt. What a jerk. What an imbecile. I didn't really get it together to ask him anything. My thinking had stalled out; I had blown an incredible chance to cross over to the other world, the dream world, the world of spirits, and to return with some really valuable information. That hardly ever happens. To anybody. What an ignoramus I am for letting this chance get away from me.

I was kicking myself unmercifully down the street, beating myself up as I walked toward Don Obdullio's present residence.

I found Don Obdullio sitting in a yard with a huge hibiscus plant. He was alone. He saw me coming, and he waved me to hurry over to where he was. "Did you find the notebook? Did you find it?" he shouted excitedly.

"Roberto Bolano," I said. "You did that, right?"

"Who?" He smiled. "Who is Roberto Bolano? I sent you the notebook. My assistant, you know, the Kid, delivered it to you a little while ago. You were asleep when he dropped it off; he did not wake you up, he told me. Who is this Bolano person?" He was obviously pleased with himself.

"You really don't know who Roberto Bolano is?"

"No idea. No idea at all. Who is he? Does he live around here?"

"You told me you couldn't do things like that, like making someone appear in my dreams."

"Right. I can't. Your parking tickets, and your airline delays, and of all things, the hurricane, and your missed travel plans, those just aren't mine to do, not my business. I cannot do those things. Making somebody appear in your dreams is just the same kind of business. It's sorcery or magic or something. I cannot do it. I was given the notebook so I gave it to you because I know you like things like that. As you already know, I certainly don't have any use for a notebook. But you do."

"Why are you doing this to me, I mean, with me?"

"What do you mean? I gave you a gift because I thought you would like it."

"Actually, it's not that. I do like the gift. I like it very much. And, really, thank you for giving it to me. I love that kind of notebook. But that's not the problem. It's the rest of it, the parts that I cannot see or understand, the other things you might be doing that are really quite scary to me. It's frightening me. It's making me think I'm losing my mind. I'm not used to having these kinds of experiences. To be honest, I was happier, I think, just being a lizard here in Tulum and minding my own business and being left alone to make up stories and write them down. Yes, I was slightly bored, having an uneventful, simple life in which nothing unusual, nothing of consequence ever happened. But at least it was quite straightforward. And best of all, it was easy for me. And entirely safe."

He smiled. "You know," he said softly, "You really should take advantage of the many opportunities that arise. You didn't talk to the man enough to satisfy yourself, to get answers to your many questions. And I know you must admire him. You would have enjoyed that. Maybe it was because you were surprised. I think that was why your thinking shut down. You probably couldn't anticipate anything quite like the dream you had. I'm sorry that your brain got frozen. Regardless, I'm sure you'll have other chances. I know you will. Those you can no doubt take advantage of."

So, he agrees with me then, I thought. He too thinks I'm a jerk, that I squandered the opportunity in the dream.

I was halfway to my house when I first realized that what Don Obdulio had just said wasn't a response to anything I had told to him. It was a repetition of what I had been thinking. I went over everything I said to him. I usually can't remember exactly who said what to whom in a conversation or in what order it was said. Usually, I just find that I have only a summary of what was said. But I was sure. I hadn't told him anything about my disappointment. How, I wondered, could he find these things out and then say them to me? Was it obvious from how I said things or moved or looked? I didn't think so. What was going on here? Was he reading my thoughts?

Then something even stranger happened. By the time I reached my house, I had begun to think that these bizarre new circumstances weren't so bad. Maybe it wasn't such a bad thing that Don Obdulio might know what was happening in my dreams. Or what I was doing and thinking about in my life. Or what was going to happen to me. In fact, just the opposite. He seemed to care what I was thinking. Yes, it was a strange sort of caring, but it did matter to him. Maybe this was a kind of opportunity for me. One that could actually turn out to be beneficial to me. Maybe he would continue to be helpful to me. After all, hadn't he healed my sarpudilla and predicted the disastrous trip to Cuba, and hadn't he found Ramirez in Playa del Carmen, and didn't he help me get paid? Maybe he was playing with me. Sure. He was. I knew he was. He had to be. That was a part of it, I thought, that he was obviously playing with me. I didn't think it was funny, but maybe he did. But, and this seemed to be a very important but, wasn't he also helping me out, trying to keep me from ending up in jail or involved in various disasters? Wasn't he trying to keep me from harm? Wasn't he actually trying to be helpful to me?

Maybe. Maybe not. I had some persistent, gnawing doubts about him. Maybe I was wrong and he was purposefully creating disasters for me. Maybe he had given me a curse. Or a spell. Or something. Maybe it was sorcery of some kind he was using on me. It could be that. Sure. But that didn't seem to be the case, that just didn't seem to be what he was doing. That just didn't seem to fit. It didn't feel dark or evil or pernicious or even scary. It didn't feel heavy and draining or dangerous or evil. It actually seemed playful. A strange kind of play to be sure, one I hadn't thought about, let alone experienced before, but it still felt like joking around, just bromiendo, just kidding. Maybe he was just a very unusual guy with a very strange sense of humor and he was also looking out for my best interests or trying to get my attention in unexpected ways. Perhaps. Some of this could seem scary and that part made me want to hide from Don Obdulio. Some of it, to my surprise, actually excited me. How could I simultaneously want to run away and at the same time want to stay? And didn't the man in Cuba tell me that Don Obdulio was protecting me, that he'd left a mark on me and that he was going to help me? And work with me? What about that? That sounded good.

And then there was that other question. And this seemed to me most strange: I wanted to learn how to do what Don Obdulio was doing. Most of all, I wanted to know how to track. And I wanted to know how the present would grow and unwind into the future. Could I do that too? Could I learn how to do what Don Obdulio was doing?

That thought surprised me. I began to think maybe, just maybe I could get Don Obdulio to show me how to do what he was doing. How did he know these many things? How did he see or sense them? The thought both excited and frightened me. Could I too do these things? What, I thought, did I have to lose? I could easily ask him to show me how to do whatever he was doing. And yes, I absolutely believed he might be willing to show me how to do it. After all, he wasn't asking me to jump into some deep cenote from which I couldn't emerge and then to drown. He wasn't trying to drive me off. He didn't seem to consider me a problem or an annoyance. He apparently liked me. He liked me in a very strange, quite unusual way. And hadn't the man in Cuba seen that he was protecting me and following me and that I'd eventually work with him?

Late that afternoon I drank a beer and fell asleep in my chair with the novel by Ricardo Piglia on my chest. My second nap of an already very strange day. A beer nap. I initially closed my eyes to focus on 9 de Julio in Buenos Aires, the world's widest boulevard, and to think about all the subways running under the entire city of Buenos Aires, like the root system of a gigantic forest, to think about what is under the world. What was under Tulum? What were Tulum's roots? What were her underground connections? How did her underground rivers flow? How were they connected to each other. And the sea. I have no idea how long I slept. At some point, my book must have fallen silently to the sand at my feet. I was finally awakened when the sun was low in the west by a huge, throbbing mosquito bite on the top of my right foot. My Buenos Aires dreams and my search for Tulum's underworld vanished instantly with my sleep. I cursed the insect, and I decided to forage for dinner in the refrigerator.

I know what you're thinking, that my refrigerator must be a mess, that it must have in it only beer, stale milk, mayonesa, mustard, cheese with mold and old, stale, hard tortillas wearing a green patina. Admit it. You imagine that the refrigerators of old guys like me who live alone are truly toxic. And disgusting. Well, you're partially right. It has those rancid things in it, sure. But tonight it also has in it beautiful tamales wrapped in aluminum foil and ready to heat and a gorgeous flan for dessert, all produced lovingly by my neighbor, Flor. This is the result of a deal we made so many years ago. I provide far more ingredients than I will eat; she makes beautiful food for me and her family from it. We both benefit greatly from this exchange. But, of course, that's probably not the kind of woman you were thinking about. No. You were probably thinking about Mari Estrella and wondering about her. Is she the one with the sea creatures in her basket? Is that somebody else? Who is it? At the time I was wondering about her too. She seemed so far away and utterly unreachable.

After I ate dinner, I realized that Don Obdullio might be willing to help me out so I went looking for him. I ran into him and El Kid at Chiquiti Mini Super on the Main Drag. They were buying a big plastic bottle of Coke. Coke in Mexico is sweetened with sugar, not corn syrup. It doesn't taste quite like US Coke. It tastes a lot like Coke did when I was a kid.

"Wish to join me for a drink?" he asked. The invitation seemed almost courtly. "I have received a very nice bottle of rum. Of course, it was a gift."

How could I refuse? I followed along with him and El Kid to a lot where I could see his hammock hanging. When we arrived, he mixed drinks for us, giving no rum to El Kid who said twice how much he really wanted some, fishing ice cubes out of a blue and white, plastic cooler. We sat on a concrete slab. There were no chairs. Again, Don Obdulio stopped us from drinking, poured some rum on the ground and said something, then offered the bottle to the sky and said something else. Then he took a sip.

I have to admit that rum is perplexing to me. I love it. Especially the way it smells. And I love how much of the sun is in every drop. And I love mixing it with fruit juice or cola or, if it's dark rum, with tonic or ginger beer. And I love how bright it is. And how warm. But I cannot forget even for a second that rum was one leg of the Triangle Trade and that another was slavery. Rum was a literally intoxicating, next step in the degradation of this hemisphere after the Cruz de la Parra. I want to remember this, even as rum relaxes me and makes my face shine. It is not really what it seems. It has an old, dark, centuries long shadow. One that is mostly ignored. But still there.

"Is there something you want from me? Something you want me to do for you?" Don Obdulio asked.

"Actually, I was wondering whether you might be able to help me with something I've been thinking about."

"Isn't she a little too young for you?" he smiled.

"Well, I really came over for a another reason also, but I think I'd really like some help with her, too. I don't think age difference matters. You know, Garcia Marquez has some very famous books he's written that involve some very old men being with some very young women, his last book, in fact, centered on that, and, well, I'm not nearly that old, and also, she's not nearly that young. You know who Garcia Marquez is, right?"

He laughed at this silly question, lifted his glass, clinked mine, spilling some of my drink, and chugged his down. And then he winked at me and laughed some more. He had no idea who Gabo might have been. And that didn't matter to him in the slightest.

"Does that mean you might help me out with this?"

"That depends," he said, "It depends on a lot of things. It depends on whether it's in the best interest of everyone. Everyone on earth. Everyone in the universe. Everyone who is here now and everyone who will come in the future."

This wasn't really what I wanted to hear. Not at all. It wasn't even an answer. "Do you know what's in everyone's best interest?"

"That depends also. Usually, you can tell if you care to."

Was he trying to keep me from pursuing him about her? At least for then. For the time being. Was he trying to deflect me? Was he telling me to stop pursuing this idea? Was he saying it wasn't a good thing to think about?

And how could he tell what's in everyone's best interest?

"You," he smiled, "like to ask questions that have simple answers. Listen. Everything is connected to everything else. You might not be able easily to see how things are connected to each other, but they all are. So anything I do to something or with someone else has effects on everything else. I just track these things, and I see what their connections are, the direction that things will go, and that tells me what can happen. Then, of course, I see whether this is good or not. Not just in my opinion, in the view of the many beings on this planet.

"You can do the same thing if you want to. Just look at what you or somebody else is doing, and see where it leads. Don't think about it. Just see where your heart says it ends up. Does it end well or not? Where does it end up?"

It seemed simple enough, but I had no idea how anyone would do that. I had no idea how I would do it. It shut me up. I didn't ask him how we were going to decide what was in my best interest. Or hers. And I didn't ask him specifically how he could be of help to me, if he ever agreed to help, to get me together with her. And of all things, and the most important, I never asked him if he'd show me how to do what he was doing.

I just dropped all the questioning. We spent the rest of the evening amiably finishing the bottle and telling stories. I don't remember exactly what we talked about. I then left to swivel my tipsy way down the potholed, swaying, poorly lit, dusty streets to home. When I got there, all was perfectly quiet. And dark. The neighbor's dog was still lying in the street snoring. The neighborhood was quiet except for the night insect noises. Miraculously, I managed to step over the dog without rousing her and to make my stumbling way through the door and to collapse into the bed.

I awoke at about 3 am with intense feelings of discomfort and wariness and confusion. I sat up in bed. I turned on the light. The insects were still conversing quietly with each other, the street was still empty. But something was bothering me. Something wasn't right. Was I drunk? Yes. Was I hung over already? Apparently. Inside my head there was pounding and thinking that was loud and irritating. And persistent. A rum headache? Already a rum hangover? I looked at myself in the mirror. I looked normal enough. Slightly drunk, but normal enough. I looked to me like my father, a sign of my age. In my head, I'm 23. In my body, that was decades ago. If I look like my father, I'm still alive. And older than 60. Still running, just a little bit slower. And a headache is completely normal, right? What is it that's agitating me anyway? Peering into my eyes in the mirror, I recognize that on top of everything else, I am all churned up. Upset. What, I want to know, is that all about?

Maybe I wished I hadn't asked Don Obdulio for help with Mari Estrella. It wasn't impossible to withdraw the request. Well, I thought, maybe I really didn't want any help. Maybe I didn't want anyone, including Don Obdulio, to get involved in my life. Did I want to be alone? Maybe I didn't want any more of his playing around with my life. Maybe I didn't want to hear any more predictions. Or did I? Maybe I didn't want any more drastic fallout from my thoughts and actions. Certainly. No more surprises. No more unforgettable dreams. Is that what I wanted? Maybe I didn't want to learn anything from him. Maybe I wanted something simpler: Maybe I just wanted to go back to how things had been before. Did I want to live exactly as I had before? Maybe I wanted just to be a lizard that sat under the flowering tree and enjoyed stories. Well, I could easily tell Don Obdullio that, I thought. I could always tell him that I had changed my mind, that I didn't want help from him after all, that I had thought it over, that I had made up my mind.

But, of course, I hadn't made up my mind about anything. And I did want his help. I started to go back to the bed. But I stopped dead in my tracks. The mirror was still there with my face in it. I needed a shave. Badly. My eyes were quite red. My nose was running. Was I kidding myself? I had no intention whatsoever of going back to how things were before. No. No chance. There was something far too exciting, far too interesting going on, something with far too many possibilities that was occurring. It was wild. I'd have to be crazy to try to opt out of it or to stop it. Why on earth would I do that? In fact, I thought, the truth might be that I wanted to step right out of my comfortable, customary, isolated way of doing things, and jump directly into this new, somewhat unusual, probably quite bizarre way of being. Maybe it was actually an opportunity. I watched my face. I looked like hell. But I saw and felt the beginnings of a smile at the corner of my mouth. I'd have to admit it. That's what I wanted. Yes, it was. I went back to bed and ultimately fell asleep.

That morning El Kid woke me up at 7 am by banging loudly on my door and shouting. I pried my eyes open. I immediately recalled the rum of the night before. And my stubbly, haggard face in the mirror. The headache was still there pounding away. It was then crouching over my left eyebrow and thumping with two hands as if my forehead were a djembe. The sun seemed far too bright and way too high for 7 am. What was wrong, what did El Kid or Don Obdulio or anybody else want at this horrible, inhuman, barbarian hour? Who knows? Hadn't I just decided that I wanted whatever excitement Don Obdullio was bringing me? Did he already know what I had decided just a few hours ago? Apparently, word travels fast when there are no words to travel.

"I need your help. There's a problem. A big problem."

Oh great, I thought. Isn't this wonderful? A big problem. No sooner do I decide to try to find out what Don Obdulio is doing and learn how to do it than he finds out and he sends El Kid to me to try to get me involved in "a big problem." The guy obviously doesn't know anything about being gradual, going slowly, working up to things. But this morning, even a small problem, a tiny one, a microscopic one would be a huge imposition. And unfortunately for me, I'm hung over. Very hung over. I feel awful. So I feel grumpy and I want to go back to bed and I don't want to deal with problems, big or small, no matter whose they might be. Couldn't we wait until noon or so? O manana?

But some calls apparently have to be answered. El Kid filled me in. It turned out that the Federales had just arrived at Don Obdulio's, and they wanted to know where the gringo kid from Alabama with the two piercings and red Che Guevara t-shirt had gone, and when Don Obdulio last saw him, and who else may have seen him. Isn't that the persistent, great Federale question, the last one, the one about who else? That's an engraved invitation to get all kinds of innocent bystanders like me involved in things we don't want to be involved in. And wasn't it great that in response to this archetypical Federale gambit Don Obdulio for some reason known only to himself felt compelled to provide them with my name and whereabouts?

It had only been a few weeks since I had seen the person they were now asking about at the paleteria. To my horror, I realized despite my headache that El Kid saw him at Super Mar Caribe, too, and then I was with him, and El Kid saw me with him and then El Kid remained in the checkout line at Super Mar Caribe. Simple denial wouldn't work. I clearly couldn't deny that I knew who the kid was, or that I had ever talked to him. But who knows what might have happened after the guy ate his melting paleta and left? I thought he'd leave town. I thought he'd never return. And sure enough, he didn't. At least I never saw him again.

I pulled on a dirty shirt, a wrinkled one that didn't smell too terribly bad, hurriedly brushed my teeth, and walked with El Kid over to Don Obdulio's present residence. Every step brought waves of nausea and sharp headache. And made me squint. And made my head pound. When we got there, we encountered three Federales with reflector sunglasses and their twin Federale mobiles. Of course, all of the lights were flashing and strobing red and blue and white. Don Obdulio was sitting on a tire in the lot. The cops were facing him, standing around him in a tight semicircle, standing elbow to elbow, like hogs at the trough. Don Obdulio was patiently explaining, probably for the forty second time, that he saw the kid one morning at 5 am, no, he didn't know what the date was, he never knows what the date is, or what day of the week it might have been, he doesn't pay attention to things like that, but he did tell the kid to go to a cenote north of town. He didn't see him after that. Ever. Didn't hear from him after that either. But, he said, the Kid saw him after that, and, and this was the crowning achievement of the morning's discussion with the agents of federal law enforcement, I, the one time gringo, was, as far as he and the kid knew, the last one to see him, over at the paleteria, that one morning.

"Whoa," I interjected "Wait a second. Hang on. What do you mean, last one to see him?" I paused. They stared at me. "I saw him and he walked away from me. I haven't seen him since. That was a couple of weeks ago. That doesn't make me the last one to see him. Not by a long shot. No way."

"So you admit that?" Boss Cop with sunglasses took a step toward me. "You admit you talked to him and saw him in town in early October?"

"What's to admit? I talked to him, and I bought him a paleta, I think it was a strawberry one, if that matters. We talked, and then he left. He didn't tell me where he was going. I haven't seen him since. I haven't heard from him since."

"So you claim you don't know what happened to him? Is that it? Is that your story? You don't know anything about what happened after that, after he walked away from you that day?"

I was not enjoying this. Not at all. My headache was raging. My eyeballs hurt. I was thinking about throwing up. Maybe I could throw up on the cop's shiny boots. The sun was getting even hotter. It didn't help matters that I really, truthfully didn't know anything at all about the person they were asking me about. And Don Obdulio was making matters worse. Through my squinting, bloodshot, painful eyes I could see that he had a small smile on his face, like he was somehow enjoying the way the Boss Cop with sunglasses was glaring at me and interrogating me and staring into my face and acting like a tough cop, which is precisely what he was. The semi-smile made me even more angry. And it made my head pound even harder.

"No, I don't know anything. What happened? Why are you asking about this? Is there a problem?"

At this, Boss Cop with sunglasses nodded to one of the other Federales. "Yes, there's a problem. The problem is," the other Federale paused meaningfully, "Death." Clearly he had been watching entirely too much television. That's what they're always saying on Univision. And they say it just like that, with the pause before the d-word. The Federale then theatrically pulled out a photo, an 8 x 11 color photo portrait of the kid. In the photo, which had cleaned him up quite a bit, he was smiling and wearing a suit and tie. It must have been from a graduation or a wedding or something. "That's him, right? That's what he looked like when you last saw him, right?"

We all nodded that, yes, it was him. I didn't try to explain that the last time I saw him he didn't exactly look like he was going to Sunday school or an ice cream social, that instead he was wearing a dirty Che t-shirt and had sticky paleta on his hands and pimples and piercings. The Boss Cop with sunglasses frowned. The frown is a favorite form of Federale punctuation, like an overused exclamation point or a sad faced emoticon. He looked meaningfully at the other Federales. "We'll be back," he announced. "We'll return. We need to get written statements from all three of you. From each of you. Separate statements." This was not thrilling news.

"Would you mind telling us what happened?" I asked.

At this the Boss Cop took off his shades. He squinted back at me. He peered directly in my eyes, he looked me up and down meaningfully, and then he spoke very slowly and very evenly and very gravely, in the kind of voice you sometimes hear at televised police press conferences when they talk about how they are working on horrible, unspeakably evil crimes, "They pulled him out of a cenote. He must have drowned. He's dead. We're not sure how that happened. Or exactly when it happened. How long ago. We'll be back to get a statement."

I imagine he was watching me to see how I would react to this news. I hoped that something obviously innocent, something like surprise might somehow show up on my stubbly face despite the hangover and the sunlight and my festering, nearly overwhelming annoyance at Don Obdulio.

I doubt I looked sufficiently innocent. The kid's demise wasn't actually earthshaking to me. I only spoke to him that once. It wasn't like I knew him. People, I thought, die all the time. In all kinds of ways. I didn't have anything at all to do with this particular death. And I didn't really know the person they would later call "the decedent." I'm sorry to admit it, but it was hard for me to act upset about whatever may have happened to him. I just wanted to go back to bed.

The Federales then marched off to their cars and drove away squealing their tires and flashing their lights.

"Nice work, amigo," I glared at Don Obdulio. "You had a great idea. You'd get rid of those pests, those tourists from far away. You sent him on a spiritual mission to that dangerous cenote. And now look at what's happened. He probably followed your crazy advice and he died in the very cenote you told him to jump into."

"No, it's not that simple." He was very calm; he spoke softly. To him none of this was a very big deal. "Nothing is ever that simple. You're angry. You don't feel well. You have a headache. Upset stomach. From drinking the rum." He smiled. "It's not what you think. Why not go home? We can talk about this later. It'll be easier to talk about later on."

This sounded like moderately acceptable advice. I didn't want then and there to try to hash out how Don Obdulio by himself, and himself alone, and not at all me, was responsible for whatever may have happened to the kid, so I took his advice. Besides, my head hurt, my eyes hurt, and I was still feeling very queasy. I went home, crawled back into bed, pulled a pillow over my eyes, and fell into a merciful, soft, deep, cotton filled abyss.

And oh did I have a dream. A vivid dream. A hangover dream so bright I can still recall it with all of its shining details.

I was swimming in a deep, cool pond, probably it was a round cenote, that was surrounded on all sides by impenetrable, lush jungle, tall trees and thick plants and hanging vines. It seemed to be a familiar cenote just off the Tulum Beach Road. I always liked this cenote. It was at ground level. You didn't have to climb into it from above. And it was surrounded by a beautiful veil of the most dense, most green forest. As I was swimming and treading water, there was suddenly a gigantic black jaguar standing at the very edge of the water, staring at me and snarling and growling and licking its chops and swishing its long tail. It had huge yellow eyes and was jet black. It was enormous. And each time I came at all near to the edge where it was pacing, it raised a large, black paw studded with long, razor sharp nails, and reached out to try to grab me by the arm. The gesture reminded me of the way a house cat might play with a dead bird or mouse. The first three or four times this happened, I hastily pulled away from the jaguar and went back to treading water a distance away from her. I hope she's not going to jump in here with me, I thought. Oh please, please don't jump in here with me. I hope she won't jump in here. I was treading water, and if I approached her at all, she turned toward me. The last time she reached out with her paw, the jaguar was really close to me and she struck out with her nails three or four quick, sharp jabs. Snap, snap, snap, snap. That woke me up. I sat up in bed bolt upright, my heart pounding from all the swimming and treading water and the fear, sweat pouring down my back, and my head drumming and throbbing. To my surprise, my arms had no wounds. My t-shirt was soaking wet. I got out of bed. I took two more aspirins. I again looked at myself in the mirror. I was a complete mess. My eyes looked beady and red. My hair was wild. My face was stubbly. And then, while I was looking at my bloodshot eyes and wondering what to do so they wouldn't hurt so much, I had the surprising idea that the kid's drowning had nothing at all to do with Don Obdulio. Or me. We didn't have anything to do with it in any sense. It had nothing at all to do with us. I had no idea how I knew this, but it was a fact. It was so. I knew it. I sighed. I went back to bed. I threw the wet t-shirt on the floor. And I slept. Soundly.

When I finally awoke at around 11:30 am, I decided I should escape from Tulum and make my way to the Si'an Kaan Biosphere Reserve. I needed some truly alone time. I wanted to go for a long walk on a deserted beach all by myself. Maybe I could get rid of the remaining parts of the hangover, and maybe I could unscramble my thoughts. Maybe I could begin to think clearly, unknot all of my confusion. Maybe I could try to sort out whatever was happening in my life and why I felt so full of contradictions about virtually every aspect of it.

My neighbor was happy to lend me the Tsuru for my journey, provided I returned it with a full tank of gas and in the same condition it was then in. Neither of these requirements seemed to be much of an obstacle. I figured that 200 pesos should be more than enough to fill the tank, even if it was then completely empty, and the car was so beat up that if it's still running and isn't obviously missing important parts when I return it, my neighbor will be pleased. There are no parking police in the Reserve. I wouldn't lose his license plates. Or anything else.

I drove from Tulum down the Boca Paila Road toward Punta Allen, a small, picturesque lobster and fishing village on a narrow peninsula where the reserve ends in a point and Asuncion Bay and the Caribbean surround it. Punta Allen is famous for sport fishing for permit, tarpon and bonefish. It has a few modest restaurants. Mostly, it's pretty and remote. And quite hot. And quiet. And you can feel, when you're there, that it is indeed far, far off the beaten track. In fact, the beaten track ends there at the water's edge. There is no dry place beyond Punta Allen.

In fact, in his famous, exploratory walking trek of the coast of Quintana Roo in the 1950's, a Frenchman, Michel Piessel, walked to this point, and then, ut oh. He couldn't get across. He had to back track to go all the way around the Bay. I can imagine how disappointed and angry that discovery made him. And how very hot the hike around the bay must have been.

All the way down the difficult, bumpy, pot holed road, there are beautiful white sand, palm tree lined beaches. The coral reef shelters the land from direct contact with the open ocean. Sparkling turquoise water reflects a cloudless blue sky. The air is filled with birdsong. The water is filled with creatures. On the right hand side of the road, growing right up to the road, is a dense, tall mangrove and behind it, invisible from the road, is the bay. Everything is incredibly green and alive and growing rapidly. Everything is also hot and brims with insect sounds and bird songs.

The jungle and mangrove themselves are quite inhospitable to people. Lots of biting insects, mud, snakes. Plants that think they are boa constrictors. Boa constrictors that are camouflaged as plants. Someplace where eating or being eaten remains the obvious rule of the day. Let's face it. Nobody goes into the dense mangrove unless there's a good reason. A really good reason.

This could be a wonderful drive. Except for one thing. It turns out that the sea water isn't really completely spotless. And that realization is always a grave disappointment. It's not really pristine. It might look spotless on first impression, but it isn't. Not really. As you drive down the road and stop at beaches you see that there is entirely too much plastic in this paradise. I cannot help but notice it. And when I see it, I am repulsed. And annoyed.

Some of the beaches that face the wind and the open sea are littered with plastic. All of the usual civilized species are there: blue plastic jugs, old shoes, plastic bags, bottles, packaging, plastic coke bottles, old nylon ropes, auto parts, light bulbs, sun screen tubes. How so? How does this happen? Garbage gets dumped into the sea from ships, from barges, from people. The sea doesn't want to be befouled by it. The wind and the sea vomit this poison right back onto the beach, from whence it came. Because nobody lives on these particular beaches, nobody bothers to pick up the piles of plastic the sea disgorges. Token, symbolic clean up efforts go unnoticed. They cannot begin to make a dent in the amount of plastic that has accumulated over time.

Unlike the beaches nearer to Tulum, which get a frequent, tidy, plastic pick up from residents, nobody owns these beaches or takes personal responsibility for removing all of the plastic, for picking it up, for returning the plastic to the appropriate stream for garbage. So it sits. And more and more is slowly added to it. The more that is produced on land, the more that ends up in the ocean, the more that arrives on the beach. Repeat and repeat and repeat again. For many, many years.

Beaches around Tulum are spotless. They are spotless solely because people, frequently owners of homes and businesses on them, make sure they stay free of visible plastic. Some of the beaches in Si'an Kaan are, I am sorry to say, quite filthy. Some might require heavy equipment to remove all of the plastic garbage that has accumulated on them.

In the Reserve, I hope a windward beach will be pristine. I park the car in the shade of a leaning coco tree. I get out of the car. I walk toward the sea. This beach could have potential. It might turn out to be breathtakingly beautiful, and empty of people, and quiet. It is all of that, but, alas, it's littered with plastic. I won't stay here. Not all of the beaches are littered, but some are. Some are quite littered. Some have debris deposited by Hurricane Wilma and by Hurricane Dean and by hundreds of other fierce storms, both named and unnamed, before and since the big ones. The accumulation of a substantial amount of plastic on any of the beaches is a plain and simple disgrace.

This upsets me. It makes me angry. It makes me sad. And the upset runs deeper than just that the beaches are littered. The litter means that the sea just off shore is also polluted with floating and sinking plastic. And this in turn means that animals in the sea, including endangered sea turtles, are imperiled by the plastic. And that the sea birds and the fish they eat are also imperiled by plastic. And, sadly, that instead of being pure, clear, turquoise sea water, the ocean is actually to some degree really a deceptive, deathly, man made plastic and salt water gumbo.

This is not real news. How could it be? We humans have befouled our ocean. We continue to soil it. We all know that. I'm reminded that when Oscar Wilde saw the convicts at Redding from a train, he was reported to remark, "Well, if that's how the queen treats her convicts, she doesn't deserve to have any." And so with us and our oceans. And our beaches. How terribly we've treated our planet.

I pull out from the dirty beach and drive a few minutes farther south. My plan is to find another beach, one that is cleaner, and to go for my planned, long, pensive walk. But first, I stop the Tsuru in the right hand lane of the narrow, sandy, two-lane, deeply potholed road. There really isn't anywhere for me to pull completely off the road. I don't want to get the car stuck in the sand, there's no shoulder. I stop anyway and put on the flashers. I have no idea whether there is anyone coming. Heat waves are rising from the road. I don't see anyone or anything coming. All I see is the road and the heat. I walk toward the mangrove. I would like to pee.

There are no cars to be seen in either direction. All I can see is the road and the waves of heat rising from it. I hear nothing but the wind softly clacking the branches of coco trees and the birds singing and the humming of the vast insect community. As I face the mangrove and begin to unzip my fly, I notice a movement in the mangrove, a shadow moving from right to left, an animal, a surprisingly large one. What is it? I stand stone still. It is larger than a big dog. It is very large. I hold my breath. It moves again slightly. And then I see it in the shadows, a large black jaguar with yellow eyes. It's only about 7 meters away from me. It stands perfectly still and stares at me. It gazes directly into my eyes. It swishes its long tail. It begins to growl. The sound of the growl is very deep and strong and loud, but the jaguar doesn't move toward me. Thank goodness. I begin to plan an emergency, hasty, unceremonious retreat to the roof of the car, as if that would help. Climbing a tree is not an answer. Running down the road isn't good either. There really is no safe place to go. I think about quickly getting inside the car and rapidly slamming the door, as if there will be time for me to do all of that. These are just a quick, bumpy stream of jumbled, bad ideas fueled by fear and surging adrenaline. I stand motionless. I am petrified. The jaguar opens its mouth wide, yawns, slowly licks its chops, and finally, finally, finally turns slowly away from me. I can feel every hair on my body standing on end. Every pore in my body has opened. I am drenched in sweat. My eyes are impossibly wide open. And jerking from side to side. My breathing is rapid and high in my chest. My heart is pounding. Hard. The jaguar turns its head further away and then she walks gracefully and slowly and quietly deeper into the mangrove. Instantly, I can no longer see her. She's again invisible. And silent. I am standing on the shimmering road in the hot sun. But now I am again alone. I have no desire at all to pee. I want to get in the car. Right away. I want to turn on the air conditioner as high as it will go, and I want to breathe deeply through my nose until my heart returns to its normal cadence.

What a huge surprise. I had been told many times by my neighbors that there are jaguars around Tulum and in the Si'an Kaan Reserve, but I had never seen one before. My neighbors tell me that jaguars give humans a very wide berth, but that they occasionally see jaguar tracks in the selva and they say that on rare occasions they have also seen jaguars when they have been walking in deserted areas at dawn or in the night. But never in broad daylight. And never near the beach. My neighbors assure me that the only jaguar you will ever see is one that wants you to see it. Otherwise, the jaguar is completely silent and so graceful that it can wander in the forest without making even the slightest sound. It kills its prey by crushing the prey's brain with its powerful jaws. To do that, it needs to be extremely stealthy and very quick and amazingly strong. It has to be able to jump high, to pounce on its prey's head and quickly deliver a crushing, mortal bite between its ears. I do not want to think about being its intended prey.

I am amazed to have seen this jaguar. And I think, well, that's the third jaguar. The other two were dream jaguars, but this one certainly wasn't. And this one apparently wanted me to see it in broad daylight. It strikes me that there is something quite odd about this. Something slightly improbable. After decades and decades of never seeing a single jaguar, I am now dreaming about them and also seeing them in the flesh. True, I am fascinated by them. I feel very lucky to have seen one so close. But I keep thinking that it's odd. Very odd. Maybe it's just some kind of a coincidence. Or something like that.

My neighbors tell me that in the old days—I'm never sure when that was, whether it was centuries ago or a few years ago—curanderos turned themselves into jaguars. This surprising transformation was the second most important function of the curandero, to turn into a jaguar and to hunt, to provide meat, to drive animals that could be eaten toward people from the pueblo who were hunting, and then to disappear. Some curanderos, my neighbors claim, only turned partially into jaguars to accomplish this task. The top part of them was jaguar, complete with huge teeth and mouth, and the bottom remained human from the heart down. Apparently, this also worked well to drive game to the hunters, but it was, they tell me, the mark of a less proficient shaman than one who could completely transform himself into a jaguar and back into a person.

I imagine that some shamans must have managed to turn themselves into jaguars, but then couldn't change back. This kind of error, one that might mythically happen to a Sorcerer's Apprentice, seems like the beginning of a strange story. I scribble on an envelope, "Jaguar, Night on Bald Mountain," and jam it into my pocket. Later, I will be angry that the reference is to Walt Disney's *Fantasia*.

The primary, traditional job of the curandero, my neighbors tell me, was to make it rain so that maiz could be grown in the interior, in the slash and burn milpas throughout the Yucatan Peninsula. If there were no rain, the corn would wither and die, and if there were insufficient rain, the maiz would be vulnerable to disease and to insects. If there were a poor harvest, the community would be without life's most important, portable sustenance and the staple of its diet. That would cause hunger and suffering and discord and weakness and illness and death. It was the curandero's job to make sure this didn't happen, to make it rain. It was the curandero's main job to thwart suffering by making the crop abundant. To intercede with Spirit for that purpose.

Making it rain was, of course, dependent on the curandero's relationship with Spirit and the qualities of the ceremony and offerings he would make. If Spirit accepted the shaman's offerings and prayers and ceremonies and responded favorably to them, Spirit and not the shaman would make it rain. It was the shaman's task only to invoke Spirit's goodwill by making the right offerings and sending good prayers and summoning the right kinds energies. Spirit would then respond with rain that could lead to abundance and prosperity and health and wellbeing. Shamans didn't make it rain. Shamans reached out to Spirit, whose grace brought the rain.

I had a long beach walk. I walked about an hour and a half. I was in no rush. I just wanted to be with myself and see how I was doing. Some things did come up. I wanted to know about Mari Estrella and whether I would ever see her again. And I wanted to know whether Don Obdulio would show me how to track. Those were the two most important items.

On my way to return the car to my neighbor, I saw El Kid sitting on a curb. He waved. He then pointed over his shoulder. In the yard I saw Don Obdulio tending a small fire. There was only a little wispy, pungent smoke, and you could smell that he was burning various kinds of herbs. "What's he doing?" I asked. "Nothing."

"It doesn't look like nothing."

El Kid shrugged and turned toward Don Obdulio. I parked the car so I could get out and see what he was up to. When I entered the yard, he was already walking slowly toward me.

"What were you doing?" I asked.

"Nothing."

"That's what he said, too, but it didn't look like nothing."

"That was a good answer he gave you. Very good."

"Well, is it a secret then? I saw that there was a small fire and that you were burning something in it. What were you doing?"

He shook his head. "Remember when I told that kid to jump into the deep cenote?"

"How could I forget? Even the Federales want me to remember all the details I can about that. I'm sure we haven't heard the last of that. Not by a long shot."

"Do you know why I told him to do that? You might think I was just trying to get rid of him, maybe even trying to kill him. It wasn't that. Not at all. I just wanted him to go away because I don't want to answer any questions about what I am doing and why I am doing it and how I am doing it. Especially from those I consider outsiders. And it's not just outsiders. It's not really a secret, it's just that the questions are about thinking and what I'm doing isn't at all about thinking. It's about something else. Something else entirely different from thinking. It's got nothing to do with any thinking." He looked in my eyes. "And it's not about feelings, either. It's not about emotions. It's about making contract with what you probably call the Divine or Spirit or the Universe. You probably have other names for what I'm talking about, but I'm sure you know exactly what I'm talking about. Let's leave it at that."

I wasn't at all sure what this "something else entirely" might turn out to be. Regardless, it seemed to me that maybe this was my opportunity.

Did I clear my throat? I hope not. "Let's say somebody wanted to learn how to do what you're doing. How would they learn it if you won't answer any of their questions?" I asked.

He started to smile. I could see his gold tooth emerging, shining. The smile turned into a laugh. He took off his ball cap. He rubbed the top of his head with the palm of his hand. He smiled broadly. "You mean you, not somebody. You are asking about you, right? About you and how you could learn from me what I do."

I nodded. "The Kid here, he is learning. He learns by helping me, being with me, doing what I tell him needs to be done. Every once in a while, I answer a question for him in words, if it really needs to be answered, but usually, it's just that I show him what I'm doing and how I'm doing it and what I'm trying to accomplish and then he helps me carry it out. He's my apprentice. An assistant to me. A helper.

Eventually, he'll be able to do all of what I can do, and more, all by himself. There are others who have learned from me in this way. In fact, I myself learned how to do what I do in this very way. Eventually, he'll be able to see all the things I see. This is how you learn. It's the only way I can teach you. There's no classrooms or books or lectures or questions or answers. It's not about thinking and talking about it. It's not about analyzing and figuring it out. It's not about the questions. Or the answers." He put his hat back on his head and folded his arms against his chest. "Yes?" He was still staring in my eyes.

"I've been thinking about what you do," I said. "You've helped me in many ways, especially healing my sarpudilla and helping me find Ramirez, so I was wondering whether you'd be willing to show me how to do some of the things you do."

He looked puzzled. "Wait a minute. Hold on a second. You want this even though you accused me before of doing malicious and evil things to you?" He squinted at me. He frowned. "What about that? You don't want to do bad things to other people, do you? That's not what you want, is it? You're not trying to get me to help you hurt anyone or mess up anybody's life, are you?" He had a slight, ironical tilt to his head. He started smiling again. "Well?"

"Maybe 'malicious' is the wrong word. Maybe that is too strong a word for me to use. But we both know that you've been playing with me for quite a while now. Let's not go into the details of what you've been up to. No. But, in fact," I said, and it surprised me completely that I would be so direct with him and that I would say something I was so unsure about as if it were a known fact, "You were even playing with me earlier today when I was in Si'an Kaan."

He smiled. "What? What's this? Yet another accusation? Playing with you? I was? I don't think so. You sure of this? Tell me how I was playing with you, what I did to you today that was playing with you."

That's when I said it. "That jaguar," I said. "The black jaguar right near the road. The one that growled at me and walked up to me and scared me to death. That one."

He paused for a second or two. He stared at me wide eyed. And then he laughed aloud. It was a delighted, melodic cackle that burst from his mouth. He removed his hat again from his head. He continued to laugh. He waved the hat around as if he were swatting bugs. El Kid started to laugh also. "Oh," he laughed. "Do you think I did that?"

He was laughing so hard he had to hold onto his knees. Tears were starting to glisten in the corners of his eyes. He continued to laugh. His face reddened. The tears rolled down his cheeks. When his laughter finally began to subside, he said, "Come and see me at 5 am tomorrow morning and bring two stones." That started him laughing again. "No, don't. Really. No need to do that. No need at all."

He wiped his face on his t-shirt. He was grinning ear to ear. "I am so happy. If you want to learn, I am happy to show you." He offered his hand. We shook hands.

He continued to stare at me. "So," he said, "Entonces. The Kid is still young. Because you are older, because you've been alive so much longer, there is something special I want you to do before you begin to work as my apprentice, as my helper. This will get us off on the right foot, to a very good start and help you quickly grow in power and perception and strength."

My face must have revealed my fear, so he continued, "You don't have to worry about it, this will be completely safe, it won't hurt you. This is very safe. I'm not trying to drive you off. There's no physical danger. I'm not trying to let you get hurt. You're not afraid of the dark, are you?"

It turned out that he wanted me "to become friends with darkness." I had no real idea why. He didn't explain it to me. Not at all. What he asked me to do was to go by myself into a particular dry, deep cave near Aktun Chen, north of Tulum and near Akumal, turn off my flashlight, and sit in the dark. If I did this several times, if I stayed in the cave in the total dark on each occasion for a few hours, I would, he said, begin to know the dark and I could then, he said, become its friend. It was important to become its friend, he said, because then I would be able to honor the dark things I didn't want to know about myself. And about others. And if I were friends with the dark, I could be a better friend to the light.

When I began to ask what all of this might mean, he put his finger to his lips, saying that I shouldn't talk. Then he turned and walked away.

The idea seemed harmless enough. Early in the morning, as if it matters at what time of day or night somebody sits in a dark cave, as if the sights there might change over time, I took a collectivo up the Highway and got off at the Aktun Chen overpass. I easily found Pedrito, whom don Obdulio told me to find, and he didn't seem at all surprised that I wanted him to show me the cave where I could sit for a few hours and be left alone. He'd be happy to do so, how was his friend, Don Obduio, would I send his very best regards?

The entrance to the cave looked like a small, round hole in the side of a hill. It was about my height, maybe a little higher, and wider than a person. There was a lot of scrubby, dry brush growing on the hill. The cave itself was nothing like the huge, dramatic, underground cave tourists can visit at Aktun Chen. It was much smaller. It was about 150 meters long, Pedrito said, and had a ceiling about 7 meters high. It was very cold. And, to no one's surprise, it was totally dark. And it had a community of bats hanging silently from the ceiling amid the limestone formations near the entrance. I found a flat rock to sit on that was back from the entrance, covered myself in a blanket, and I turned off my flashlight. It was completely dark.

My jacket and the blanket were keeping me warm. It didn't much matter whether my eyes were open or closed. There was nothing to see. There was no light. Within seconds my brain was chattering away, thinking and wondering, rehashing the past, speculating about the future, planning and analyzing, jumping nimbly over the present, which was just me sitting in the dark in the cave on a rock, with my mind darting around. Wild, crazy, active monkey mind.

After only a few minutes, I was finished sitting. Really. It was enough. I was ready to leave. My butt was beginning to get cold. And tired. The rock was hard. It was dark. Remind me what the point of this was, ok? To become friends with the dark. Well, obviously that wasn't happening. Not yet. So I made myself sit. This was not easy.

Eventually, after quite some time with my mind spinning round and around, I just gave up. That was all I could do. At any moment half of the planet is in darkness. And every day half of the time on average is in darkness. And if you look up, peer far into the heavens, there is far, far more darkness than light. Deep under the seas it is always dark. So too in closets, cupboards, boxes, empty boots, under beds. Humans found fire and electricity to elbow the darkness away, to shove it back into the far corners. To get away from it. But we all know that we come from the darkness of the womb and that when we close our eyes and sleep, the darkness can no longer be held at bay, that it always returns. And then there's the matter of dreams and death and wondering about them. And eventually the dark inside of a coffin or a grave or an urn.

When I stand with my back to the sun, and I look down at the ground, I see some of my personal darkness lying on the ground just before me at my feet. My shadow is darkness's constant beachhead in the light. Nothing is more persistent than this darkness. And, of course, my personal darkness is not solely external: it includes an ocean of unacceptable thoughts and conduct, all of which I usually battle in vain not to reveal, to suppress, to hide, to stifle, to ignore.

So I find myself sitting in the cave. In the absolute dark. Eventually I begin to see and feel all of the darkness. How, I wonder, can I possibly be as friendly with ubiquitous darkness as with the sun's enlightenment? How? I will return, as Don Obdulio has asked me to.

I return again and again. While I sit, my mind refuses to just be in the dark. It squirms. It tries to see whether it's the same in the cave with my eyes open or my eyes closed. It turns out these are different. My mind also turns to events that happened years before. I think of old girlfriends, distant lovemaking, conversations, classrooms, my parents. They are all as alive in me as they were forty years or more before. As I revisit them in the darkness, I sometimes make sounds. These sounds are involuntary. Shame. Embarrassment. Joy. Happiness. All of these sounds emerge into the silent cave. As a reflex, I try to stifle the sounds. But why? The bats don't care, nobody else is near me, no one can hear me. Nobody will ask me what I was thinking that elicited a groan, or a cry, or sighs, or moaning. From whom am I in the habit of hiding these emotions? Is it from somebody outside, or is it from myself, or both of us?

One second I'm in the cave in the dark. The next I am in the back seat of a car making out in a high school parking lot. The next I am 30 years later thinking about my gangster life just before I came down the highway to Tulum. Then I am in tomorrow. And what I will be doing. And then I am speculating about Mari Estrella. What she might say. What her body is like. And Don Obdulio. And whether I will ever be able to track. Enough. Enough. Enough. It's exhausting. I'm back in the cave in the dark. And then I'm immediately somewhere else. Again.

I wish I could tell you that something phenomenal happened from sitting in the cave. That would make things much better, much more exciting. It would make this story different. Maybe even coherent. But instead, I'm sorry to admit, it didn't. I just sat and was in the dark and I experienced that and I thought about what it might mean to be "in the dark." And I tried to carry with me in my daily life that I was going to be a friend of the dark, just as I am a friend of the light, and I tried to see what difference that made in my perceptions. I think all of this has maybe made me slightly less fearful and perhaps a little bit more compassionate. Maybe. But I don't want to exaggerate.

When I came home from the cave late one afternoon, the curandero was sitting in my yard. He was sitting in my plastic chair, under the flowering tree with a beer bottle in his hand. He stood up. He came over to me and looked into my eyes. "How's it going at the cave?"

"Well, I'm trying to sit there," I said. "It's harder than I thought it would be. But I'm working on it. Is something special supposed to happen after a while?" I asked.

"I don't know," he said, "Hmmm." He paused. He looked at me some more. "Well," he said, "I think you've done that enough for right now. Please don't do it any more unless you want to, ok?" And that was that.

No, he didn't give me a little diploma with ribbons, or a medal for sitting in the dark. In fact, he didn't mention it again to me.

A few days later in mid morning, Boss Cop showed up again. His uniform was crisp and he was wearing his reflector sunglasses, but this time he was uninspired. "Look," he said to the three of us. "We need to complete these written statements. We have to have the right paperwork. I need you all to cooperate. We just need to have something to put in the file, we need to show that we followed up and we investigated and we talked to all the relevant people. That would be the three of you. And that you gave us whatever information you had. Understand?" In other words, it was only a formality. He had other plans, there were no doubt others whose day he wanted to enrich and he didn't want to spend a lot of time with us on paperwork.

I dutifully took the form from him. He handed a form to El Kid and another one to Don Obdulio. Then he folded his arms across his chest to wait. "Please just write briefly what you told me yesterday."

El Kid looked at Don Obdulio, Don Obdulio looked at me, looked down and looked at the paper. Said El Kid, "Probably you should write out Don Obdulio's statement for him, then he can make his mark on it when you're finished. You should read it to him first. I will write my own statement."

"You making a full confession?" I asked Don Obdulio. "You going to explain how you went out to the cenote, hit him over the head with a hammer, and then drowned him?" He grinned at me. Boss Cop, however, didn't think this remark was at all funny.

"Please, no kidding around, let's not waste any more time on this than we have to, let's just fill out the forms and get it over with. Please. No bantering. No joking. Let's get to work. Let's finish this up."

We were all only too happy to comply. We finished the forms and handed them to Boss Cop, who dutifully read each of them through, and said, "Humpf." He folded the forms neatly in half and placed them in a metal file box.

Don Obdulio then spoke. "Please, just one question," he said, "if that would be ok. When they found him in the cenote, what cenote was that? It probably needs to be purified."

Boss Cop didn't bat an eyelash at the concept that Don Obdulio might have in interest in purifying a cenote, in making a limpia. "It was on the Boca Paila Road, south of the intersection, toward Si'an Kaan. The first of those twin cenotes. Across from Los Lirios, the ones behind the fence. The first one you get to. Do you know where I mean?"

We knew what he meant. We thanked him for the visit, and we all waved goodbye to him as he strode importantly to his Federale Mobile. I hoped I'd never see him again. Ever.

"Hah," said Don Obdulio as soon as Boss Cop had driven off. "Were you listening to him? Did you just hear that? Did you hear what he said? The Officer said it was South on the Boca Pila Road, and you know very well where those twin cenotes are. They are not North on the highway to Playa del Carmen. Did you hear that? Did I tell you that before or didn't I? Did I tell you it was not the cenote I sent him to? He just told you it wasn't where I sent him. He confirmed what I told you before. Didn't I tell you before that this wasn't what it appeared to be? It wasn't the deep cenote, the one where you have to jump in. It was one of those at ground level that are like a small, round pond."

I knew it well. It was the cenote in which I had just had a scary meeting with the black dream jaguar while I was treading water.

"Please," he told El Kid. "Get materials for purifying the cenote and bring them back here. And you," he said talking to me, "please borrow your friend's car for a few hours so we can purify the cenote. We need to go there this afternoon and have a ceremony. Right away."

I walked over to my neighbor's. I was sure this was going to be a gigantic problem. I was sure he wouldn't part with the car, even briefly.

"Manuelito," I said, "I need to borrow your car again. Can you lend it to me?"

"You? What for this time? Didn't you just use it? Didn't you just take it all the long way to Si'an Kaan? You're going to wear it out. It cannot handle that kind of use, really it cannot. It's quite fragile. And old. I'm afraid it might die. From overuse. From being driven too much. I have no idea where I might get another one. Or how I would pay for it. You, of course, wouldn't be willing to help me pay for it, would you?" He wasn't smiling.

I wasn't sure what I wanted to tell him. I wanted to have him lend me the car, but I didn't know how many details he would want to know. "Well, Don Obdulio, you know who he is, right? He wants to do a ceremony off the Boca Paila Road, and I agreed to get him there. With your car, if that's OK."

"Why didn't you just say it was for Don Obdulio? That's different, you can always use the car when it's for him. Don't even put gas in it. I will happily do that for him whenever he needs it. I consider it to be an honor." I was astonished. I'd never heard such a thing from Manuel before. He immediately fished in his pockets and handed me the keys. He was honored by this request? I was extremely surprised.

This was how my first few weeks helping Don Obdulio went. Mostly, I sat in my yard, drank a beer or two, smoked a wonderful cigar and tried unsuccessfully to return to my previous, normal, boring lizard's life. I began to think about stories set in Tulum, in the jungle, on the beach. I began to imagine them. I had a fleeting idea about writing about my life in the States. I thought about telling some true stories about Don Obdulio, as if years before I hadn't inadvertently told far to many of them. And I thought I might be able to sell a piece about Tulum. But I never quite got settled in to my own rhythm of doing nothing, into the feelings of torpor, into gently harvesting the stories and writing them down. I was sitting at the river of stories. Yes. I could see it rolling into the sea. I'd begin to fall asleep, or I'd be walking around the house and the yard dreaming, or I'd be reading, or I'd be writing, or drawing, and El Kid would show up. This would interrupt whatever story was then swimming toward my net. The net would disappear and the story with it. And I would find that both had vanished as if they were only a dream. And I would never be able quite to get back to them. They'd be gone.

One afternoon at about 4, I was sitting in my chair scribbling. There had been, in my story, a terrible murder in Tulum of a man who ran a small newspaper. A newspaper like a weekly shopper in the United States. The man, who was driving an SUV, had been shot at point blank range by a man riding on the back of a motorcycle. The shooter and his driver got away. Nobody could identify them, because they had masks. And nobody could identify the bike. Or the weapon. It all happened too fast. The case had been assigned to a Mayan Federale detective, who because of a paucity of any other clues, began sifting Tulum's people searching for a motive for the killing. Was the man shot because he criticized the new, municipal government and its mayor? Was the man shot because he was extorting business owners, telling them that if they didn't advertise sufficiently, there would be many critical stories about them that would hurt their business? Those were the only two theories. Meanwhile, all of those with a motive were happy: there was no more criticism of the local government, and there were no payments for "advertising," and there was, as you might expect, little cooperation with the investigation. Most people with a real motive were, of course, secretly delighted.

Troubled by the crime, and wanting desperately to solve it no matter who was responsible, the detective was running out of ideas and getting nowhere fast. His bosses claimed that they wanted the crime solved right away. He wasn't so sure they wanted it resolved. There were times when resolving crimes was in nobody's interest. That's when he started being visited while he was sleeping by the old dream jaguar. The dream jaguar at first frightened him by growling and clawing at him, but after many nights of having the dream jaguar interrupt his sleep on multiple occasions, the cop realized that dream jaguar knows how to find the killer and is willing to tell him how to solve the case. All the cop has to do is get the dream jaguar to show him how to proceed.

At this point in the story, I was pacing the yard, opening the refrigerator door, staring at the sky, mumbling, walking around, up and down the block, trying to coax a twist out of what I had. Yes, the jaguar would point the cop to somebody. Except that this would have to be the wrong person. The jaguar got it wrong even though it was an old, experienced dream jaguar. But the detective's confrontation with this wrong person, a confrontation in which potential violence and actual menace is writ large, would lead the cop immediately, directly to the real killer and the real motive, which has nothing to do with politics or extortion or anything we might suspect. No. It has to do with a sexual assault, several years before, on a gangster's present lover. The gangster had no idea where the rapist went. Turns out he went to Tulum. The gangster hears about this. The dream jaguar's clue leads via the wrong person to the right one.

Just as I walked back to the chair, to get all of this written down and draw diagrams so that I could see whether it made any sense, El Kid arrived to interrupt me, to help me lose the thread, to distract me, to make things complicated and blurry and confusing. And to help me lose any of the logic of the tale, if there ever was any. When I saw El Kid, I immediately shouted, "Oh no, not again." He started to laugh. "We have an errand to do," he said.

El Kid was thoroughly enjoying these unannounced visits. Would I be sober? Would I be stoned? Would I be wearing clothing? Would I be sitting at the computer? What would he find in my house? Surprises abounded. He'd come to the door and pound with his fists. While he was pounding, he'd shout, "Senor, we have to run an errand!" If there were no answer, or if the answer didn't come quick enough for him, or loud enough, or clear enough, El Kid would come into the yard to find me. A very special treat. Would he get to wake me up by touching me and nearly giving me a heart attack? Would he get to shout in my ear? Would he find me enjoying a book I didn't want to put down, smiling about it? Would he find me daydreaming? "Senor, we have to run an errand."

Anyway, I decided to go back to the cave five or sixth more times on my own even though I had "graduated." It didn't matter that Don Obdulio said it was enough; I thought I wasn't quite finished, that it might help me. It was still really hard just to sit in the dark. Harder still was trying to make friends with the darkness. I've spent about six decades trying in one fashion or another to hide darkness, trying to appear to be acceptable. Now all of the dark ideas and feelings and memories were coming out from under the rocks I had so carefully put on top of them to hold them in place, to keep them hidden from others and myself. My memories and feelings were flooding me. I was angry, or I was sad, or I was terrified. Or filled with regret. Or shame. So I tried to make friends with these feelings, too. It was not easy. When I couldn't make friends with them, and often I couldn't, I tried to make friends with my wanting to make friends with them. Some of what I remembered was quite painful to me even though fifty years had passed.

"Darkness, my friend. I'm here to visit you, to see what is not illuminated. To bring into awareness what I have been trying to ignore. What I've been trying to cover up. To shine awareness on what you conceal. To see what you are holding for me. Please let me be your friend. Please let me see or feel or know what I need to. And also, thank you for all that you have done for me for so very long by keeping things I could not bear hidden. And for covering up what I thought was ugly. Please let me know or see or feel what I need to. I am happy to honor all of these things for the ways they have helped me live this long."

This talking, this sort of entreaty or prayer, seemed to help me. Eventually sitting in the cave was almost comfortable, and I found that I could sit for a while. Yes, my thoughts, and feelings, and memories were still quite disturbing. Yes, I still made involuntary sounds. Yes, events of decades before were as alive in the cave as they were when they happened. Maybe more so. For reasons I don't fully understand, I pressed on anyway.

When I wasn't sitting in the cold darkness with a theater full of distant but compelling events shouting and carrying on in my head, I was trying to write and I was running errands for Don Obdulio. Most of these errands involved gathering the materials needed for making offerings. And materials for making a fire. And various symbolic materials to burn. Sometimes it was corn and other kinds of grains, sometimes it was herbs, cinnamon and cacao, sometimes it was tequila. Or rum. Or wine. Sometimes it was candy, or cookies, or pictures from magazines. There were all kinds of things that Don Obdulio would ask us to get, depending on what the purpose of the ceremony was.

What he did for each ceremony was always unique. He never seemed to do the same thing twice. Yes, there were parts he repeated, like how he began and how he ended ceremonias, those were always virtually the same. But apart from that, each ceremony was brand new. Each responded to what Don Obulio understood was necessary to fulfill its purpose.

He was quite clear about some things. First, he insisted that we never use candles. Fires were required often, even small ones were good. But candles were unacceptable.

"Why don't you use candles? They use candles in the Mayan Church."

"I told you please not to ask questions."

It emerged later that candles were brought to this hemisphere by Cortez. Before that there were no candles. And no chimneys. Was Don Obdulio trying to keep his ceremonies connected to his pre-Columbian lineage? He wouldn't tell me.

Second, he insisted that El Kid and I always pay attention. Don Obdulio didn't really give any instructions about what to do when he was performing the actual ceremony. He told me only that the ceremonies were extremely important, and that he needed us to pay very strict attention to what he was doing. To stay focused on what he was doing and to hold in our hearts the reasons why he was making a ceremony and to remember at all times what the purpose or intention of the ceremony was. That was it. He sometimes called it "holding the intention." And no talking. Ever. No jokes, no banter, no sounds. Nothing, no matter what happened. And no getting distracted. Ever. No daydreaming. No thinking. No discursive thought. No planning. Just pay attention. This is sometimes far easier said than done.

Sometimes there was more than a single purpose. The three of us traveled in my neighbor's car to the twin cenotes. The purpose, we had already been told, was to purify the cenote. Because there had been a drowning, Don Obdulio told me and El Kid that it was also important "to send home the one who died, if he hasn't already left the cenote. He should not linger there any longer. He should leave."

I wanted to ask questions about all of this. How would he know whether that person had already left or was still hovering? How would he send him home if he was still around? How would he then purify the cenote? What exactly needed to be purified? How would he know it was pure again? What would happen if the person remained? On and on and on. I didn't ask any of these questions. I had agreed not to.

When the three of us arrived, we took all of the materials out of the car and started clumsily hauling them to the cenote. There was a lot of stuff of many different kinds and many different bags and in many loose containers. The things we needed were strewn into the car and totally disorganized. This may have looked something like emptying a Shriner's clown car. There were all kinds of things in the back seat and trunk and in the space below the back window. And on the floor. We unloaded the car and picked up most of the bags. But before we could walk 50 feet, people started showing up. A woman from the house

149

near the cenote greeted Don Obdulio, "I'm so happy you are here," she called out. Two construction workers driving a heavy truck piled high with bags of cement and concrete blocks stopped their truck in the road and put on their flashers. "Don Obdulio, how can we help you? Can we carry some of these things for you?" And a taxi driver without a fare stopped. "May I watch you, Don Obdulio? May I come along?"

Don Obdulio acknowledged these people and invited them all to come along and to help him with the ceremony. They all seemed delighted. And they all seemed to know exactly what to do. I didn't have much of an idea; they all seemed to know full well what he was doing. And its importance.

Don Obdulio only used about a tenth of the material he had us carry to the cenote. He began by greeting all of the six directions and welcoming them and their spirits to come and participate in the ceremony. He only burned some of the sticks and he scattered and burned some of the corn. And the cinnamon. He lit the charcoal for the copal and sent up sweet plumes of smoke. He said some prayers to each of the cardinal directions, and he made a small fire and burned things in it. He made many offerings to the past, present and future. He blew the conch. He rang a bell. When he was finished burning the offerings, he offered thanks to the six directions and the spirits for supporting the ceremony, and then told us it was OK to leave. So, of course, then everyone had to lug all of the many unused items back to the car when the ceremony was finished.

"You know," I told Don Obdulio once we were in the car, "We didn't need to bring all of the things to this ceremonia. We could have only brought what you knew you were going to use."

"Oh, no," he responded, "We could never do that. That's not possible. I don't know what I'm using until I start the ceremony and inquire of Spirit what is needed by Spirit. What if Spirit wants me to use something I don't have with me? I cannot bargain about that. I cannot stop and go and search for something that's needed. If it's needed, it's needed. Right then. I have to have it because I have to use only what's needed and I have to use it only when it's needed. There aren't any substitutions. Or trades I can make. So I have to bring all kinds of things I might need to the start of each ceremonia just because, to be honest, I have no idea what Spirit will think is appropriate until I begin and ask what is needed and find that out."

"Have you ever needed something you didn't have?"

Don Obdulio paused. I thought he was going to tell me to stop thinking and stop asking questions. Instead, he just smiled and turned on his heals. And walked away.

Later that evening, I drove to Soriana in Playa del Carmen, a huge big box store, and purchased four plastic cartons to fill with Don Obdulio's supplies so they could be easily carried from wherever he kept them to a car and then to his ceremonias.

The next morning I showed the cartons to Don Obdulio. He thanked me and said it was a good idea. Then he said, "Let's leave these cartons here for now." I immediately knew that he would never use them.

"I'm wondering whether you would mind answering a question for me," I said. "I want to be able to track. I just need to know the starting point to do it. What's the beginning?"

"Very well," he said. "I will show you the starting line. Did you just have a thought about these very nice boxes that you brought me?"

"Yes, I thought that you will never use them."

"Perfect. Very nicely done. You did it perfectly. Just keep doing that. Exactly that, and you will track wonderfully." He then turned on his heals and walked off.

Over time, this became an elaborate, fun game we played often. Don Obdulio would ask me whether I had any thoughts about someone or something. I'd respond with whatever jumped into my head. He'd say something like, "Juan is thinking about going to Chetumal this weekend. What do you think about that?" I'd say whatever jumped into my head. Sometimes the information I gave was right, other times wrong. Sometimes I didn't have any thoughts at all, then Don Obdulio would say, "What does the dark think of this?" or "What does the moon think of this?" I'd wait and see what thought emerged and then I'd tell him what those thought. Again, sometimes right, sometimes wrong.

A weird thing. When what I "tracked" was right it had a certain way it felt to me. It fit in a certain way. If the answer I got didn't feel that way, it was most often wrong. I knew it when I said it: it didn't have that special feeling. So I played around and tried to find out what would give me the "special feeling." If I asked myself, "What does the darkness think about this?" it usually produced the feeling and the answer tended to be more accurate. But it wasn't precise. I'm just at the beginning with this. I'm just playing around with it. I believe that eventually I will learn how to do it well. In fact, when I ask the darkness, I know that I will.

"What about Mari Estrella," Don Obdulio asked me one afternoon. "Will you ever see her again?" He smiled.

"Yes," I told him. "I will."

He asked when. I said, "Pretty soon."

He smiled at this response. That didn't mean it was correct. It just meant that he was having fun. Then he changed the subject. As he always did. There was nothing to dwell upon.

"We have to go up the coast and look for the right spot for a ceremony I will have to do in the very near future. We need a spot that goes out into the sea and is made of rock and will be good when it's time for the ceremony. It's not time for the ceremony right now, not yet, but we have to find the place that will be right for it in the near future. And we have to get the place we find ready for the ceremony. Can you leave in a few minutes?"

I didn't ask what kind of future ceremony Don Obdulio was talking about. Or why he thought that a ceremony might be advisable at some time in future. I just got ready so we could go.

The three of us walked to the intersection with the traffic light at the North end of Tulum, and we hailed a collectivo. It was cheap. And quick. We got out about fifteen minutes later at the entrance to Tankah 3.

Tankah 3 is a small, mostly expat community of expensive villas facing a bay. It has many vacant lots both on the sea side and on the selva side. It has two restaurants, Blue Sky, an Italian restaurant that has a good pizza oven and very good Italian seafood, and Casa Cenote, a beach bar that has Mexican food and drink. Casa Cenote got its name from the Manatee Cenote that is just across the road from it. As far as I know, the cenote has never had a manatee in it. It has some fish in it, yes, but no non-human mammals. I don't know why it has its name. Nobody I ask knows why either. Some old timers insist there were once manatees in the cenote. I think not.

"We have to walk," Don Obdulio said. So we began to walk down the long, straight, dusty, dirt road from the highway toward the beach. It was a long, dusty walk. Eventually, we came to a security station.

"We want to go out to the point," Don Obdulio told the guard. He pointed toward the North.

"You can have access to the beach," the guard said, "There is public access. But each of you will have to leave your ID here and pick it up when you leave."

"I don't have any ID," said Don Obdulio. "Nor does he," he pointed to El Kid. Evidently, I was not a problem. Yet.

"Maybe if I leave my entire wallet here with my ID and my money that will be enough?" I asked. "I'm sure I'll come back and get it and that I'll have these two with me then."

The guard wasn't so sure. He wasn't going to deviate from what he had been told to do. He wasn't making any decisions, he wasn't going to jeopardize his job. He radioed somebody else to come to the security station. He asked us please to wait.

Shortly, a man who must have been the supervisor rode up on a small motorcycle. "What's wrong?" he asked the guard. The supervisor looked us over. We must have looked completely disreputable. Don Obdulio's clothing was in tatters as usual. He was wearing flip flops and looked like he was utterly destitute. I needed a shave. Badly. I too looked totally disheveled. And El Kid looked shifty, like he'd steal anything that wasn't tied down with heavy chains. "Oh, I know those two," the supervisor said, pointing to Don Obdulio and El Kid. "I know them forever. They're ok. Is there a way I can be of any help to you, Sir?" he asked Don Obdulio with a nod.

A discussion about how his family was, and his kids, and how grown up they were now led directly to Don Obdulio hitching a ride on the back of the motorcycle while El Kid and I walked slowly out to the point on the beach. It was a long hot walk until we took off our shoes and walked in the surf. That was much, much better.

North of Tulum there are several points where rock and coral reach from the coast out to and actually touch the reef. The reef runs right up to the tips of these points. These points have no trees, and only low growing plants, small shrubs, and a few vines. Mostly, they are brown and black and beige colored rock formations that are embedded with a huge number of fossils. And there are many large pieces of broken coral and rock that have been stacked up on them. These broken pieces have been slowly eroded and pitted by the sea and the wind. The tide sometimes covers the point during storms and the high of tide, so in many places there are small sea creatures holding on to the rocks and coral or living in wet spots or holes. And there are many small tidal pools close to the sea with small creatures and little fish in them. There are also low spots in which sand has accumulated. The point feels in some ways like the surface of the moon or a desolate planet. The rock is not smooth, it has brittle, sharp edges and points and it has many holes in it. It is otherworldly. And hot.

When we first approached the point, I noticed that there was an osprey in the sky, circling the bay, flying low, looking for food. I pointed toward it. Don Obdulio said, "That's good." Then, up ahead on the point, there was a large, dead tree trunk that had floated across the sea and been beached on the point. It had no bark. Its skin was smooth. It had no branches. It looked and felt for all the world like a dead, shiny whale. As if it had until very recently been swimming in the sea as a mammal. There were, of course, other branches and trees on the point, but none as large and drawing as much attention from us as this one. And none attracted my displeasure like this one. Don Obdulio looked at it. He walked around it. He stared at it. "It won't work here," he said. "This is not the correct place for us."

It's a good thing Don Obdulio could make up his mind quickly. Although there was a strong breeze from the sea, the point is in direct, hot sunlight. The bright sun was reflecting off the sea and radiating off the rock. It was slowly cooking the inside of my head as well as the rest of me. And especially the bottoms of my feet. I was ringing wet.

We retraced our steps all the way back to Highway 307 and hailed another colletivo for another ride North. We exited after about 10 minutes at the sign for Oscar y Lalo's Restaurant, the Sahara Café, and Jashita Hotel, and another long, dusty, quite potholed road toward the sea.

For many years Oscar y Lalo's was a Riviera Maya landmark. A large restaurant on the beach at Paradise Bay, it was expensive, but the food was good and the location was completely spectacular. It was a location for making Mexican beer commercials that would air in the US and in Mexico. It looked like what the Mayan Riviera was supposed to look like. The bay was sparkling, shimmering turquoise and it was surrounded by selva. From the restaurant, no buildings were visible. There were pelicans. And shore birds: herons, egrets, cranes. A few kayaks might dot the bay. And most important, there was the illusion of an unspoiled limitless paradise. Lalo, its now departed owner, presided over the place from a hammock in the middle of the room. But then Oscar y Lalo decided that the land surrounding the restaurant, including a cenote, should be developed and, incredibly, they decided to move the restaurant from its fabled location to, of all places, Highway 307 across from the former entrance to the Bay.

Yes, developing the land might bring in huge fortunes some day. Yes, opening up on the highway would assure that maybe tour buses would stop. But the people who lived in villas on Bahia Soliman, the bay south of Paradise Bay, who used to walk to Oscar y Lalo's, drink and eat heavily, and then weave their ways home on foot using flashlights were gone. The subdivision has not been built. So ended an era.

Oscar y Lalo was a restaurant before the first house was built by North Americans on Bahia Soliman. The original resident lived in a motor home. Then came the first house, now known as Nah Yaxche, round, with its tall palapa roof supported by a tall, clean tree trunk, incredibly simple and airy. Just one story. And not air conditioned. Then came other houses. Initially, all of the construction beginning in the mid-1990's was low impact and had a very special, very ecological aesthetic: louvred, wooden windows with screens, palapa roofs, jungle plants, minimal concrete, outdoor showers. Ceiling fans kept the homes cool; air conditioning wasn't needed. The idea was to be in the spectacular nature of the bay, to invite it in, to embrace it. Many of the initial owners seemed to be former hippies of one kind or another, or eccentrics, or nature lovers. They were all people who had found paradise and wanted to bask in it.

But over time, larger and larger homes began to be built. These larger homes were much like those built in Tankah 3, if not more extravagant. They all had glass sliding windows and glass sliding doors and air conditioning and large swimming pools and were primarily made of cement, not wood. They were tall. They had second and in some cases, even third floors. And they filled their lots to the very edges. They towered over the surrounding trees. And the bay. This followed a disastrous building tradition imported from just to the North.

The first place in the Mayan Riviera in which there was rampant overbuilding was Akumal, the "home of the turtles," about 20 minutes to the north of Bahia Soliman. Many, many condominiums were built on the bay. And many shops and restaurants. Huge houses were built both on the bay and in the interior. There were small hotels and bars. And dive shops. And the place became very much the North American enclave in the Mayan Riviera. Of course, it paid homage to Mexico. But who are we kidding? It was an expat enclave for the most wealthy and probably the most unadaptable. And then, despite the efforts of those who were concerned about the impact all of this rapid, dense development would ultimately have, it became obvious that the reef in Akumal was slowly and irrevocably dying. It was too late to reverse the process. It was a process you could call Akumalificacion: gigantic homes filling their lots, their windows closed and their air conditioners running, the nitrogen from their waste seeping slowly but inexorably into the bay, slowly but surely exterminating the coral, killing the reef, destroying the environment, befouling paradise.

Yes, I sound like I'm complaining. But if I didn't complain about this, would I be able to complain about anything else in the world?

These magnificent edifices that clashed so thoroughly with the emptiness and what had previously been in Tankah 3, in Akumal, in Bahia Soliman were, of course, at one time, magnets for burglaries. How could it be otherwise? Mexican laborers built these fabulous mansions usually by mixing cement in the street or in a very few cases by using a small cement mixer. They then carried the cement in joint compound buckets up ladders to pour it into hand made, wooden forms. Repeat and repeat again. Repeat all day long. Repeat for weeks. They cut rebar with a hand saw. They dug the holes for swimming pools with shovels. Hand shovels. Not backhoes. If something had to be dismantled, they used hammers, not jack hammers, to break it apart. If something had to be lifted, they gathered together and as a group lifted it. There was no heavy machinery. They worked from 7 am until sundown six or seven days a week. The contrast between their lives and the lives of the owners of the palaces they built to architectural specifications stood in sharp, obvious contrast.

The workers didn't have 60 inch flat screen TVs and iPods and computers and Rolex watches and nice cars and nice clothing and cash and jewelry and US$50 tequila. And, of course, they told their neighbors about the incredible things they had seen in the new homes they were building in Akumal and Tankah. It was as if they had visited the set for "Lifestyles Of The Rich And Famous." Only this wasn't reality television. Word spread. How could it not? Eventually, it had to reach the wrong ears. It had to reach the ears of someone who would wait until a home seemed to be unoccupied and pry open a second floor window or door. And carry off whatever could be found. It made perfect sense.

There is now private security in Bahia Soliman and Tankah 3 and Akumal. There had to be.

The three of us walked the road toward Bahia Soliman from the highway. After about 200 meters, an animal began to cross the road. Was it a raccoon? No, wrong kind of tail. Wrong kind of body. Wrong color. It turned out to be a coati, called "chic" in Mayan or "tejon" in the local Spanish. Don Obdulio immediately stopped walking. El Kid and I stopped as well. "Wait," he whispered. The coati slowly crossed the road and entered the mangrove on the south side of the road. We waited. Then a smaller, younger coati crossed the road, evidently following its mother. We waited. A third, small coati crossed the road. I looked at Don Obdulio. Were there more? I had heard that coatis sometimes traveled in daylight in packs of a half dozen or more. He paused, he smiled. Two more crossed. Then he said, "OK, let's go."

When we came to the end of the road, there was a tall fence on the left, telling us to stay off of the property of the former Oscar y Lalo's or else we'd be reported to The Authority, whoever that might be. And on the right was the security shack for Bahia Soliman. As we approached the shack and the chain crossing the road, a guard in blue came over to us. "Weren't you just at Tankah 3?" Yes, we were. We wanted to go to the point, same thing here. "No problem, sirs," says the guard, "I'll show you the best way to get there."

The best way, it turned out, was to squeeze through Oscar y Lalo's fence and walk up a sandy road, and then turn left and walk up the beach out to the point. The beach had a path of sorts between the tree line and the thick piles of coral deposited there by storms. The beach toward the point was strewn with coral, there was little sand. The sand had the texture of ground coral. At the shore there was rock, like the rock on the point, sharp, but pitted and with holes. Lizards were everywhere on the coral and in the rocks. The bay, to our right, was sparkling turquoise and blue, and the breeze came toward us from the sea. Small plants were beginning to grow in tufts on the coral, slowly beginning to break it down, slowly turning rock into sand. Some of the plants had small yellow flowers; others, purple. They also had razor sharp burrs. And vines were beginning to grow across the top of some of the coral and rocks. Some of the vines had pink flowers like morning glories or moonflowers.

On the point, we found the usual detritus. Plastic, tree limbs, lumber, old rope. A small rusted refrigerator. Tidal pools. Patches of sand. Many small sea creatures clinging to coral and rocks. Small fish swimming in wet spots. The sound of the ocean crossing the reef was a loud, low, constant, rumbling. Don Obdulio looked around. He walked around. He turned around. He stood stone still. He raised his arms over his head and closed his eyes. At last he spoke, "This is perfect. There are some things you need to do. The most important is to gather whatever wood there is here that can be burnt. Nothing too big. Or too wet. No logs. Old pieces of furniture are fine. And stack it up over there on that hillside so that when we come back it will still be here. Put it right there," he pointed. "So it will be high up on the bank and out of the wind. It has to be high enough that it won't get wet, even at the very highest of high tides. We need enough sticks and wood to make a good sized, very hot, tall fire. And be sure to collect enough small twigs and sticks that we can quickly start the fire when we want to."

He watched us begin our work. He didn't do anything to help. Instead, he waved to us, "I'm leaving. When you are done, and you should be in an hour or less" he was talking to me, "take our friend here up to Akumal and buy him a fish taco. You know the place. And a Coke. I know he likes that a lot. It's in recognition of all the good work you will both complete in my absence and your doing it so well I do not have to check on what you did later on. So I won't have to come back until it's time for the ceremony." He then turned and walked away. Evidently my abundant wallet was expected to buy these few things. Don Obdulio didn't offer any financial aid.

La Loncheria is in Akumal, which also has the most expensive, most gringoized mini super, Chomak. It is essentially a lunch counter on the access road. In the back room is the kitchen. It seems always to be open. And it always has a wide spectrum of patrons: vacationers and owners of houses in Akumal, taxi drivers, maintenance workers, shop owners, travelers. The food is good and quick and cheap.

After we ate, it was time to walk back to the highway and find a collectivo back to Tulum. The intersection of the road to Akumal and the highway has changed drastically over the years. It used to be just a crossroads. Then it became a circle. Now it is an elaborate intersection with the main highway with a bridge, a pedestrian walkway over the highway, access roads and a retorno. We found the logical spot for a south bound collectivo to stop and waited only minutes before being picked up.

As the collectivo sped down the highway past Chemuyil toward Tulum, to my great surprise, in fact to my utter amazement, I saw someone standing at the side of the road in the middle of nowhere, near Chemuyil, whom I very much wanted to talk to. "Wait," I told the driver. "Stop. Right here. Stop. I have to get out. Right now. Please stop." He managed to pull over and to stop about 200 meters later and drop me off on the shoulder of the road. The driver looked at me like I was crazy and mumbled something. This was not a spot where there was ever a reason to stop. He didn't say, "Good riddance," but he was grumbling and made the same face.

I said goodbye to El Kid and started walking back toward Akumal on the side of the road facing the oncoming traffic. The sun was really bright and hot. Cars were whizzing by. I was squinting. I was immediately drenched. When I got closer, I called out, "Hey, what are you doing here?"

She looked up. It was Mari Estrella. She was wearing a pale yellow t-shirt and jeans and sandals. And a baseball cap. She was still as beautiful as ever. That was good. Her lips were wonderful, and her smile delighted me. That was good. "Hi," she said. She said it as if it were not really big deal that I had encountered her. That was not so good.

Well, even if she wouldn't say it, I would. "I'm quite surprised to see you," I said. "I was riding by in a colletivo and thought I saw you. I wasn't sure it was you, but I got out anyway. To see."

It turned out that she was in Akumal briefly to meet with some more experts about turtle habitat. And she was then on the side of the highway photographing some of the despachos, the small monuments and chapels that had been erected over the years at the sites of auto fatalities. To nobody's surprise, because of the way Highway 307 had been, and because so many people had to walk on its narrow, dangerous shoulder, there were a quite lot of these small shrines between Chemuyil and Tulum. The government has tried to eliminate the fatal accidents with a huge overpass and high fences at both Chemuyil and Akumal, but the many monuments will endure.

Would she like to have dinner tonight? I knew of a lovely place in Akumal. That would be nice, she said. That was good. She didn't seem at all surprised by the invitation. That was good. She smiled. That was good. We made a plan. I'd see her that evening.

I stopped another oncoming collectivo, waved good bye, and rode off toward Tulum. She continued to look at a small cement monument with unlit candles and a shiny picture of the Virgin of Guadalupe. She fiddled with her camera. I watched her out the rear window of the van until she vanished in the heat.

I thought she was beautiful, even more beautiful than I had recalled, and I was amazed at the good fortune of seeing her at the side of the road. What a wonderful coincidence.

As I rode down the highway in air conditioned comfort, it occurred to me that this apparent string of events, the trip to Akumal, the ride back to Tulum, miraculously seeing her at the side of the road, stopping to make a dinner date with her, all of those many coincidences obviously had Don Obdulio's fingerprints all over it. He, of course, hadn't told me, as he doubtless could have, that I would have a surprise on the trip back from Akumal. But no, he didn't say anything about it. He didn't utter a peep. But to me it didn't matter, it felt completely like Don Obdulio's intervention. I had asked him to help me out, yes, and apparently, he had. Yes, when I told him I wanted to see her again and had asked for his help, he changed the subject. But, apparently, I thought, he had gone ahead and was going to help me out anyway. Evidently, Don Obdulio had determined that my seeing her was good for me and for her and for generations to come. I wasn't going to argue with that. Not one bit.

I decided that it would be fun to take her to dinner at La Lunita in North Akumal. We could walk there from where she was staying. It's a beautiful restaurant on the beach, tables with white table cloths under the cocos, candles, the moon shining on the calm water of Akumal's Halfmoon Bay. The drinks, especially the margaritas, are good, and the menu is mostly well prepared, Mexican seafood. There's an excellent tortilla soup. There are coconut shrimp. There are many styles of fish. It had great potential, I thought. It could be romantic. I thought romantic might be a really good idea. OK, I admit it, that was exactly what I wanted.

The entrance to the restaurant is on the first floor of a condominium building. When we arrived, there was already a large group of people, maybe twelve of them, at a long table near the beach on the far right side of the restaurant. They had several small kids who were running around, and the adults at the table, who were from somewhere in the Midwest, were giggling and laughing raucously. Many margaritas had broken their volume controls. The day's sun had fried their electrical circuits. And now they had missed an exit and were well on their way on the caraterra to blithering drunk. Their conversations were almost entirely shouts. And their children competed with them to be heard. They were loudly discussing how terrible something was. I have no idea what.

Alarmed, worried that the romantic atmosphere I had sought out and was prepared to pay for, was endangered, I looked carefully at their table to see whether they had eaten and might soon be on their staggering way out the door. I hoped so. But that was not quite the case. No such luck. The waiter came and began preparing flaming drinks for them, as they loudly oohed and ahhed. I was sure these drinks and probably dessert would make them even louder, that there would be even more shouting and braying laughter before they finally stumbled into the dark.

Maybe we should move further away from these people, I asked. Maybe we can stay outside—I didn't want to eat dinner inside the restaurant, I wanted the beach—if we move a little. Maybe that will make this better. We moved to a table at the far left boundary of the restaurant, near a stone wall. The change was more cosmetic than effective. We ordered some drinks. That would help, I hoped.

At this point, one of the red faced Midwesterners began to deliver an angry and impassioned oration about how he'd been coming down here for years and how the lazy and stupid gas station attendants continued to try to rip them off and how he wasn't having any of it and the next time and blah blah blah.

And his besotted confreres all joined in, that, yes, that had happened to them and blah blah blah. And he was right. And the answer to this was blah blah blah. And how did they, I wasn't sure who they might be in this case, allow that to continue and blah blah blah. And while they were doing this, hablando blah blah blah, their kids were shouting excitedly about something, which their parents were ignoring, while they shouted to each other and called out to their parents to be answered.

What they were complaining about: a by now famous gas station rip off. You get 200 pesos of gas and you give the attendant at 200 peso note. He folds it over and shows you a 20 peso note and demands another 180 pesos for the gas. You're a gringo, maybe you did give him 20 and not 200. Right. That's called getting ripped off for 180 pesos. It's an old story. So old, in fact, that the new Pemex station on

Tulum has a big sign permanently painted on its exterior wall as a direct response to this story that says, "Somos Honestos."

The loud complaining was all a very bad omen. I have to make a small confession here. It's probably not necessary to tell you. The reason why I wanted to take Mari Estrella to dinner was obvious. To me. And most probably to her. And definitely to you. It was certainly not complicated. In fact, it was quite basic, our age differences and everything else sociological, including geography be damned. This much was completely clear to me when I initially saw her at the roadside. It was the renewal of a fantasy I had before, way back at La Nave and again at Playa Paraiso. It was something I had been hoping for and had even gone so far as to solicit Don Obdulio's metaphysical and spiritual assistance to obtain. So I was beginning to get frustrated. Very frustrated. And worried. It looked to me like the Midwesterners were working effectively to thwart me and ruin my plans, by creating a toxic, carnival atmosphere, one that would send us both home disappointed, with bitter complaints on our lips, wondering why the Universe had so strongly blocked our mutually desired getting together.

I reached into my pocket and held onto the white bag with its black stone. "Please," I thought. "Please help me out." Then I thought that it wasn't the stone's purpose to work out my romantic desires. I shouldn't ask it to shut these people up and/or send them home. Perhaps a spacecraft could arrive and suction them out of their seats and abduct them. I certainly would not miss them. Or report them missing.

Undeterred, we tried to block out their rumpus. We drank our drinks, and ordered second ones, and I asked Mari what she did in real life, when she wasn't working on tortugas. How was I to know that this too would turn out not to be such a good idea? She had been a television journalist in the Caribbean but gave that up a few years ago, and now she was writing articles about travel in the Caribbean and things, like the despachos, but her real interest was in writing poetry. She wanted to be a poet. A real live poet. She loved to write poems.

That's funny, I had written travel pieces. I still do. That was always fun for me. You got to talk about places you visited and enjoyed. And you got paid a little for writing about them. Was she having any luck selling these stories? Yes, sometimes, but she really wanted most of all to write poetry.

What kind of poetry? I asked. Could she show me? This, of course, sounded promising to me. It was as if she had offered to show me something private, something intimate, something that revealed her—dare I say it?—her soul. Of course, I'd be happy to read them, I said. The reptile in me immediately thought that this was, indeed, a positive a development, one that led directly and inexorably to what I wanted.

But nothing is that inexorable. I didn't expect that then and there she'd immediately pull a notebook out of her bag. And that she would hand it to me. "Is this your poetry?" I asked moronically. It was a notebook with handwriting in it. Lots and lots of dense handwriting.

"Here's where you can start," she said, opening the notebook and turning pages, looking for the right place for me to begin.

"Should I read it out loud?"

"I think it's best like that." I stared at the page. I couldn't read it. I couldn't see it well enough in the dark, romantic candlelight to make out any of the words. I'm just old enough that my eyesight will not let me read this page in this light. And I didn't have my glasses. I called over the waiter. A small problem, did he have any reading glasses I could please borrow? No, he was very sorry, he didn't have any. Sometimes one bad idea leads to another. Not to be thwarted, I walked over to the table of the loud Midwestern inebriates, did they have any reading glasses I could borrow for just a moment? One of them handed me a pair, "That's what happens at a certain point to us old guys," he opined. Was this drunken gentleman daring to make a critical social commentary about me? Yeah, thanks a lot. Then I returned to the table with the borrowed glasses.

I wish I hadn't been able to find any glasses. I could have explained that I wouldn't need them if only there were a little more light, that it was the darkness that made me need glasses, and maybe I could have worked my way into reading the poems at her place, where I was sure there was bright incandescent light, but no. I didn't do that. I didn't think of it. And when I started to read the poems out loud, I knew that the evening might be going to turn out to be a complete and utter bust. A miserable failure. I wasn't going home with anybody, young and beautiful or not. No. I was going to end up riding the collectivo home with a bunch of exhausted workers and drunks. Alone. And the next chance I was going to give Don Obdulio an enormous earful and a piece of my mind for playing such malicious games with me. And, of course, he would deny that he had done anything. At all. He would insist he couldn't do such things.

To make the recounting of this painful dinner poetry reading a little shorter, and to show mercy for you who are reading this, I am not quoting any of these "poems" to you. I am not going to write them down for you. But I can describe them. They all rhymed. The rhymes were not clever. I hate rhymes anyway, brilliant or not. I also hate cliche. The poems were all relatively short. They had a sing song meter. At least they did when I read them. And I don't like sing song. Their sentimental content would fit perfectly in the most cloying, commercial greeting cards. I didn't like that at all as far as poetry goes. I did rather like the open heart of someone who thinks the world is like this. But the poems were, in a word and in my critical judgment, terrible. At least I thought they were. Their author, however, in addition to her other many redeeming qualities, which I've mentioned before, had a remarkably sweet, very kind, extraordinarily compassionate view of the world. These poems in other words weren't exposing her inner lizard. They were revealing her inner saint. I found that extraordinarily endearing. And unbearably erotic. How completely unlike me.

Look, I have no problem whatsoever with sleeping with beautiful women who are bad poets. I have no problem with that at all. How could I? If I don't get involved in their poetry, that's great. It doesn't matter. My problem, and it may seem to be quite a trivial one to you, but let me assure you it is important to me, is with being dishonest, with lying, in this context. Yes, I have told bazillions of lies in many other contexts. But I absolutely hate telling lies for my personal gain when intimacy is involved. I don't like that. I will not do it. Call me crazy if you must. Call me an inconsistent, grandiose lizard. Whatever you choose. That's how it is.

And to make matters worse, and to help keep me honest, I don't have a good, solid, serviceable poker face. My emotions usually show immediately on my face. I cannot suppress this, and I don't want to learn how to. So when I read the poems, my expression must have shown what I thought of them, that I really disliked what I was reading. A third round of margaritas didn't really change this or mollify it. Even that couldn't really paralyze my face. In other words, it was probably as clear as window glass that I didn't like the poems. At all. It was fine that I didn't like the poems. I just didn't want to have to lie about the poems or anything else to advance my agenda for the evening. That just didn't seem right to me. Call me crazy if you must. I imagine that there are lots of people for whom the end justifies saying almost anything. Especially when the end is intimacy of some kind. But alas. I'm just not one of those people. I'm inflexible about this.

And as if that weren't enough, after we had eaten and I had read about eight uniformly terrible poems, she asked me, "What do you think of these poems?"

This was a test, I thought. It was absolutely a challenge. A test from the cosmos, from the universe, perhaps from Don Obdulio himself, but not personally from her. From whatever vast intelligence rules the Universe I was being served up a Big Test. And I knew it immediately. I don't really like being tested because I'm aware of how easy it is to fail this kind of test. You can fail this test even if you get it 99.7% correct. And my fear of failing this sort of existential test and my desperately wanting to pass it, I am sorry to say, shows up in what shrinks call projection, in my thinking that somebody did something to me. That somebody was somehow the perpetrator of something. And that I was a victim.

I didn't initially think this test was brought to me by Don Obdulio. That didn't cross my mind. Was it her? Why did she have to ask me this? Wasn't it obvious what I thought from my face? I didn't want to be mean. Or rude. And I especially didn't want to be dishonest. I know full well that when others have read things that I have written and expressed their dislike or even their contempt for them, I have felt devastated. And hurt. And I sometimes wanted to run away and hide. I felt I had wasted their time, and I was embarrassed that what I had asked them to read was in their opinion so very bad. So in response to her question, I wasn't going to tell her the obvious, that she shouldn't quit her day job. And I also wasn't going to tell her how great her poems were in the vain hope that through praise of them I might end up in her bed. That seemed completely despicable. And even too reptilian for me. I wouldn't do that.

I took a deep breath. I paused. I must have sighed. And I told her that really I wasn't a good person to ask about these poems, that I wasn't a poet or a big reader of poetry or a poetry critic or anything like that, and that I also wasn't really comfortable with how very sentimental they seemed, with the display of the emotions she was talking about. So, I said, I'm not really the person to ask about this. And blah blah blah blah.

There was something about La Lunita that night that induced enormous amounts of hablando blah blah blah blah. In other words, I definitely didn't lie to her. I didn't not tell her the truth. Please note that I did not fabricate. I was kind. It's true, I almost lied. I was sorely tempted. But almost doesn't count. This isn't horseshoes. Ultimately, I didn't lie. I didn't fail the test. I was delighted and, in fact, totally relieved that I hadn't told her a single lie about the poems. Or about anything else. I really didn't want to say anything to her that later would open the door to my kicking myself down the road. And I struggled, but I didn't fail. What a relief.

I paid the bill, and I said I'd walk her home. She'd like that, she said. On the walk, we held hands. That was absolutely great. She had small, soft hands with thin fingers and short nails. I liked her hand and how they felt in mine. I also liked how it felt when our shoulders touched occasionally. It was dark, but the Caribbean sky was filled with a zillion stars. We stopped in the middle of the street to stare up at them. We stood shoulder to shoulder looking up. There were billions of stars, no moon had yet risen. We stood silently. We both wanted to see even more stars. We crossed over onto the beach to look up and out at the stars over Half Moon Bay. Again, we stood shoulder to shoulder looking. Occasionally there was a shooting star. I have no idea how long we watched the sky over the sea, how long we stood there staring at the sparkling canopy.

When we arrived at her place after a long, somewhat potholed, somewhat inebriated, somewhat extended by star gazing walk in the dark of North Akumal, I told her it was great to see her again. I was sorry that the other patrons had been so loud and obnoxious at the restaurant, that it really was usually quite a nice, quiet, relaxing place. She thanked me for dinner and the time together. She enjoyed the stars. And the walk. Did I want to stay the night?

Actually, I did. Very much. I don't think she initially knew how very much. After all, I had been thinking about her quite obsessively for some time. Since La Nave. And I'd asked Ramirez and Don Obdulio about her. And I asked Don Obdulio to help me out with her. And maybe she was also the person the tall man had seen in Cuba. And anyway, I found her really, really attractive. She was occupying a large corner office in my mind before we had dinner, before we had any drinks. And standing here at her door, my desire for her was sweet, and overwhelming, and passionate.

She came close to me, so I kissed her. Her lips were like cumulus clouds, and her body fit beautifully against mine. No more words. We went inside the house. She took my hand. I followed her up the stairs all the way up to the roof. The roof was flat. The stars were everywhere. We spread a blanket and lied down on it to stare up at the vault of heaven. We lied side by side, holding hands, watching the cosmos slowly wheel by over us. We were silent. Eventually, the strong force between us and the stars and the milky way overhead and the rising moon and the sounds and wind from the ocean reflecting the stars and the gentle flowing of time pulled our clothing from us and pulled us toward each other in a deep embrace that fit us perfectly. We became a small planet, turning, spinning, swirling, following the moon across the sky, joining the flight of the millions of stars across the Caribbean night.

The next morning on the long, hot walk from distant North Akumal to the highway I had plenty of time to think about the evening and to talk with myself about it. It was so delicious. It was so wonderful. We would definitely see each other again. Soon, but we didn't know exactly when. She had meetings. Then she had to transport a case of still unhatched turtle eggs quickly to the island called Desde Desdemona before they hatched out. I had her cell phone number, she had mine. She was leaving on a plane in two days with the eggs, but she'd be back. Maybe we could meet again before she left. She had a white, Toyota rental car, she could drive down to Tulum to visit. I wanted to see her, I wanted to show her the old museum I lived in. I thought she might like sitting in the yard under the purple tree. Maybe I could find for her where the poems around here were, in the ocean and in the clouds, and could point her toward some of them. Maybe I would tell her how I harvested stories. This was something I would happily share. But we didn't make a firm time or place. We'd call each other. Hasta pronto.

It was still quite early. I was walking against the arrival of all of the many workers who would make Akumal function. They lived across Highway 307 in Akumal Pueblo. It was about 7 am. Unlike me, they seemed rested. Their clothing was clean. They were ready for the day's work. I had a silly grin on my face, and a small headache. I wondered whether those approaching me would see that my heart and hands were radiating a green color. Could they see that just around me there was the softest, warm cloud. I was sleepy. I would need some sleep when I got home. But I felt great. I was happy. And there was something new and special about the world.

I arrived at home just before 8 am. At about 10, I was awakened by the loud sound of a loudspeaker truck. It didn't sound like the mango and papaya guy who came every week, it didn't sound like the Telebodega truck, telling me of their great, one time only deals on major appliances. I couldn't make out what the words were. There was no political campaign going on at the moment. It was entirely too early for this kind of racket. What in the world was it? I pulled on my pants and opened my front door. Then I could hear the message, and it was quite simple.

A hurricane is coming so you have to leave. You have to be out of your house and leave town before this evening. No excuses. No one is to stay behind. For any reason. Go to high land or go to the shelter at the school. This is important. This is an official order. Then it repeated itself. Over and over again.

On a practical level, there were some things that had to be done immediately so that I could leave. These included throwing away everything in the refrigerator and freezer today. Right then. Yes, you could wait and see whether the storm knocked out the electricity, but in this hot, very humid climate it's better to throw away perfectly good food than to come back to a refrigerator that has not had power for a week and to try to clean up the mess. That is a most disgusting, nauseating task, one that is done exactly once, if at all in a single lifetime. The other steps to be taken were simple: close and tape the glass windows. Put up some plywood on the ones facing east and south. Put the important papers in a plastic box, lock the house, and leave town toward Coba and Valladolid by whatever conveyance might present itself.

Coba isn't really a town. It's a location in the jungle that has beautiful Mayan ruins, a tall pyramid, the tallest of the Mayan ruins, Mayan roads, temples, and other buildings. Until the mid 1970's getting to the location was close to impossible for outsiders. But when the Mexican government decided to build Cancun, it also decided that the ruins in Coba should be unearthed, that a road should be built, and that the site could be a tourist destination. That was a brilliant plan. The pyramid is tall, far taller than the trees, and from the top you can see much of the green Mundo Maya.

Valladolid, beyond Coba, is a colonial town with a main square and a cathedral and some hotels. It is far enough inland that most storms do not do it great violence. And beyond Valladolid, are Chichen

Itza and beyond that Merida, all places that are safe from hurricanes coming from the southeast that are making landfall in Quintana Roo.

Some people like to sit storms out in Tulum. They stay at home and pray. Or they rent a room at a hotel made of cement, buy ice and liquor and rolling papers, and ride the storm out. It usually takes only a day for a storm to pass through. Afterwards, nothing works. There's no electricity. No running water. No plumbing. Food spoils quickly. I personally don't like the idea. It is no fun to be in Tulum after a storm when there is debris and broken glass all over the street, the electric wires are dangling everywhere, cars are stuck in deep water and won't run, and there's nothing good to eat anywhere. And no way to keep food cold. I prefer just to leave.

As I was getting finished on my basic, often mentally rehearsed storm preparations, El Kid arrived and started pounding on my door. I answered the door immediately. "Senor," El Kid said with a grin, "Today we're supposed to make the ceremony at the point."

"It has to wait just a little bit. I've got to get the house sealed up and get ready to get out of town. After I do that, I can help make the ceremony. It won't take me long. Particularly if you lend me a helping hand."

El Kid had no interest in being the helping hand. He sat down at the kitchen table and started to rummage in the cereal box on the table. "Don Obdulio knows that there is a hurricane coming this way, and we're supposed to make it turn, turn it away from Tulum, turn it to the sea. So we need to do that today. We need to do it soon, so that the storm has time to turn before it is too close or arrives. The ceremony is about protection from the storm, of people, of property, of the town."

"Well, it's your lucky day then. Eat anything you find here. Go ahead, eat as much as you want. Whatever you don't eat is going into the garbage."

What was the emergency? What was the rush? I assumed there was plenty of time. I went outside and looked at the sky. It was still clear, blue, beautiful. There was not a cloud. It was hot. There was a lovely, soft, warm breeze from the east. Yes, I heard the warnings from the loudspeaker truck, really I did. But there was no sign of a storm, much less big, angry, black clouds filling the sky. Didn't that prove that there was plenty of time? And couldn't the ceremony wait until I got the house securely closed up? Yes, it could wait just that long. But evidently not much longer than that.

El Kid, who was then eating cereal, and tortillas with jelly on them, and huge globs of Nutella off a spoon, repeated with a full mouth that we really needed to do the ceremony as soon as we could. I hurried. I quickly finished sealing up my house and throwing out the garbage, and we then hurried over to the yard where Don Obdulio was folding up his hammock and giving it to some people for safekeeping.

"I am somewhat surprised that we found you at home this morning," he said.

"Well, it had your fingerprints all over it," I responded. "I really want to thank you for all of your help. Magnificent. Gracias, gracias, gracias, gracias. This was really amazing, much better than other things you have done for me. Entonces, muchissimas gracias. That was really a wonderful event, for which I deeply, deeply thank you." I was gushing.

He laughed out loud at this. "So, again, you think I did something, made something happen, right? I know you liked it. But you insist I did something to make it happen. Sometimes you accuse me of doing things. But today you are giving me credit. Both are wrong. I'd like to hear what it is all about today. I bet you think I did something to your life. That I made something happen for you. You might have liked it, but that's not the point. It's the same whether you like it or you don't. I didn't do anything. I didn't. But we don't have time right this minute to talk about your compliments, or what is the same, your complaints about me doing things in your life or for you, whether they are things you like. Or you don't. Forget about what I have and have not done. I haven't done anything. We can talk about it later on, maybe, but right now we need to be going out to the point. We have to get going. We have to do the ceremony. And we don't have a lot of time to do it. It has to be done pretty soon. The water really is rising quickly."

We commandeered the Tsuru, filled it with materials for the ceremony—the plastic boxes were, of course, nowhere to be found—and headed North on Highway 307 to Punta Bahia Soliman. It took about 25 minutes to reach the security point. We parked the car. The security guard greeted us, "I've been expecting you. I heard the weather report. The water is already rising quite a lot."

We picked up all of the material for the ceremony—I wished again that I knew what Don Obdulio did with the four boxes—and we headed for the point. There was still no storm in sight. Anywhere. The sky was blue all the way to the horizon. However, the water was high, very high, already higher than the usual high tide. Some of the rocks at the shore were already under water, and the path between the trees and the water was becoming more narrow by the minute. The sun was so bright. And the breeze didn't carry the slightest hint of a big storm. If the storm was coming from the southeast, you would have expected to see something on the horizon. But there was nothing to see. The horizon remained bright. And clear. And blue.

The rocky point was already starting to shrink. The water was steadily rising and filling all of the low points. We quickly built a large, hot fire and Don Obdulio began the ceremony. There were only the three of us. First, he called out to all of the directions, calling in the spirits and beings of the six directions to support his medicine, to carry our ceremony, calling them by their very many names, reminding them and us of their power and how they used their power, asking them to be with us and please to help us. Then he made offerings to all of the directions and to all of the spirits and gods and energies who were involved in rain and storms and wind and water, and also to all of those involved in restoring orderliness, in making peace, in creating beauty and harmony and safety, and to the gods who in ancient times were called Chac and Kukulkan and so many other names. And ultimately he spoke a prayer as he made offerings to the East and the South and to the storm itself and to the energies and beings that controlled the storm by placing objects in the fire and burning them:

> In front of you I offer my copal, this is for you . . . Be with us again with my offering of cinnamon, and cacao, and corn, and tequila these are all for you . . . In front of you I make these my gifts, again, for your happiness. And your use. For you . . . I have placed these before you and for your happiness in this fire, look at me and see that I am giving these to you, these gifts for your happiness, for your grace, look at me and see that I am giving these to you, gifts for you and the spirits and powers of the storm and the wind and the rain and the flood that is coming toward me now. It is not here yet, but it is coming. And I ask that you turn this storm away, turn from our village, from our town, from our children and from us, that they are not surrounded by and injured at all by the storm, that it does not imprison us

in water and mud and wind and broken trees and broken buildings, that the storm turns, turns away, and walks gently away from us and that when it sees us in the distance, when it sees our fire, when it knows we are here, it gently turns its strength away from us, and it turns, and it shows us its side and then shows us its strong back as it goes away from us.

The ceremony did not take very long. When it was finished, Don Obdulio told me to wait with the fire until it was burned out, until it had completely consumed itself, until it was just hot ashes, and all of the offerings and prayers and wood were completely burned up as much as it could be consumed and the flames were completely extinguished. Then he told me to sweep the ashes into the ocean. To bow to the ocean, and to walk away from it and not turn back to look at the ocean or the fire or the ashes.

He would drive the car back to my neighbor's house. He would travel with El Kid. I had no idea he could drive. Then, he told me, after the fire was finished, I should go immediately to the Coba Road and hitchhike toward Coba and Valladolid. El Kid and he were leaving now in the car, which they would return to Miguel, and then they were going to the school for shelter, they would be just fine there. They turned and walked away. They left. "I want you to go toward Coba," he said. "Wait on the road. Go to the West. Stand on the road going west."

I stood by the fire and watched it burn down. It didn't take long. A tail of brown, wispy smoke rose high in the blue sky and then vanished. The water in the bay continued slowly and gently to rise. All of the homes on the bay seemed to be closed, and all of the people seemed to have already left. It was a beautiful beach day. The sky remained blue. The breeze was gentle. The sun was bright. The only sign of an oncoming storm was the high, rising water. There was not a single other visible hint of an approaching hurricane. When the fire was out, I used palm branches to sweep the ashes into the sea, and then I left. I did not turn back.

When I left the point, I walked the beach until I came to the security point. There was one man in a blue shirt still there, he was closing up the security point. He said, "Vaya con dios." I waved at him. The dirt road to Highway 307 was still dry, but the water in the mangrove had clearly risen and was beginning to lap at its edges. Soon it would cover the road and seal off all of Bahia Soliman and the houses there until the storm's waters ultimately receded.

There was a lot of traffic going South on Highway 307 toward the Coba Road, and there was very little going north. I stopped a collectivo and said I wanted to get off at the Coba Road. So, apparently, did all of the other passengers. When we reached that intersection with the stop light in front of the San Frarncisco de Assis supermarket, we all got out. The driver said he was going to make one more trip from Tulum to Playa del Carmen and then Cancun, and he was then going to drive his van west toward Chichen Itza on the toll road to find shelter. We wished him good luck.

Past the San Francisco Supermarket and some other buildings, there were about a dozen people standing at the side of the Coba Road, each was trying to catch a ride. I was one of them. None of the cars looked like they had any room for another person. Or another box of possessions. The sun was still bright. There were still no clouds.

I noticed to my dismay that I didn't have anything with me. I had left my cell phone at the house. It had Mari's number in it. I couldn't call her. I had a wallet with some money in it. And I had the keys to my house. I was wearing my only clothes. I didn't have water. I didn't have food. I didn't have a suitcase. I didn't have anything. Period.

Look at me, I thought. Just look at me. I have apparently become one of Don Obdulio's many clueless followers. How else could I get in this position? I might have to be away from my house for a week. Or more. I have no real destination. I have no hotel reservations. I have no idea where I am going or how I am getting there or where I will end up. Regardless, it all seems just perfect. It doesn't seem to matter to me. I am doing just what Don Obdulio told me to do. This is the Coba Road. I am standing on it. I am traveling to the west.

After trying unsuccessfully near the intersection to get a ride for about half an hour, I decided that maybe it would be a good idea to begin walking away from the other people, away from the coast, away from the storm, toward Coba. After walking about 20 minutes at the side of the road and being a quick hors d'oeuvre for the selva's many foraging mosquitoes, none of whom were leaving, storm or no storm, and with many seemingly full cars passing me, I turned to hitch a ride. About a dozen more cars passed me before the white Toyota rental car stopped.

September 9, 2010
Bahia Soliman, Tulum

18536036R00112

Made in the USA
San Bernardino, CA
18 January 2015